W9-DBS-957

ALL I WANT

All I Want

ALL I WANT

A Novel

DARCEY BELL

THORNDIKE PRESS
A part of Gale, a Cengage Company

Copyright © 2022 by Seven Acres, LLC.
Permission to use portions of the lyrics of "Wouldn't It Be Loverly" from *My Fair Lady* granted by the Alan Jay Lerner family, The Alan Jay Lerner Testamentary Trust and The Frederick Loewe Foundation, as their interests may appear. All rights reserved.

Thorndike Press, a part of Gale, a Cengage Company.

ALL RIGHTS RESERVED
This book is a work of fiction. Any references to historical events, real people, or real places are used fictitiously. Other names, characters, places, and events are products of the author's imagination, and any resemblance to actual events or places or persons, living or dead, is entirely coincidental.

Thorndike Press® Large Print Thriller, Adventure, and Suspense.
The text of this Large Print edition is unabridged.
Other aspects of the book may vary from the original edition.
Set in 16 pt. Plantin.

LIBRARY OF CONGRESS CIP DATA ON FILE.
CATALOGUING IN PUBLICATION FOR THIS BOOK
IS AVAILABLE FROM THE LIBRARY OF CONGRESS.

ISBN-13: 979-8-8857-8016-2 (hardcover alk. paper)

Published in 2022 by arrangement with Emily Bestler Books/Atria Books, a Division of Simon & Schuster, Inc.

Printed in Mexico
Print Number : 1   Print Year : 2022

To Denise Shannon

All I want is a room somewhere
Far away from the cold night air
With one enormous chair
Oh, wouldn't it be loverly?

Someone's head restin' on my knee
Warm and tender as he can be
Who takes good care of me
Oh, wouldn't it be loverly?
— FREDERICK LOEWE, *MY FAIR LADY,*
"WOULDN'T IT BE LOVERLY?"

PROLOGUE:
THE COMMUNITY CHRISTMAS TALENT SHOW

A woman tiptoes out onstage, sideways, like a crab. The audience applauds. She's wearing a funny hat shaped like a pastry tart, an old-fashioned wasp-waist jacket, a long skirt, and sensible shoes. And she's carrying an umbrella. An open umbrella indoors? Doesn't she know it's bad luck?

She closes it. Her smile is coy and flirtatious. Tendrils of gray hair peek out from the edges of her dark wig. Her heavy makeup makes her look like a clown-faced Mary Poppins.

I recognize her from somewhere, but the wig and makeup are confusing. The audience knows. They're laughing. They love it.

She stands at the microphone and waits, as if for an orchestra to start up. There is no orchestra. She's on her own. She frowns. She seems distracted, totters a little. Is she ill?

She begins to sing. Her voice is wobbly

but clear. A good church-choir soprano, a cappella and very slow, like a record played at the wrong speed, threatening and dirge-like:

"All I want is a room somewhere."

Seven words. That's all it takes. My adrenaline spikes. I lay both hands flat on my belly.

Stay calm. Stay calm. Stay calm.

It's not Mary Poppins.

It's Eliza Doolittle. Eliza Doolittle from *My Fair Lady.*

I recognize her. I should have known right away. Why didn't I? Because it's too perfect. Too strange. But it's true. She's singing the last song I want to hear, the song I heard in my head all last summer.

Why does Eliza Doolittle need an umbrella? And why is she singing so slowly?

"Far away from the cold night air."

I'm struggling to put the fragments together. I'm missing the piece — the critical piece — that might solve the puzzle.

Earlier, in the Nativity pageant, there was . . . the girl and the baby. The baby looked at me. He knew he'd seen me before.

"With one enormous chair."

She reaches into a huge carpet bag slung over one shoulder and pulls out a doll. It's a baby doll, with a frilly bonnet and a bow around its neck. A black bow. She turns it to face the audience, but the doll has no face, just a jagged wound surrounded by a stained white ruffle. Its face looks as if it's been chewed off by an animal, leaving two ragged holes, extruding stuffing, where its eyes should have been.

I feel as if someone's pushing me into a gigantic armchair. I'm a child, a child's doll, drowning in the upholstery. Struggling to breathe. I'm Alice in Wonderland, shrunk to the size of a mouse.

She points the doll at me, then dances it in the air in time to her slow, menacing song.

I'm having a waking nightmare. I'm not myself. What does *myself* even mean?

I watch myself — I watch *her* — doing things I would never do.

I jump up. My chair scrapes, loud.

Everyone turns. Let them look.

It's my house.

The theater is inside my house.

I live here.

I stand facing the stage.

Eliza Doolittle is looking at me. She knows

that I know. She waves the doll in my direction.

Something terrible is happening. But why is it happening to *me*?

Someone is dead or about to be dead.

"Oh, wouldn't it be loverly?"

She stuffs the doll back in the bag and opens the umbrella again, raises it, and twirls around. She misses a step, almost trips, catches herself. When she stops, she's staring out at the audience. Staring at me.

I hear someone scream. Who?

It can't be me. I never scream.

It's me.

I turn. Who hears me? Who can help?

Faces float around me like headlights in the dark, like bulbs on a Christmas tree. They drift in and out of focus, a theater full of worried strangers wondering what to do about a massively pregnant woman, standing there.

Screaming and screaming.

CHAPTER ONE:
THE BIRTHDAY

Six months earlier: June

Emma and Ben are celebrating her thirty-fifth birthday at Ray's, their favorite restaurant, in a newly gentrified section of Crown Heights. Ben orders a half bottle of wine. Emma takes one sip from his glass and gets a contact high. She was never a big drinker, but she'd liked sharing a bottle of wine with Ben and doing shots with friends. She'd forgotten that first hint of a buzz, how everything gets more interesting, how softly the restaurant noise begins to hum beyond their circle of light.

Since she was a teenager, she's spent so much effort on *not* getting pregnant, it came as a shock when she changed her mind and then it wasn't automatic. Nothing, nothing. Two miscarriages and then, just when she and Ben were about to ask around about a fertility doctor, the little stick turned pink again.

Both of them think but don't say that this baby might never have siblings. But who knows? Maybe they'll like being parents. Maybe the second one will be easy.

Emma's annoyed when Ben orders swordfish, which she can't share because the mercury content is so bad for the baby. Her doctor was clear about that. Ben's a good person, he loves her, he's smart and decent and fun. One in a million. So what if he wants swordfish?

Ben catches a glimpse of her fleeting discontent. She's glad she's married to the rare guy who actually pays attention.

He says, "Wait no. I'll have the chicken. If I get the chicken, will you have some, Emma?"

The idea of chicken is slightly sickening, but Ben's thoughtfulness pleases Emma. "Go on. Get the swordfish. I'll get the pasta. I'll have plenty of food."

"If you're sure," says Ben. "Okay, back to plan A."

Emma orders pasta with fresh peas, mint, and bacon.

She wants all the bacon but eats half.

"I should have told them to hold the bacon."

"Enjoy yourself, Emma. Live large. It's your birthday. Relax. It's not like you've been eating bacon every day. Or ever, lately."

Nothing makes Emma more tense than being told to relax, but her vague discomfort vanishes when, over the delicious fresh corn and maple ice cream, Ben tells her about the house.

Neither Ben nor Emma is doing exactly what they'd wanted or planned to do with their lives, but they like what they're doing, so fine. They'd both changed direction before they met, so they can't blame each other for making them give up their dreams.

Ben had wanted to be an actor, but he's become a theatrical producer. This year, his hard work has paid off. *No Regrets,* a hip-hop musical based on the tragic life of Édith Piaf, is a Broadway hit.

The show sells out every night and gets standing ovations when the chorus sings "Non, Je Ne Regrette Rien" as the two stars cross the stage, rapping about how Piaf was abandoned by her mother, went temporarily blind, prostituted herself to pay for her little daughter's funeral, became famous, lost her great love in a plane crash, destroyed her liver and died young. As the cast takes its bows, a film of Piaf's funeral — one hundred thousand Parisians! — ripples on the closing curtain. The audiences is in tears.

Emma and Ben were introduced by a mutual friend named Laura, who — only after Ben and Emma fell in love — realized she was in love with Ben and stopped speaking to them both. Laura's bad behavior was just one more thing they had in common. At the beginning, they were always discovering things they both loved. Bach and Gillian Welch. The songs of Édith Piaf. When Ben came to Emma with the *No Regrets* hip-hop idea, she *got it* right away. She remembers the night he told her. High fives. Champagne. All-night sex.

One thing they'd always liked was watching old movies in bed on Ben's laptop. Thigh to thigh, the laptop balanced, straddling them, it was hot. Their favorites were forties black-and-white detective films and anything with Robert Mitchum. They held each other during the tense parts. They laughed. It was fun.

On their second date, at Emma's Greenpoint apartment, in bed, they'd watched the original *Cape Fear,* and afterward Ben told her, apropos of nothing, "There's a saying: 'You can't make a living in the theater, but you can make a killing.' " He'd said it like a promise.

Now he's made the killing. He's gone into business with his college friend, Avery, and Avery's wife, Rebecca. Last year, Ben's father died suddenly and left him more money than anyone ever dreamed a guy who'd owned a company selling restaurant equipment could have stashed away.

Emma had wanted to be a painter. Her work — big washy landscapes based on photos she took in Central Park — was old-fashioned. No gallery was showing anything like that. She didn't believe in herself enough to keep going. It was childish to blame her parents, but she did. Her parents always said she wasn't resilient or tough enough to handle rejection. They probably imagined they were protecting her from some inevitable disappointment. Her mother had been a psychologist, her father a corporate lawyer. Mom had suggested that Emma might want to think about becoming a teacher.

"I hope you marry a rich guy, sweetheart" was the last thing Mom said to her, on the morning she and Dad were killed by a semi that jumped the divider on the Long Island Expressway. They were on their way to see a doctor. Mom's personality was changing. She'd gotten forgetful and uncharacteristically short-tempered.

An uncle helped Emma sell her parents' house in Oyster Bay, and the money paid for art school and Emma's move to New York City.

She'd dropped out of art school before she met Ben. When he started making money, she was glad, of course. But she didn't like the feeling of having followed Mom's last words of advice.

Ben had asked if she wanted to start painting again. He'd support her. She knew he meant it. He would help her find a studio and pay the rent. He'd never make her feel guilty or pressured. He would really look at her work, take her seriously, notice the details she was most proud of.

But by then she'd found something she liked: a job teaching art at a charter school in Queens.

The pay was okay, no benefits, but Ben has good health insurance. She adored her students. Teaching was fun. But she didn't love the subway commute, or the paperwork, or fighting the administration for every crayon. Her getting laid off and getting pregnant was a chicken-and-egg situation. Both things happened at once.

Someday she'll go back to teaching, but for now she likes the idea of staying home, taking care of the baby when it comes, reading books she's always wanted to read, maybe painting a little.

At her going-away party, the other teachers hugged her and said she could try to come back as soon as she got tired of being cooped up in the house with the baby. The moms said that. The others said "We're so happy for you."

The baby is due in early January. A New Year's present, said Dr. Snyder.

Ben has been bored at work lately. No interesting projects have come in. He's admitted to wasting a lot of time online, checking out home rentals and real estate in places where they will never move. As internet addictions go, it seems harmless, even sweet. He's fantasizing about their future, about places their little family might live.

They've talked about moving to the country after the baby is born. Their Upper West Side apartment is spacious and sunny, but it's a sixth-floor walk-up, and Emma can't see herself lugging a stroller up and down the stairs. Moving will make life easier, and they can afford it.

They could find a larger, nicer place in the city, with an elevator. But the country will be a clean break. Something new. Light and air and sun. Vegetables from the garden.

Ben can work half the time from home, on the computer, at least until a new project gets going. For now he can get away with spending a few days a week in the city. They'll keep their city place, and Emma will go into town for medical appointments.

She'll stay at their apartment during the last weeks of her pregnancy.

It will be an experiment. They can always move back to Manhattan. But what if the city turns its back on them? It's happened to people they know. No one and nothing, not even a city, likes being left.

Until now, the move to the country had always been a vague *what if.* But that's all changed.

Ben has found the house. Online.

Emma hasn't seen him this excited and happy since the night she told him she was pregnant. They'd called out for Chinese food, which they ate in bed. They watched *The Maltese Falcon* and hugged each other and laughed until two in the morning.

"I've only seen the house listing online, but Emma, it's beautiful. It's not just a house. It's a mansion. Eleven thousand square feet."

Ben's so fired up, it's warming the air

between them. She can't help remembering that night he told her about the Piaf play. His eyes glittered then, too. It's as if he's looking into a crystal ball, seeing the future. Their future.

"It's twenty miles from Luxor, one of those ghost towns in Sullivan County. The house has been empty for more than a year, since the death of the last of three ancient sibling hermits who let the place fall down around them."

"Okay, that's creepy," Emma says.

"I know," says Ben. "But listen. It gets better. Before the hermits, it was a rest home and dry-out clinic for actors and actresses, directors and producers, Broadway stars who'd had nervous breakdowns or were drinking themselves to death. Rehab, we'd say now. One of the photos in the listing . . . Emma, *there's a theater,* a half-ruined abandoned theater, *inside the house.* The residents put on plays to amuse themselves and speed their recovery."

"Is *that* in the listing?"

Ben hesitates, just a beat. "No . . . I figured it out. Why else would they have a private theater?"

"Our own theater . . ." Emma tries to imagine it. A scene from a Russian movie . . . red velvet curtains . . .

21

"So, I called the Realtor." Ben pauses, maybe to see if Emma's annoyed that he's taken things this far without consulting her. Actually, it's fine with her. A phone call doesn't mean much, and she's been preoccupied lately.

According to Ben, the Realtor admitted that the house has a *kinda dark backstory?* That's why it's such a *fabulous* deal, plus the fact that, *well, frankly, to be honest . . .* the place needs serious work?

Ben makes a silly face when he imitates the Realtor's Valley Girl upspeak.

"She actually said, 'Bring your architect!' She sounded like a twelve-year-old. Everything was a question. Not the sharpest crayon in the box. But Emma . . . our own theater. How amazing is that?"

Ben orders coffee, Emma asks for peppermint tea, and as they wait for their drinks to arrive, Ben keeps imitating the squeaky-voiced Realtor. "Okay, I'll be honest? I mean . . . you'll find out sooner or later? My company could get, like, sued if you, like, have a problem?"

Ben is still an actor at heart. For a moment he *is* the girl Realtor. Emma blinks. He's Ben again.

"Find *what* out?" The waiter brings Ben's coffee and Emma's tea. She stirs a half teaspoon of sugar into it, then, guiltily, a half teaspoon more.

Ben says, "When the doctor who ran the show-biz rehab clinic died — his wife passed away some years before — the house went to his nephews and niece, two brothers and a sister, one whose face had been burned off in a fire. Each one crazier than the next. The siblings lived there, and, one by one, died there. Nobody knows what went on in that house, but it was definitely dark."

The Realtor — Lindsay something, Ben has forgotten her last name — said she was *not* going to speculate. "Like maybe there are bodies buried in the cellar?"

"Let me get this straight," Emma says. "She was trying to *sell* this house?"

Ben laughs. How handsome he looks in the golden light.

"Maybe she was joking," he says. "Or covering her ass."

The house has been on the market awhile. It's cheap, it's a deal. But it's a project. More than likely, a gut renovation. Lindsay had shown it "maybe twice."

"In other words, never. Not once. No one will go near the house. No one but us."

Emma thinks, *It's crazy, all right.* But as Ben talks, she can feel her resistance fading away. It's so important to him, and she does

23

want to see the house. At least take a look. Maybe this could be great. A challenge, that's for sure. Mostly she just likes the sound of Ben saying *No one but us.*

"I kind of love the idea of it," she says.

Who wouldn't? Most people wouldn't. She and Ben would.

"A house with a theater," she says. "It's so . . . romantic. So nuts. It'd be so *like us.*"

"Exactly," Ben says.

He orders a grappa that Emma covets. Well, maybe just a drop on her lips, for old times' sake.

He goes on about the house and its history. The light in his eyes is the same light that Emma feels shining in hers, or is hers a reflection of his? It really *is* a terrible idea. But it might be a dare they have to take. They'd be daring themselves and each other. And the whole logical, sensible world.

Ben takes out his phone, scrolls till he finds the listing, and hands it to Emma.

Emma swipes through the photos. "It looks like a set for a low-budget production of *The Phantom of the Opera.*"

"Crazy," said Ben. "Am I right?"

Everything that might keep a sane person from considering the project is precisely what attracts them. The crazy idea makes them happy, grateful they've found each other. It's partly why Ben loves her, and Emma wants him to love her. She needs him to love her and the baby. She's read about men who feel excluded from the close bond between a mother and child. She doesn't want that to happen to them. She feels certain — fairly certain — that it won't.

The lights dim, sparklers blaze, the waiters sing. Emma's forgotten this part. The surprise cake. But it was inevitable. Embarrassing, but fine.

Ben joins in. He can actually sing. Happy birthday, dear Emma. He grins at her, his eyes bright with love. Emma feels it all through her body. No one tells you that pregnancy will shoot you up with weird aphrodisiac hormones.

"I love you," says Emma. "Let's check out the house. How soon can we go see it?"

Chapter Two:
House-Hunting

June

Rounding a sharp curve, Ben clutches the steering wheel, and Emma sees, through a clearing in the woods, a girl standing in a field.

She's knee-deep in the wild grasses, near enough for Emma to see but too far away to see clearly. A few trees with yellow-green leaves fringe Emma's view. The girl's face comes in and out of focus. Emma probably wouldn't have noticed her if Ben wasn't going so slowly around the corkscrew curves in the rutted driveway.

A baby straddles the girl's hip. Seven months old? Eight? Emma's been paying closer attention to babies lately, but she can't always tell. Something about the way the girl stands — feet apart, hips swayed back — reminds her of Depression-era photos, those hollow-eyed moms and kids. The girl's pale hair is lanky, ragged. Her shapeless white dress glows with a ghostly sheen. Her age is hard to tell: maybe a womanly thirteen, maybe a childish twenty.

Their eyes meet across the distance. They see each other: Emma knows it. Even the baby seems to be staring at Emma, or maybe just at the moving car. Emma's read that babies can't see very far. But somehow she is sure that this one can.

The road turns, and when it turns back again, the girl has disappeared.

The car skids on a slick of mud, and they come heart-stoppingly close to running into a gigantic oak, growing right by the side of the road, directly on a curve. The branches overhang the blacktop, and the gnarled burls overhang the edge of the roadside.

Emma says, "What an amazing tree!"

Ben says, "That amazing tree almost killed us."

It would be easy to miss the curve and hit the oak. Really easy in winter. It seems like a bad sign. The road doesn't want them driving up it. The tree is blocking their way. Emma thinks of saying that to Ben, but she hesitates, knowing he'd say she was being irrational.

She can't help herself. "Do you think this driveway is a bad sign? Like maybe the house doesn't want us here?"

27

"Of course the house wants us," says Ben. "It knows we've come to save it."

How did the girl and the baby get here? There's not another car anywhere around. The only way in or out is along this driveway. There are no neighbors, no one — according to Ben — for miles.

Another sharp curve in the road pitches Emma against Ben's shoulder.

He puts his arm around her, then slips it out from behind her back and puts that hand back on the wheel.

"Easy," he says. "Hold on. Be careful."

"I . . . don't know," she says. "Are you . . . sure about this?"

"Our own theater, remember?" says Ben. "Anyhow, we're just looking, right?"

They're here to look at a house. Emma needs to pay attention. Forget the girl and the baby.

They're just looking.

All the way up from the city, Emma and Ben have been so anxious it's made them giddy. It's partly because they suspect that buying this house would be a giant mistake. It *is* cheap, but it needs a ton of work, and they know there's always more work than you expect. All that square footage and fifty acres in the middle of nowhere. That's prob-

ably why they've been entertaining themselves by trying to remember every film
about a happy urban family who buys a
country house with an evil past, vengeful
spirits bleeding through the walls, and a
dead girl inside the TV. It turns out they've
seen a lot of them, if they think back far
enough.

"*The Amityville Horror*," says Emma.

"Does *The Exorcist* count?"

"That's not a haunted house, it's a demon
girl."

"Worse," Ben says. "You can get the
demon out of the kid, but you can't get the
blood out of the walls —"

"It can be done," says Emma. "But it's
harder. You need a specialist exorcist."

She loves it that they can still amuse each
other, even if their laughs sound a little hollow. A little forced. Well, sure.

The traffic on Route 17 clears up, the
stores and strip malls thin, and they're on
the road, in open country. There are trees
to look at! It's beautiful! They're in nature!

In the silence that falls, Emma is somehow
sure they are both thinking the same thing.

Buying the house would be a giant mistake. But there's something weirdly sexy
about making a giant mistake together. So
what if Emma is pregnant? It's as if they're

driving off a cliff, hand in hand, like two lemmings, like Thelma and Louise.

They have enough money. If they hate it here they can flip the house and go back to the city. They would never admit this, but now that they are . . . comfortable, they need to believe they are still the brave young couple who met and fell in love. The slightly edgy rebels. Or maybe Emma needs to *pretend* to believe it. She needs to pretend for Ben's sake, and sometimes for her own, that having a baby won't change her from a person into a mom.

Pregnancy has already changed her. She's more fearful than she used to be. Also, more superstitious. She notices black cats, doesn't walk under ladders, throws salt over her shoulder. Will she teach her child to be suspcious? It seems like bad luck to imagine that far into the future. Sometimes, like now, she *can't* imagine. She just can't picture how it will feel: another person with them in the car.

Ben says, "I'd love to see *The Shining* again, wouldn't you? Let's see if we can stream it. We could watch it in bed. Like the old days."

Old days? It hasn't been so long. Things only changed when Emma got pregnant and sleepy. So far Ben has been sweet about tell-

30

ing her, in the morning, what she slept through. But *The Shining*? *Now?* When they're thinking about buying a house in the middle of nowhere? Ben's got to be kidding.

Emma says, "This might not be the ideal moment to watch a family moving into a giant house —"

"Hotel."

"Fine. A giant hotel that drives the dad so crazy he tries to axe-murder his wife and kid."

"Sorry," says Ben. "I thought —"

"Plus. it's terrifying. I'm not sure the adrenaline would be great for the baby."

"Forget it," says Ben. "It was just an idea. There's other stuff we could watch." He sounds so disappointed. And surprised.

"No, we could watch it. We could, Ben. We could watch *The Shining* . . . I didn't mean . . ."

This is exactly what she didn't want to become, didn't want to sound like: the cool person Ben married transformed into a quivering, pregnant wreck. Anyhow, she and Ben have watched *The Shining* a half dozen times. She wouldn't want to watch it even if she wasn't pregnant.

"Never mind," says Ben. "We don't have to watch the goddamn *Shining.*"

31

Emma wants a do-over. Can't they go back to joking about *The Exorcist*?

"Sorry, Emma. This driveway is a bitch. We're going to have to get someone to plow this in the winter."

He sounds as if they've already decided to buy the house. Was that another thing Emma missed?

The driveway *is* scary. Emma tells herself to stay focused. It's as if she needs to keep them on the road by the sheer power of her concentration.

How did the girl and the baby get there? And how did they disappear?

"Who was that?" Emma says.

"Who was what?" Ben is an excellent driver. Calm. It's one of the things Emma loves about him. She hopes all this bouncing around isn't harmful for the baby. She knows better than to say that.

"We'd need four-wheel drive," he says. "Or a pickup truck. A pickup! Finally!" He takes one hand off the wheel and fist-pumps the air.

Finally? How could Emma not have known about his secret desire for a pickup? Maybe every man has it, like a late-onset gene. Don't ask where they'll put a baby in a pickup truck.

"Didn't you see her?" Emma says.

"I saw us not slamming into that tree."

"A girl and a baby were standing out in the field."

"Now you're scaring me, honey," says Ben. "There was no girl. No baby. There couldn't be. We're beyond the middle of nowhere. You could scream and nobody would hear you. Joke. You do realize you dozed off for a few minutes?"

She's been doing that lately. Taking little catnaps. Her eyes get so heavy they close on their own. Dr. Snyder has reassured her that being tired is normal. Plus, she's given up coffee.

Another curve, then another. It seems unlikely that she could sleep through *this*. Could pregnancy make you hallucinate? That must be way down the list of symptoms. She'll google it later, even though she swore to stop googling every twinge.

There's probably no internet service out here: another serious problem. Did Ben even ask the Realtor what fixing *that* would involve?

As soon as the driveway straightens out, Ben takes his hand off the wheel and reaches across the console and takes Emma's hand. She loves it when he does that, loves that he's still doing that after five years of marriage, and now with her being pregnant and their maybe buying a house, settling down and growing up in all the ways they swore they never would.

Before Ben decided that social media was a huge distraction and waste of time and closed all his accounts, his Twitter handle was PeterPan87. The house is part of that. Fixing up a huge old house is a young person thing. A never-grow-old thing. Ben's three years older than she is. They're on the cusp of middle age.

Ben likes the house's dark, theater-connected history. He's talked about it almost nonstop since Emma's birthday dinner. Despite the wife, the baby on the way, their newly easy life, it makes him think he's still a pioneer, a bad-boy rebel. He still has the vision, the energy — the balls — to make this happen, to take a weird piece of theater history and make it his own.

Fixing up the house would be the opposite of why most people move to the country — for peace and quiet. He wants things to be *less* peaceful, more complicated. As if a new baby won't make it complicated enough. He wants the most difficult, magical thing. A haunted mansion with its own theater.

Emma wants to be comfortable and safe. But despite the inconvenience and the risk of a major renovation, the idea of the house is exciting.

She's never stopped being interested in Ben, in how his mind works. In his Don Quixote pie-in-the-sky *maleness,* to which she feels a little superior, a little more . . . grounded. But she loves the feeling of surrender, of seeing where something takes her. It's a little like sex. She trusts Ben. She loves him.

They are in this together.

One last turn and there it is, a gigantic three-story Victorian hunting lodge with a sweeping tiled roof and four triangular turrets, one on each corner. Dusty mullioned windows line the facade. In front of the house is a huge porch that curls around, above a foundation wall of rounded river stones, practically boulders. The house goes on forever with its slightly serpentine curves.

"Can you believe this? Are you seeing what I'm seeing? That's what *I'm* talking about," says Ben.

"Why are you whispering?" says Emma.

The house is much larger and grander than in the photos. It could be magnificent. It *is* magnificent.

Ben says, "We agreed. If we don't like it,

35

we fix it up, flip it. Kaching. It's an investment."

A tree has fallen through the porch roof and crashed onto the floor. Emma sees that, and at the same time she sees what the house could be. What the house is now.

For a moment she has the strangest thought: She's glad her parents and Ben's are gone. Buying this house is exactly the sort of thing your parents tell you not to do.

And they'd probably be right.

Is it bad luck to think that?

Just because she's pregnant doesn't mean she isn't brave. Her parents got that wrong. Maybe she wasn't brave enough to hear some snotty art-gallery intern enjoy telling her that the gallery wasn't showing work like hers, but she's brave enough to move into a haunted wreck in the middle of nowhere.

Minutes after they arrive, Lindsay — Emma assumes it's Lindsay — drives up in a new Prius. Slight and doll-like, with blond blown-out curls, Lindsay slides out of the car. Her filmy, short, flowered summer dress hikes up over her perfect tanned legs.

She looks like a dandelion, thinks Emma, but a dandelion with a steel stem. Where does that thought come from? Why is Emma

36

feeling mean-spirited? It's not like her to distrust another woman just because she's young and pretty.

Halfway through her long, vigorous bony handshake, Lindsay catches Emma looking at the hiking boots that only a young person with great legs could get away with. How did Emma expect a country Realtor to dress? Like a weather forecaster at a local TV station.

"I'm so glad you guys are wearing sneakers," Lindsay says. "I meant to tell your husband, but I forgot? God knows what you'll find. Mud. Raccoon poo. I know I don't sound like a Realtor? But I believe in honesty. Saves everyone trouble in the long run, right?"

Her voice matches Ben's imitation, though not as high and reedy, and she speaks in sentences, not questions. Okay, half sentences, half questions.

Lindsay flashes them a winning smile: a country girl trying to please. Emma and Ben try to make their faces do something appropriate.

They appreciate her being up-front about the house's problems. They believe in honesty too.

"The house is a train wreck, but a super-cool train wreck. Ridiculously beautiful if you like that grand-hotel/haunted-mansion horror-film kind of thing. Like, you know, *The Shining*. The scariest movie ever, right?"

"That's such a coincidence," Ben says. "Emma and I were just talking about *The Shining*."

"Scariest movie ever? Nightmares for weeks? All right then," Lindsay says. "I told your husband the background stuff, some anyway."

"He told me," Emma says. "Thanks."

"So, okay, we're all on board here? You can see what *is* there. And what isn't. Can I be totally honest?"

Ben and Emma nod. How can they say no?

"Add seventy-five thousand onto whatever renovations you might be thinking. I'll let you guys do the walk-through without me. I know it's not like TV shows where the Realtor trails the couple, telling the camera how hard it is to make two people agree when one wants modern and one wants vintage, and the wife wants the double sink."

Emma says, more sharply than she means, "This is not about a double sink."

"Oh, no. Gosh, I didn't mean you. You guys are way too cool for that. Just be careful. We *really* don't want anyone, like, falling through a floor?"

38

Emma says, "I'll be careful. I'm pregnant." Why did she say that? Maybe because it seems like something you say when you're house-hunting. You're not just buying a home for yourselves but for a growing family.

"I know you are. That's so great."

"You know?" Emma doesn't show all that much under her baggy lightweight hoodie, but she looks down at her belly as if to make sure.

"Your husband told me on the phone. He's so proud and excited."

Emma's supposed to smile and not be annoyed at Ben for blabbing their personal information to a stranger. She's supposed to be proud that Ben is proud. And besides, Emma just blabbed it before she knew that Ben already had.

"Then you guys need to be extra careful. Don't trip over anything. Really."

"We'll be cool," promises Ben.

"Go for it," Lindsay says. "Take as long as you like." She's talking to Ben, in a low voice, as if she's talking about sex and not a house tour. Take as long as you like. Corny, but whatever. Let her flirt with Ben. Lots of women do. He's a rich producer, and he's good-looking, though maybe not what a girl like Lindsay would think is movie-star hot.

39

If they move here, they will never have to see her after the closing.

Ben grips Emma's elbow as they walk up the front stairs. They step lightly across the half-ruined veranda. By the time Ben unlocks the front door with the key he'd gotten from Lindsay (a good sign, the house hasn't been standing open), they feel fairly sure that the floors won't collapse, though the fallen-in porch roof doesn't inspire trust.

It's like a house in a dream. In fact, it *is* the house in a recurring dream Emma has every so often. The houses in her dreams are always different, yet she knows she's been there before. The rooms ramble on, long corridors open up into vast domed spaces, like the naves of churches, then into rooms like wood-paneled saunas, then into modern rooms with dazzling light.

"I've dreamed about this house," Ben says.

"Me too." Emma can't remember if she ever told him that. She tries not to tell him her dreams. She doesn't want to bore him.

Unlike the shadowy house in her dreams, the real house is surprisingly light inside. The thick dust glimmers, motes sparkle in the air. In the front hall a double staircase spirals up to the second floor, creating a huge violin-shaped space beneath a leaded glass skylight, high above.

40

"Jesus," says Ben. "It's the freaking Borromini Chapel."

Ben's told Emma about the Church of Sant'Ivo, the seventeenth-century architectural wonder in Rome. In fact, he's told her so often she feels as if she's been there. She knows that its beehive space makes you feel as if your soul is being sucked upward out of your body.

"Better than Borromini," says Ben. "That skylight looks like it's in good shape."

"This is so beautiful," says Emma.

Ben says, "I should be checking for water damage, but I have to say, I'm sold."

Emma says, "Let's assume there's major work. That way we won't be surprised." She's imagining living here. They haven't even gone past the front hall. But she gets it. She sees it. She's been here in a dream. If not exactly here, then someplace like it.

The theater is as big as a ballroom. The floor is polished dark wood. A chandelier with half its crystals missing tinkles like wind chimes in the draft.

On one end of the room is a stage, behind which is a theater set, painted with topiary trees, flower beds, and statues, like a French garden, like the grounds of a royal palace. There are several uneven rows of folding

41

chairs, and more chairs stacked against one wall.

Ben bends over and grabs his knees as if he's out of breath. Then he stands up and says, "Emma, I'm blown away. Who has a theater in their house? I'll bet there's no place like this in the world. And this is happening. To us. It's real. We could have it."

Emma's *never* heard him sound like this, not even when he told her about the Piaf play.

The walls are bright red, pocked with white plaster splotches. There is a row of sconces just above eye level, ceramic hands holding glass globes made to look like flames.

Emma says, "Look! The Beast's palace."

In Cocteau's film, *Beauty and the Beast,* Beauty arrives in the Beast's palace and finds herself in a corridor lit by disembodied hands holding candelabras. Emma and Ben streamed the film, on Ben's laptop, in bed, soon after they moved in together. Neither remembers who persuaded the other to see it. They agreed it was like having the same dream: a woman, a beast, a hall lit by disembodied hands.

"We'll both be Beast," Ben says now.

"We'll be Beauty," Emma says.

"You will." Ben takes her hand.

42

Down the hall is the pantry, long and deep, shelves interrupted by high rectangular windows.

Ben says, "It's like some postapocalyptic *Downton Abbey*."

"*Remains of the Day* meets *Blade Runner*," Emma says.

Painted battleship gray, the cupboards are filled with crockery, bowls and vases, platters large enough for Thanksgiving turkeys. Emma's afraid to pick anything up, or even look closer. But she can see that it's all beautiful china from the forties and fifties.

There's a store in their neighborhood that sells stuff like this, in large lots, sometimes in barrels, but expensive. And here it is, a houseful. The real thing, untouched.

"Do those dishes come with the house?" Emma's voice is shaking with desire.

"We can ask," says Ben. "Look. A fifty-year-old can of tomatoes."

"Botulism," says Emma.

"We can Botox each other," says Ben. "And stay young forever."

"Two vampires," says Emma. "The Addams Family. Morticia and what's-his-name."

"Gomez. You know that, Emma. I know you know that."

"I used to," Emma says with a shrug. Did

43

she? Did she ever?

They walk through the pantry into the kitchen.

The first thing — the only thing — Emma sees is the vintage stove.

It's enamel, the beautiful, pale toothpaste-green color that kitchens used to be. There are four gas burners and two ovens with beautiful chrome handles.

Once, after Emma had dropped out of art school and was waitressing and moving from cheap apartments to cheaper apartments, she saw, in an antique shop, a stove from the 1930s.

Of course, she couldn't buy it then. She didn't have the money even if she'd had a real kitchen or a permanent place to live. But she's longed for it ever since.

When she pictured a life in the country, she imagined cooking on that stove. It's still one of her most cherished and comforting fantasies, whenever she lets her mind wander to something guaranteed to calm her and cheer her up.

And here it is. The stove she'd fallen in love with all those years ago. Maybe she dreamed about houses like this, but this is the actual stove of her dreams.

Did she tell Ben? She can't remember. Pregnancy's playing wicked tricks on her memory. Does Ben understand the crazy coincidence? He's glancing around the kitchen. She can't catch his eye.

"The stove!" she says. "Did I ever tell you how I saw one just like it, years ago? Do you realize how amazing this is?"

Ben's hardly listening. "The stove? I wonder if it still works."

He doesn't know. She *didn't* tell him. It *is* a crazy coincidence. She doesn't want to tell him now. She doesn't want him to think she's the kind of person who falls in love with a stove. Question: Who buys a house because of a stove? Answer: Emma.

"It's a beauty," he says. "But let's leave it open whether we want to keep it or maybe get a brand-new Viking."

"I want that one," Emma says.

"Okay, fine," says Ben. "Then that's the stove we'll have."

She flips the light switch, and a neon coil stutters on, over the table. The light buzzes, and so does the giant housefly that flings itself against the bulb until it drops onto the peeling linoleum floor.

"This place is a train wreck. Lindsay was honest, all right."

"Easily fixed," Ben says. "Cosmetic. The structural stuff is what —"

"Even the structural stuff can be fixed."

45

They're daring each other to go for it, rise to the challenge, take the bait of the house.

Emma says, "This place is too beautiful to let go. A *theater,* Ben." She imagines their kids, their future kids and their kids' future friends, putting on plays for their proud parents.

Let's go upstairs. She imagines saying that on warm summer nights after they've eaten the wonderful meal they cooked in this kitchen. The baby will be asleep. They'll finish their wine and go up the staircase hand in hand and go to bed and . . . what? Lately she sometimes fears that Ben is losing interest in her. He wants her less often than she wants him. Supposedly Elvis Presley never had sex with Priscilla after she got pregnant with Lisa Marie.

Laughing, they separate and each take a different side of the staircase and meet on the landing above. They walk along the corridor as if they're expecting something to jump out at them and say *boo.* Some of the bedrooms are very small and furnished with metal cots and ripped mattresses spewing stuffing. Stained lace doilies are draped over the bedstands.

One of the bedrooms is palatial, with a soaring ceiling and tall French doors looking out the back of the house, onto a field

46

with a view of the Catskills. The doors open onto a balcony.

"The master," says Ben.

"Got that."

"Waking up here . . . Imagine . . ."

"I know. Though we'd better get the porch checked for structural damage."

"We will," Ben says. "Meanwhile, the baby will have twelve bedrooms to choose from."

"I was thinking we'd put it in the one right next to ours."

"Duh-uh. I was joking. Promise me you won't lose your sense of humor when you become a mom. I've seen it happen to women who used to be funny and then . . ."

Not me! Emma wants to say. But why should she reassure Ben? He should be reassuring *her.*

Emma says, "You do know that moving here would be insane with the baby coming and —"

Ben's already in the hall. "Watch out." He opens a trapdoor in the hall ceiling and grabs the pull-down stairs that lead up to the attic.

Emma is proud of how strong he is. And how considerate. When the trapdoor releases a dust cloud, he tells her to stand back.

Ben says, "Are you sure you want to go up there? It could be nasty."

47

"I'm sure."

He turns and helps her follow him up.

Bands of light filter in through the windows of the cavernous attic. Everywhere there are overflowing cardboard boxes, piles of boots encrusted with dried mud, belts and gloves white with mildew, broken furniture, sweaters chewed into lace, buttons, hair clips, ribbons, bottles with illegible labels, tennis rackets, bowling balls, garden tools, ancient telephones. Emma would have expected the smell to be awful, but it's pleasant. Like a combination of moth balls, maple syrup, and furniture polish. She feels like the first explorer who discovered the early cave paintings. It's like an archaeological dig. Like excavating the remnants of a vanished civilization.

A pigeon dives at them, its wings beating like helicopter blades, so sudden and violent that Emma jumps.

"Don't be scared, Little Person," Emma whispers.

Little Person. That's how she thinks of the baby.

She and Ben haven't decided if they want to know the baby's gender. She secretly hopes for a girl. She wants to teach a girl whatever she's learned about being one.

Maybe part of the reason they're delaying

learning if the baby's a boy or a girl has something to do with the fact that they've been fighting — well, fun-fighting — about names. They can't agree. If it's a girl, Emma wants to call her Iris, after her favorite flower. If it's a boy, she wants to call him Henry. Ben wants to call a girl Ruby. And call a boy Sam. Emma can give in on Sam. That was Ben's dad's name. But she's holding firm on Iris.

"Don't be afraid, Little Person. It's just a bird," she says now.

"It's just meningitis," Ben says. "Isn't that what pigeons carry?"

That sounds like something *she* would have said, and Ben would have called her neurotic. She's learned to watch what she says to avoid his gentle but still crushing disappointment. "That's what I was wondering. About pigeons."

Ben says, "It's nuts here, right?"

"It used to be a mental hospital," says Emma.

"A celebrity dry-out clinic isn't exactly a mental hospital."

Emma looks around at the boxes of . . . things. *Dry-out clinic. Rehab.* The word that comes to mind is *asylum.*

The attic would terrify a child — and upset most adults. Pigeons, mice, rabid bats,

49

for all she knows. Even a toddler, too young to understand that all this was left by people who lived and maybe died here, would sense the terrible sadness.

Yet something makes Emma want to own it. She wants it to be hers. She wants to come up here whenever she likes. She wants to be alone here, to explore, to find out what secrets the attic is keeping. The attic is the essence of everything that attracts her about the house and everything that scares her.

It's warmer up here. The stifling air doesn't move. Emma feels her eyelids get heavy. She has to stop taking these catnaps. She needs to ask Dr. Snyder if there's something harmless she can take to help her stay awake. She doubts whether there is. Anything like that would affect the baby.

She's asleep on and off all day and awake at night. Some nights she doesn't sleep at all. Some nights she wanders into the living room and lies on the couch and cries. Why? She doesn't know. It's as if she's scared of something besides the birth.

Something that hasn't yet happened.

Something about to happen.

Ben says, "We could open a vintage shop. Help pay off the mortgage."

"I thought we were paying cash."

"Jo-oke."

50

"Sorry. I keep missing the punch line."

"Don't apologize, Emma. This whole insane project is my idea."

"It's both of ours. You know that."

Emma's attention has drifted to a box of letters and journals. Whatever these people wrote has been waiting for her to read it. If only she could take it with her now. In case they decide against the house, she could still read them. What if the place is bought by someone who tosses it all in a dumpster?

Emma can't steal the box. Ben would have to help, and she'd have to sneak it past Lindsay. Emma looks out the window. Standing on the weedy lawn, Lindsay is slapping at something that must be biting her bare legs. As if she senses that she's being watched, she raises her eyes to meet Emma's, and Emma thinks about the blond girl with the baby in the field.

Leave this place, Emma thinks.

Run as fast as you can.

And at the exact same time she thinks: *This is where you belong.*

She wants these journals and papers. She wants to spend time here, waiting for the baby, dreaming about the future, seeing into the past. She wants to cook on that stove.

In a horror film, this would be where the young couple buys the old house, and within twenty minutes the ceiling is dripping blood and the walls are squirming like sacks of jumping beans. . . .

"Earth to Emma," says Ben.

"I want it, I do, but I don't know . . . Look around, Ben. It's a lot."

Ben says, "It's not like we're going to be passing this stuff hand to hand and tossing it out the window into a dumpster. There must be lots of guys around here could use a construction job . . ."

The good news and the bad news are the same. It's a bad idea. And they want the house.

Ben backs down the ladder and tenderly helps Emma follow.

He says, "Do we want to see the theater again?"

"No," says Emma. "I don't want to see it unless it's ours."

They agree not to seem too excited. They can probably negotiate the price even lower.

But when Lindsay greets them on the lawn and asks how they liked the house, Ben and Emma say, at the same time, "Amazing." They're supposed to say, "Well . . . we don't know."

But they do know. Lindsay can tell.

Ben says, "I guess it does need a little work." Emma laughs. Lindsay doesn't.

"*How* close are the nearest neighbors?" Emma asks. Ben said miles.

"Miles," Lindsay says. "Miles and miles."

Emma takes a deep breath. "This strange thing happened, when we were driving here. I saw a blond girl, a teenager maybe, holding a baby on her hip. She was standing in the field."

Lindsay furrows her brow and makes an intense show of thinking but comes up empty. Mystified. She looks at Ben. Did he see the girl? Ben shakes his head and shrugs. It annoys Emma: He's throwing her under the bus. But he didn't see the girl, so why should he say he did?

"I don't know who that could have been," Lindsay says. "I haven't seen anyone like that anywhere near here. Sometimes the heat and humidity make everything kind of shimmery and weird? Sometimes the shadows do strange things. One day I thought I saw a billion frogs hopping on the road? I stopped and got out. And guess what?"

Does she really mean for them to guess?

"What?" says Ben politely.

"There were no frogs on the road."

Emma saw a girl in a field, not a frog on the road. A silence falls.

"Well, then," Lindsay says. "Why don't we continue this conversation in my office?"

Lindsay gets in her Prius and drives off, and they follow. Lindsay drives slowly, checking her rearview mirror.

Any second thoughts vanish as Emma turns to see the house disappear, and Ben watches it shrink in the rearview mirror. They can't stand to leave it. They can't bear it that the house isn't theirs. They hate to think they might lose it. It will become the lost paradise that will haunt Emma's dreams. It's their house. They're meant to live here. The rising Broadway producer and his family were destined to live in this place where Broadway stars came to make their lights shine brightly again.

Lindsay works with her parents. Her mom, Sally — glasses, curly gray hair — is the receptionist. Ted, Lindsay's dad, has the ghost-town-Realtor version of the corner office. Obviously, their workplace doesn't get lots of traffic. Ted and Sally are thrilled to meet Ben and Emma. According to Lindsay's dad, he and "Mother" knew it would take adventurous, creative young folks like Emma and Ben to see the potential of Hideaway Home.

Ted does a funny thing with his hands, every so often wiping them on his pants, like a tic.

"Hideaway Home?" says Emma. If Ben ever calls her Mother, the marriage is over.

"That's what the doctor named it. And maybe the three . . . seniors who inherited it called it that, if they called it anything. Anyhow, that's why we turned Hideaway Home over to Baby Girl. Mother and I figured she'd connect with young people like yourselves."

"Hideaway Home?" repeats Emma.

"It was still a rest home when I was a kid. The locals went on calling it that when the . . . elderly siblings took over. Seeing as those three Looney Tunes were *really* hiding away. Hiding *out.* Didn't you tell them, Lindsay?"

"Sure, Dad. I've got a real estate license, remember? I didn't want to scare them off, but I knew they'd find out. Like they just *did.* Da-a-a-d."

"And then it sat empty for a while. Kids used to go there to party, including Baby Girl —"

"I never partied there," Lindsay says petulantly. "No one ever partied there. That's *his* fantasy."

"Have it your way, Baby Girl. So what do you two think? Ben? Emma?"

"It's . . . a project." Emma is talking to Ted but looking at Ben.

"I have a gut feeling you guys are up to it. Up *for* it," Lindsay's father tells Ben. "Listen . . . I know this is off the subject, but . . . can I ask what mileage you get on your Volvo?"

"Twenty on the road, less in traffic."

"That's why we got Baby Girl the Prius. Save the planet for her kids and their kids. When and if she has kids. Well, anyway, nice to meet you. It's a special property. You won't see anything like it again. And . . ." He pauses for drama. "It's a once-in-a-lifetime deal."

Lindsay's office smells mildly of carpet rot. It's furnished with office-supply store furniture. An unobstructed view of the parking lot. Poor thing. Lindsay probably didn't imagine herself working for her dad. How does Emma know? Maybe that was Lindsay's lifelong ambition.

"So what are we thinking?" says Lindsay. "Full disclosure." She holds up her right hand. "I was going to say 'Girl Scout's honor,' but they're making the Scouts gender-neutral. It's 'Scout's honor' from now on. Did you guys know that?"

Ben laughs. He's either charmed or faking it, Emma can't tell. "Scout's honor, then."

Emma says, "I think I read about the Scouts thing . . ."

"Of course you did," says Lindsay. Is this *child* patronizing her? Emma lets it go. If they want this to work smoothly, they'll need to keep it cordial with Baby Girl.

"Scout's honor, then." Emma gazes out at the empty lot.

Lindsay says, "I kind of like the view? In case there's an active shooter?"

"What?" says Emma.

"Jo-king." Lindsay directs this at Ben, which makes Emma want to kill her. "Excuse me a sec, I need to go to the ladies'. Unless you want to go first, Emma?" She looks at Emma's belly and beyond it, presumably, at her bladder.

"I'm fine, thanks."

Ben takes one of the uncomfortable chairs while Emma looks around. The only personal items in the room are a scatter of framed photos — snapshots of Lindsay by the ocean or on a ski slope or in a national park with her parents and a boy who — from picture to picture — grows up into her tall blond brother, always out of focus, scowling, turned away from the camera.

Several pictures show Lindsay kissing a dark-haired young woman, or the two of them leaning close, romantically, in front of various scenic red rocks and waterfalls. The happiness on Lindsay's face in those photos

57

makes Emma like her more, even when Lindsay returns and announces, "This is your lucky day!"

Being told it's your lucky day is almost as bad as being told to relax.

"I checked my texts and found one from a high school friend who's come back to town and started a construction company. Usually they do high-end period home renovations and luxury homes, but they've been stiffed on a job that was supposed to take them through the summer. By now all the fat jobs have gone to their competitors. All that's left is building decks for crappy aboveground pools.

"This guy is the answer to all your problems. I mean, like . . . the problems you'd have if you bought the house? The problems you *won't* have if you hire him. He can make it happen, and it won't cost you an arm and a leg. Where does *that* expression come from?"

Lindsay's gaze drifts toward the window. Emma wonders if she's high. That's Lindsay's business. As long as she's together enough to broker a deal and a contract. Maybe she's nervous. She can't have been in this business long. Maybe this is her first real sale.

"Sorry about the aboveground-pool

crack," says Lindsay. "I don't want to sound like a snob. These are my people up here."

"No worries," Ben says, a phrase Emma has never heard him use. In fact, they've talked about people who say "No worries." They hate it. Everyone worries.

"I could get them to do an inspection report. Up here the contractors double as home inspectors. It's probably not by-the-books legal, but that's what we're looking at unless you wait months for some dude from Middletown to make it out here when he's got other jobs in the area."

"The local guy would be fine," says Ben.

"Should we discuss the price?" Lindsay says.

"Not if we can get it for around three hundred," Ben says. The asking price is four hundred thousand. "Then no discussion needed."

"That's a big knockdown," says Lindsay. "Like, a *historic reduction?*"

"It's a project," Ben says. "I assume the bank owns it. I'll bet the bank wants it off their hands."

"You married a smart guy," Lindsay tells Emma.

Emma smiles and shrugs. Might as well be pleasant.

Lindsay says, "It can't hurt to ask. I'll

check it out. Stay tuned. I'll call you guys tomorrow. Maybe later this afternoon."

"That would be great," says Ben.

"The baby's due in January." The words slip out of Emma. She has no idea why she said it except that she wants Lindsay to know what a bad idea this is and how quickly everything has to happen.

"Cool," Lindsay says. "You have that pregnancy glow."

Emma hates when people say that. Usually it's women with better skin than Emma's.

Lindsay says, "It's like you're lit from within."

"Like the Madonna," says Ben.

Lindsay gives Ben a puzzled look. Does she think he means the rock star?

"Sort of like Madonna," she says. "Only less slutty."

For the next few days Emma and Ben talk about the house, and don't talk about the house. Even when they aren't talking about the house they're talking about the house. When they aren't talking about the house, they're thinking, *We're not talking about the house.* They know when the other decides, *Let's do this.* Or, *Let's think about it more.* Or, *We're nuts.*

60

Lindsay said she'd call the next day, but she doesn't. They both want to call her, and they both think it's smarter to wait and not seem overeager.

Three nights later, just when Ben and Emma are really starting to worry, Lindsay calls. Ben puts her on speakerphone.

"Awesome news! The bank says they'll go down to three hundred and twenty thou. Like I said, a historic reduction? Totally one for the books."

"Deal!" Ben says. Only then does he look at Emma.

Lindsay says, "I can send over the inspection report, but the gist of it is that, structurally, the house is in better shape than you probably thought."

"Go for it," Emma tells Ben.

Neither of them can breathe after Ben gets off the phone.

Emma says, "I don't know why this is scarier than getting pregnant."

Ben says, "Babies are portable. Houses aren't."

"We won't regret it," Emma says.

"Little Miss Mind Reader," Ben says. "That's what I was thinking."

Lindsay says she can't believe how fast this deal is going to closing. She's never seen anything like it. The bank is thrilled to have the property off their hands. Everyone's going home happy.

Jeb, Ben's lawyer, reads over the contract and the inspection report. He says they won't learn anything from going to the closing. He can handle it, and if anything comes up — any surprises — he'll call. They're dealing with the bank, so there won't be any sentimental handoff with the previous owner.

There are no surprises. That afternoon, Jeb shows up at Ben's office with copies of the keys. Emma's waiting for Jeb there. Ben and Emma Instagram themselves grinning like maniacs, holding the keys to their new house. Emma hasn't seen Ben smile like that in a while. Not since she told him she was pregnant. No. That isn't true. He'd looked like that when he'd told her about the house.

Emma rubs her belly and orders herself not to think about Elvis and Priscilla. Ben will love her *more* after the baby comes.

The contractor's name is JD. He is blond, lanky, embarrassingly handsome. Emma and Ben watch him park in the driveway and slide out of his spotlessly restored sky-blue 1979 Chevy pickup. If buying the house is the last scene of *Thelma and Louise,* he's the young Brad Pitt, only taller. He walks toward them, slowly, taking his time, looking beyond them at the house. Well, sure. He's a contractor. For now, he's more interested in the house than in them.

"What's so funny?" Ben says.

"He's like the guy in those movies where the newly divorced middle-aged wife has an affair with the hot young contractor and gets over the husband who ditched her. The hunky carpenter from central casting."

"Uh-oh," says Ben. "You do know I'm not planning to ditch you."

"Good. Then I don't have to have the healing affair with the contractor."

JD's movie-star looks make Ben competitive. He can't help it. Emma wants to hug Ben and say she loves him, that nothing else matters. *What* doesn't matter? Ben is nice-looking. A little vain, maybe, now that he's started losing some hair in the front and can't get away with not wearing his glasses.

Ben is going to hire JD no matter what JD looks like. And JD seems competent, honest, sensible, and pleasant, which Emma appreciates since she is the one who will mostly be here during the renovation. As soon as part of the house is reasonably habitable, Emma will try staying upstate.

She wants the light and air. Maybe it's the baby wanting what the baby wants.

JD shakes their hands, making all-business eye contact with Ben and a more complicated eye contact with Emma. He's used to women reacting to him. It's not his fault.

Anyway, he goes back to checking out the house. It makes it easier for Emma to look at him. She thinks she's seen him before. Maybe they've passed him on the road or in the gas station or . . .

JD says, "Can I tell you something without you deciding I'm too crazy to work on your house?"

"Go ahead." What else can Ben say? When someone says "Can I tell you something?" you can't say no. JD is the perfect mix of clumsy and awkward, confident and tough enough to undercut the handsomeness and make himself more appealing.

Ben says, "We wouldn't have bought this place if we weren't crazy."

JD waits a beat. "So . . . great. We're all nuts. The thing is . . . I used to have fantasies about this place. I used to imagine working here."

"Were you ever here?" asks Emma. "I hear this place was where local teens went to drink and smoke weed. That's what Lindsay's dad said —"

64

"Was he kidding? We wouldn't go near this place on a bet. What did Lindsay say about me?"

"That you're good at what you do," says Ben.

"That you'd solve all our problems," Emma says.

Emma shrinks under JD's long look. He's trying to figure out if she's difficult. If she's messing with him. Then he laughs.

"Lindsay's a piece of work. But she's right. I'm your guy. Besides which, I might be your only guy. All the other guys have jobs, which I would have too, if my clients hadn't lost all their money and stiffed me. I felt sorry for them, even though they're grifters, and I'm out of a job. But as they say, sometimes bad luck has good luck hidden inside it. Bad luck, my job dries up. Good luck, I get to work on your awesome house. If you hire me."

Sometimes bad luck has good luck hidden inside it. Emma likes that. She won't tell Ben they should talk to other contractors, get other bids. And it's clear that Ben doesn't want to.

JD says, "Like I said in the inspection report, it's in better shape than you'd think. You could use a new roof in five years, but it's holding up for now. New furnace definitely. Foundation's solid. Basement doesn't leak. The chunk of the porch roof that fell in didn't take anything with it. Definitely a new refrigerator. Dishwasher and laundry, etcetera. Plumbing and electrical, that costs. And cabinetry is expensive. The three hermit weirdos must have been more together than anyone knew. They kept the place from collapsing. It could be amazing, but you know that. We keep the beautiful old stuff but make it modern enough to be comfortable."

He's so sure he's getting the job. He's already saying *we*.

"The stove?" says Emma warily.

"Good as new. How strange is that? They don't make them like that anymore. Your grandkids will be cooking on it. There's some gunk needs to be scraped away, but once school lets out I've got an army of high school kids I hire. Everyone insured and bonded. And convinced they're immortal. I mean . . . I try to make them wear masks when they use toxic stuff, but it's a struggle."

Toxic? Emma can't be up here if the house is a superfund site. She says, "You know I'm pregnant, right? The baby's due in January."

"Lindsay told me. Congratulations. If

66

we're planning to use anything harmful I'll warn you. You can be somewhere else that day."

Emma's grateful to JD for not making her feel neurotic. Unlike Ben, she thinks guilt- ily, who never misses a chance to make fun of her worries.

"I promise we'll have this place cozy long, *long* before winter."

"When can you start?" asks Ben.

Shouldn't they talk it over? But why wait? The clock is ticking. The baby isn't inter- ested in construction delays.

They discuss costs, which seem reason- able, just as Lindsay promised. Though a bit more than seventy-five thousand. Ben doesn't flinch.

It's their money, though it's more Ben's money than Emma's. It's a good thing she'll be up here. She'll do what she can to keep the costs down.

"How about tomorrow morning?" JD says. "Bright and early."

Suddenly they hear a screech that seems to come from the attic.

Emma jumps.

"Feral cat?" says Ben.

"Feral something," says Emma.

"Bats? Rats?" says JD. "From plumbing

leaks to ghosts in the attic — you two can relax. It's my problem now."

CHAPTER THREE:
SETTLING IN

Late June

Two weeks after the closing, Emma packs both cars with some basic kitchen stuff, clothes, towels, sheets, blankets and pillows, her laptop, and some books. Two cars for two people isn't very ecological, but it will give them freedom if one needs to go back to the city, or if they both stay upstate and need to run errands in different directions.

She and Ben celebrate their first night in their new home with the all-night sex they used to have before she got pregnant.

Ben says, "Am I out of my mind, or is the smell of Sheetrock superhot?"

The house is a construction site, but JD has carved out a livable space — living room, bedroom, bathroom, part of the kitchen. The mattress and the refrigerator Emma ordered arrived the day after she called. Amazingly, the water pump just needed minor adjustments, and one phone call got the gas turned on. JD seems to know what to throw out, what to leave, what to ask Emma and Ben about before carting it off to the dump. The nasty mattresses and metal bed frames disappear from the upstairs rooms, but the attic is untouched.

Every morning, JD shows up with a dozen boys in the back of his pickup.

Looking out the window, Ben says, "Those kids aren't wearing seat belts. Are we sure the guy's indemnified?"

"He said he was. And we have insurance. Plus, look, he's driving really slow." It's kind of a role reversal, Ben being the worrier. Both of them like it. It's new.

The kids worship JD. They compete to do anything he asks, no matter how tedious or menial. Scrape the cracked linoleum off the mudroom floor? Sure! Under JD's supervision, they swarm the house while still respecting Emma and Ben's privacy. They remind Emma of Santa's elves, or the mice sewing Cinderella's ball gown.

"Good news, you probably noticed, you've got wireless," JD tells them. "You need to set up the router. The installation costs extra . . . a rush job, but I assumed you guys would think it was worth it."

Ben says, "Oh, man, we do. That would

70

have taken six months in the city."

He slaps JD a hearty high five. JD looks past him at Emma, who doesn't like fighting the impulse to roll her eyes, she and the handsome contractor gently mocking the dorky husband. Ben isn't dorky. He just acts that way around JD.

They're planning to stay for a week, ease into the house. JD says there's so much that needs to be done, he can stay out of their way.

Around noon on Monday Ben gets a phone call from Avery, his producing partner. An interesting project. The backer who's bringing it to them wants to meet today. He's rich enough to call the shots.

"Is this new?" asks Emma. "How come you never mentioned —"

"New to me," Ben says. "I told you. It just came up. Shit like this happens in the theater. Things happen in ten seconds, or never. Those are the options."

Does Emma want to go back to the city with Ben?

"I think I'll stay," she says.

It's only when she says it that she knows it's true. She feels an almost physical craving for this place, this light, this air. If it weren't such a beautiful day, maybe she would feel different. But leaving would be wrenching. She wants the clear light, the breeze, the smell of the purple flowers whose names she doesn't know. Just being here makes her feel expansive, as if something inside her is growing along with the baby, as if she's becoming more generous, more . . . something.

Ben says he'll be gone a night, maybe two. Standing in the driveway, he holds Emma close and kisses her for a long time.

Emma hopes JD isn't watching. Or maybe she hopes he is.

As Ben pulls out of the driveway she has a moment of panic, where she wants to run after him crying, *Don't leave me!* She imagines him hitting the oak tree, a momentary fantasy that seems so real she can almost hear the crash.

Nothing bad is going to happen. Ever since they started talking about the house, she's given herself a series of dares that she has to take. She dares herself to stay here alone.

The birdsong is constant, symphonic. The steady, reassuring thump of JD's hammer and even the whine of power saws marks time in a pleasant way. It signals progress. The dappled sun feels hot on her hair. It's pleasantly cool in the shade. She walks

72

down the driveway and stands in front of the house.

It's impossible to believe that this gigantic, beautiful place is hers. A house, a baby, a husband she loves. She has no right to be this happy. She looks around for wood to knock on.

She plans to poke around in the weedy yard, but winds up eating the last of the good bread and cheese they brought from the city, then goes upstairs and lies down. Just for a few minutes! She falls asleep to the sounds of JD and his crew calling to one another.

Her maddening ringtone punctures the dream she forgets immediately on waking.

"Emma, listen." Ben's practically hyperventilating. "Sturgis came to me with this project he wants to do, it's a reboot of *Peter Pan,* but with an all-female cast, Lost Girls instead of Lost Boys."

"Wow." Emma can hear how fake her enthusiasm sounds. "Isn't Peter Pan always a girl?"

"Sure. But the Lost Boys are always boys. Trust me. Sturgis thinks it can make money."

Emma thinks she knows who Sturgis is, she's supposed to know who Sturgis is, but at the moment she can't remember. And it's too late to ask.

"I know that it means I'm going to have to be in the city a bunch. But you can go back and forth. You can have the best of both worlds."

"I like it here," says Emma. "It's fine." She'd imagined being here with Ben. She feels a quick stab of disappointment, then something takes its place. Curiosity. How will it be without him?

"Are you sure you're okay? What about at night? If you feel the tiniest bit weird, or scared, or the tiniest bit anything, I swear, call me and I'll drive right up and get you. My phone is always on."

"I have a feeling I'll sleep like a baby," says Emma. "And the baby will sleep like a baby."

The first night, she goes around locking the doors, double-checking, shutting the windows, turning lights on and off, looking behind the shower curtain. She even tucks a kitchen knife under her pillow. But after a while the silence seems like a blanket she can pull over her, and the sounds — an owl in the distance, frogs from a nearby swamp — sound like an orchestra that only she can hear. She's not at all scared. Little Person is

74

keeping her company. An angel is watching over them.

How comfortable her bed is, how reassuring the night noises. The cheeping of the frogs is regular and soothing. She falls asleep and dreams about a house. But unlike the houses she visited before in dreams, this one is friendly, bright, and welcoming instead of dim and befogged by loss. The house is filled with people having fun, but it's not confusing, like parties in dreams. Then the dream changes, and the house fills with peacocks, then lambs, then furry animals. Emma is sitting in a chair, nursing a baby, and the animals kneel before them like the beasts in a Nativity painting.

She's awoken by sunlight beaming through her windows. She opens the balcony door — JD has told her that the balcony is solid enough for now, but he'll reinforce it later — and steps into the brilliant green morning. Dew glitters on the leaves, and light shines through the white petals of the late-season daffodils that have come up on their own. Sun pinks the delicate blossoms of a cherry tree growing wild in the woods. A cardinal and a bluebird perch on the railing. A hummingbird flies past, buzzing so loudly she mistakes it for a giant bee. A blue jay roosts on a branch, looking at her for so long that she wonders if she's still dreaming, until its flies away, and she knows she is home.

She goes downstairs and makes a cup of ginger tea with the electric teapot she's brought from the city. It feels good to have life simplified, pared down to what she needs. She eats a slice of bread with butter — not the fancy imported butter Ben insists on, but perfectly good, normal butter.

Then she goes and sits in the theater. They've asked JD to tell his guys to clean it up, get rid of the dust and scraps, but otherwise leave it alone until they decide what to do. She sits in the third row of folding chairs, expectant and excited, as if she's waiting for a play to begin. She tries to imagine the place full of people who played on Broadway until they ran into . . . problems.

The only time Emma ever acted was in her high school Christmas pageant. She'd played the angel Gabriel. All she'd had to do was raise her arm over the girl playing Mary and say, "Fear not, the Lord is with you." Everyone wanted to play Mary. They chose the blondest, prettiest girl. No one wanted to play Gabriel, especially after someone said that the angel was actually a boy.

76

Fear not. Fear not.

Emma isn't afraid.

She thinks about the three hermits. Had they come into the theater? Signs of their presence are rarer than remnants of the clinic. Or maybe JD has already tossed things he knows she'd rather not see. He's thoughtful of her that way.

Emma goes upstairs and makes her bed. She'd like a nap but resists the impulse.

Outside, she finds JD tearing down the rotten back steps so he can replace them with new ones. He's shirtless and it's hard not to look at the muscles shifting under his bare, tanned back. What a cliché. She and Ben joke about it. But the jokes make her so uncomfortable, you'd think she *was* sleeping with the contractor.

Does she have a crush on JD? She's shy around him in a way that reminds her of how she'd felt around boys she'd liked in high school. No, junior high.

She just likes to be around him. He has a distinctive smell. Like wood chips and fresh sawdust and soap and something piney. She loves being near enough to him to inhale it, at the end of the week, when he gives her the invoices he saves in a blood-colored manila folder. She likes standing side by side, as if they're working together — which they are, though he's doing all the labor and all she's doing is making small decisions and writing checks.

But that's not all. At first, she spends a lot of time wandering from room to room, trying to get a feel for each space. What could it be like? What color should it be? She makes lists of things she wants Ben to bring up from the city. Her copy of *The Joy of Cooking.* She imagines baking projects, berry cobblers and cinnamon coffee cakes. She orders books about famous gardens that might inspire her to think about the land around the house, most of which is overgrown except the circular driveway and a large, ragged circle in back that one of JD's workers mowed. She orders two art books of watercolors, one by Sargent, the other by Ensor. There's something in them she needs to see.

So far one of her favorite things is to go through the closets of dishes that did in fact come with the house. The bank certainly didn't want them.

Standard hotel china, Fiestaware platters, gold-rimmed teacups and saucers, dessert plates encircled with thick, embossed flowers. She washes each piece lovingly and tries to find it a place that, she knows, will change when JD builds new cabinets.

She searches for the most beautiful dishes online and feels a little shock when she finds them. Sometimes, a little guiltily, she checks how much they cost. Some pieces are quite valuable, but she would never part with them. It would be like losing a childhood toy, or one of the ticket stubs — she still has them in a drawer in the city — from a play or film she went to, early on, with Ben.

One warm afternoon she's reading on the porch when she looks up and sees JD — shirtless, of course. All she can manage to say is, "Don't you worry about ticks?" How prudish and no fun!

"Ticks don't like me, or they would have got me by now. It's weird how bugs like some people and not others. I had a girl-friend, we used to go into the woods, and she'd come back covered head to toe with bug bites, and I wouldn't have one. Not one. She used to be pretend-angry about it. But I think she really was angry. I mean, she wasn't the sanest person in the world —"

Emma feels a little spike of jealousy. She doesn't want to think about whatever JD and his crazy girlfriend did in the woods.

"That's kind of unscientific," she says.

JD puts down his crowbar and looks at

79

her. His shrug isn't dismissive. It's just a shrug.

"It's worked for me so far."

"Knock on wood," says Emma.

JD says, "Speaking of which, a lumber delivery's coming today."

"Fine. Let me know how much. . . . Listen . . . Is it safe to cook on the stove?" So far she's been living on fruits, raw vegetables, food she's brought from the city.

"Sure," says JD. "It's all hooked up. Go right ahead. That stove is awesome. Every time I look at it, I see some Norman Rockwell mom baking apple pies."

"That's the idea," Emma says.

"Cook yourself something delicious," JD says.

Emma takes a deep breath. "Hey, can I ask a favor? Can I borrow a mask and gloves?"

A few days before, she'd seen the workers using masks and gloves when they stripped paint off the staircase to reveal the burnished oak beneath. When the oak began to appear, JD called her to see. Amazing! Then he suggested she go for a ride, in case the fumes rose to the bedroom. She'd been reading a depressing novel about the end of the world. So, yes. Sure. She went to the supermarket. JD left all the windows open.

The boys will wait to finish the job till the next time she goes into the city.

"Sure, why?"

"I've been wanting to go up to the attic. Poke around."

"It's filthy up there."

"That's why I want the mask and gloves."

"Just don't trip on anything. That attic is a dumpster fire. We should have thrown all that stuff out by now."

Emma likes it that JD says *we*. Is she included, or does he just mean himself and his helpers? She reminds herself: It's her house. Her decision.

"Hold off on that, okay? I want to see what's there. I'll be careful." Emma's touched that he's worried about her. Well, sure. How would it look if his client got hurt on his watch?

There's something she wants to ask him, but she can't remember. She's always forgetting things lately. She puts a pen or coffee cup down, then spends twenty minutes looking for it. At rehearsals she's gone to with Ben, when actors forget their lines, they just say "Line" and the script person gives them the line. She wants someone like that in her life.

A few nights later, she wakes from a deep

81

sleep and knows she's not alone. Something or someone is in her room. She can't see it, but she feels a presence. It's breathing, thrumming in the air. A bird. Please let it be a bird.

Terror pulses behind her eyeballs. She turns on the light.

Something is flying around the ceiling, bashing into the windows and walls. It's gigantic. An eagle, a hawk . . .

A bat. There's a bat in her room. She grabs her phone and runs into the hall and slams the door behind her.

It's 10 p.m. Not all that late. She fell asleep early. She needs to call someone. Ben can't help her, but if she could talk to him, it might calm her down. She dials his number. It goes straight to voicemail. He doesn't pick up. He said he always keeps his phone on. And until now he has. How could anyone not answer a call from his pregnant wife, alone at night in the country? Has he forgotten about her? Likely he's gone to bed early, too. He often turns off his phone at night. She'll have to remind him.

Maybe she should go downstairs, but the couch hasn't been delivered yet, and there's nowhere to sleep. The floor is hard and dusty. Ouch.

Then she remembers JD saying to call

anytime, day or night, if she's worried or anything goes wrong or there's any kind of trouble. That's what's happening now. He can always not answer, or tell her to tough it out, he'll be there in the morning. Through the door, she can hear the bat, bashing into the walls. She wants to be in her bed. She wants the bat out of her house.

She's about to call JD when she remembers something that happened a while ago ago.

She'd been sitting on the porch when JD came tearing out of the house. He was pale and sweating, his hair stuck to his forehead.

Emma's first thought was that one of the helpers, the kids, had been injured. Oh, please, no. She'd feel responsible, and Ben would blame her for hiring JD, even though it was just as much his idea as hers. Just let everybody be all right, and she'd deal with whatever she needed to.

"What's wrong?"

JD hadn't noticed her. He looked more embarrassed than troubled.

"Nothing for you to worry about. One of the kids found a dead mouse in the wall. And I've got a thing about mice in the walls. I don't know. The smell . . ."

"It's awful," agreed Emma. One of the cheap apartments she'd lived in, before Ben, had a serious mouse problem.

"We have all the windows open and the air blowing through so you probably won't notice it. It's just a thing I have. Maybe from my childhood, I don't remember. I need a second to get past it, then I'll go back to work."

"Take your time," said Emma, but JD was already gone, leaving her thinking that it was sort of attractive, this sign of weakness in the big, strong contractor. A dead mouse!

Now the memory keeps her from calling JD to help her get rid of the bat. If a dead mouse freaked him out, how will he deal with a bat? Except that the bat is very much alive.

She calls JD.

The phone rings a half dozen times. He sounds groggy, and it seems to take him a moment to remember who she is.

"Wait a second," he says. She hears footsteps. Is he taking the phone into another room? Is someone there? The girlfriend who got all those bug bites in the woods? Why should Emma care?

She apologizes for bothering him, for calling so late, for —

"What's wrong?" He knows she wouldn't be calling at this hour unless it was important. He probably hopes it isn't something he's done, a short in the wiring, a blown fuse, a plumbing leak . . .

"There's a bat in my room."

"A bat?"

"A bat. I don't know what to do. I'm terrified. I . . ."

"Don't move. I'll be there in fifteen minutes."

Emma checks her watch. He's there in ten. He must have been speeding. Emma feels like bursting into tears when she hears his truck pull up in front of the house.

Only when he walks in and finds her huddled on the floor near the door does she realize that she's wearing her thinnest nightgown. She's practically naked. He looks her up and down, not lecherous or creepy, just looking. His eyes pause on her rounded belly, then shift back to her face.

She wishes he wasn't looking at her. She's glad that he is.

There's a bat in her room. That's why he's there. He hasn't come to look at her or make her feel something that feels uncomfortably like desire.

"Relax," he says. "Don't you hate it when someone orders you to relax? I know a bat swooping around your head is maybe not the most calming thing in the world. Just stay here. I'll be right back."

He goes upstairs. Emma waits. She hears him walking around, then nothing . . .

A short time later he comes downstairs.

"All clear. The coast is clear."

"Did you kill it?"

"I opened all the windows and he flew out. He didn't want to be there any more than we wanted him there."

"God, I can't thank you enough. Thank you, thank you —"

"One thank-you is enough." JD smiles his slow, irresistible, ever-so-slightly practiced smile and puts a brotherly arm around her shoulders — or maybe it would feel more brotherly if her arms weren't bare. "See you in the morning, bright and early. Try and get some sleep, okay?"

"Okay," Emma says.

Chapter Four:
Rapunzel

Pulling down the staircase to the attic takes less upper body strength than she expected — certainly less than Ben made it seem. Everything's under a thick layer of spongy dust. Good thing she's wearing a mask.

She paws through old-fashioned manila folders. Paper crumbs sprinkle out. At last, she finds a black-and-white notebook, a child's composition book.

The pages are dimpled, thickly covered with old-fashioned handwriting. A neat, flowing cursive, with extra swirls on the lowercase *j* and a double flourish on the capital *M*. No one writes like that anymore.

The ink is an unusual color, a bold, garish peacock blue, only slightly faded with time.

Emma opens the book to the first page.

Rapunzel; or, The Girl in the Tower
ACT I, SCENE I.

THE YOUNG WOMAN is alone in an institutional bedroom. A theater poster on one wall. She sits on the edge of a neatly made bed.

THE YOUNG WOMAN: I feel like Rapunzel, if Rapunzel was unwed and pregnant. Everything happened so fast. One minute I was flying high, on Broadway, in the spring of 1957, in the chorus of *My Fair Lady*!!
    Meanwhile. I was in over my head, in love with a world-famous actor. Mr. H.
    And now I'm put out to pasture, in a loony bin run by a crazy doctor and his wife, their nasty staff, and a cast of bleary old theater types with red eyes and shaky hands. They look like they're all auditioning to play Marley's ghost in *A Christmas Carol.* I swear I can smell brimstone and hear chains clank when they line up for waffles at breakfast. My heart breaks for them, but I can't watch them zombie-shuffling to their tables. I used to be so kindhearted! Maybe life is making me hard.
    They feed us a lot of sugar. It helps

the alcoholics. But I get a special diet, with more fruit and vegetables. Mr. H. is paying for every strawberry. I've lost weight. Everyone's upset with me, though they try to hide it. They want me fat.

My real life seems far away, though in my mind, I'm still the hopeful ingénue who got off the bus from Cincinnati and walked toward Times Square. Bright lights! The Big Apple!

I did what all those girls do. I found a roommate, a temp job, a basement apartment with a view of passing shoes. I went out for auditions. And even after all the noes, even after the casting directors looking straight through me, I was happy.

Hundreds of talented girls read for *My Fair Lady.* They traveled miles to sing and dance and Cockney-accent their hearts out. Everyone who got called back imagined a miracle: She was up for Eliza Doolittle! Her — and not Julie Andrews!

It *was* a miracle. I was one of the lucky ones.

I was a Cockney market girl, singing "Wouldn't It Be Loverly" behind Julie Andrews. I'd been sprinkled with fairy dust, touched by a magic wand.

Everyone noticed the first time Mr. H. fixed me with that gaze.

One night in the chorus dressing room I found a note from Mr. H.: *Meet me after the show for dinner.* Everyone — even innocent me — knew what *that* meant.

Mistakes were made.

Probably it was my fault, because he was my first, and the truth is, I didn't always know what exactly was going on down there.

I trusted Mr. H. to take care of it. He was such an organized person. So in control. He knew his lines before the first read through. He knew where babies came from — and how not to have them.

I wasn't his first girl. He was married and had a steady girlfriend who was rumored to be ill. But I couldn't help hoping I would be the last. What a stupid chicken clucking her way into the fox's lair!

I suspected he'd got other girls in trouble. He was so calm when I told him. He had a plan.

I had to fake a drinking problem, so I'd need to go to a rest home. That's what I'd tell the producers, not that anybody cared. I'd slur my words. I was an actress. Favors would be called in. He and the show would work it out.

He would pay for me to take the cure in Dr. Fogel's Hideaway Home. He said the only reason I'd never heard of it was that I hadn't been on Broadway that long. Welcome to show biz, doll! He called me "doll." He called every woman "doll."

I would have the baby at Hideaway Home, which had excellent doctors, and I'd come back cured. Delivered! The child would be adopted by a loving family. Hideaway Home would arrange it, everything perfectly legal. I could return to the show. No one had to know. Everyone and everything — Mr. H and me included — would take up where we'd left off.

A plan with a lot of holes in it. I see that only now.

THE YOUNG WOMAN touches her pregnant belly with both hands.

THE YOUNG WOMAN: Dr. Fogel examined me. Mr. H. looked on. The doctor ran his hands over my stomach. He was looking at Mr. H. There was something creepy in Dr. Fogel's touch.

I was glad that another woman was present. Mrs. Fogel. It was supposed to be comforting, but she reminded me of the evil housekeeper in *Rebecca,* one of my favorite films. It was all straight out of *Rebecca:* the house, the secrets, the whispering in the halls.

Mrs. Fogel seemed kindly. But the minute Mr. H. left, her true self emerged.

Emma closes the book. She can't read any more. Why did this woman — there's no name on the book, and Emma's already thinking of her as Rapunzel — write this? Like a play. Maybe just to record it, to remember. Or to stay sane. Why does anyone keep a journal?

She doesn't want to take the book downstairs. It belongs in the attic. She'll come back. She'll keep the mask and gloves.

At first Ben calls three times a day, then two, then one. He sounds cheerful, and Emma's glad. He's gone from wasting his day on the internet to being busy much of the time, but it's — more or less — fine with Emma. She's glad when he enjoys his work. He's in a better mood, more patient and affectionate.

On the phone, Ben says, "Are you sure

everything's okay?'

"I went up to the attic."

He told her not to, but she did. Fine. Let him know she doesn't do exactly what he tells her. Remind him that she sometimes does the opposite of what he tells her. She's not going to mention the book. Emma shouldn't even be reading it. That poor girl didn't write it for Ben — or for her.

"I wish you wouldn't go up there," he says. "I specifically asked you. Who knows what you're breathing in. What are you doing up there?"

Why is that word *specifically* so annoying?

"I'm just looking at stuff. Old books. Diaries."

"Diaries? *My Former Life in the Bright Lights and How I Wound Up on the Skids,* by Tipsy Ingénue."

"Something like that." Emma fake-laughs.

"Are you eating okay?" asks Ben.

"I thought I'd finally try out the stove." Even with the go-ahead from JD, she's been hesitant. "I'll start with something simple. Maybe an omelet."

She hears something in Ben's silence. Is he worried that the old-fashioned stove might malfunction and burn down the house with Emma in it?

Whatever he's thinking, he doesn't say it.

93

He's not going to make more rules for her to break.

"Be careful. Call me later. And . . . bon appétit."

"Thank you," says Emma. "I love you."

"I love you too," says Ben.

"I miss you," Emma says, but Ben has already hung up.

Emma buys eggs from a little farm stand where you take a carton of eggs and leave four dollars in a metal box. The honor system. That means there must not be a lot of recreational drug use around here, though at one of the last city parties she and Ben attended, an unkind friend — a former friend now — told them that Sullivan County was one big meth lab. Conversations like that were partly why Emma had left the city. She was tired of people saying mean, aggressive stuff they think is smart or cute or funny.

Before leaving the city, she wasn't aware of making careful plans, but it turns out that she brought what she needs. A copper bowl, a whisk, a frying pan. Salt and pepper. Bingo!

She misses Ben. But they'll enjoy lots of meals together. Anyway, she isn't alone. She and Little Person are eating dinner. There will be many such nights, mother and child enjoying a quiet supper in the soft evening light while Dad works in the city and comes up as soon as he can.

She separates the whites from the yolks, beats the eggs before folding the mixture together. She's read a new recipe online: The trick is to cook the omelet slowly, with a lid.

Suddenly she smells a harsh acrid odor. Something is burning. Dear God, she's all alone here. Ben will never forgive her if the house burns down before they really move in.

After a few endless seconds, she finds a piece of paper on fire under the burner behind the one she's using. She pulls it out from the metal grill and slaps her palm down on the black burning edges, singeing her hand but saving enough of the paper for her to be able to read it.

It's an invoice.

Mid-Hudson Antiques and Auctioneers.

Vintage stove. $900.

It's stamped: PAID IN FULL. But there is no name . . . no recipient.

Emma checks the date. The stove was bought only a week or so before she and Ben came up to see the house. Someone — Ben — ordered the stove and had it installed

95

before that first visit.

Emma must have mentioned her obsession with the stove she coveted, and Ben was taking a gamble, surprising her with the stove of her dreams to help persuade her to buy the house. If it didn't work, he hadn't lost all that much.

But how strange of him not to mention it. Isn't it normal to want credit for doing something nice? Maybe he was afraid it might make Emma feel manipulated by his playing on her desire for a vintage stove. It was sweet of him to remember. Most men don't even listen. Ben not only heard her, he went to great trouble and expense to make her dream come true. And he's too modest to want praise, or thanks, or appreciation.

If that's how he wants it, she won't let on that she's found the receipt. She won't mention it. But it bothers her. Maybe it's just that she and Ben have always been so close, with no secrets, or none that she knows about. She hates keeping anything from him — even if it's about a nice thing he's done for her — secret.

Later, on the phone, she says, "I cooked dinner tonight."

Once more she thinks she hears the slightest note of . . . anxiety in his voice.

96

"What did you make?"

"An omelet. Like I said."

"And . . . how did the stove work?"

"Great, except that I burned myself a little." She might as well tell him. He'll be coming up tomorrow, and she has a bandage on her hand. She's surprised by how much it still hurts. She called her doctor, who said take Tylenol, but she doesn't have any, so she's toughing it out.

"God, Emma. Be careful. How did you do it?"

"I . . . thought the handle on the pan would cool down sooner than it did. Stupid me. It wasn't much of a burn. The stove's awesome. The omelet was delicious. I wish you were here."

"I do too," says Ben.

RAPUNZEL. JUNE 1, 1957

Well, so much for seeing my life here as a play. It no longer seems like a fun drama. I'm writing this as a diary now — no one will ever read it. Dear Diary. For my eyes only. Read at your own risk.

Emma closes the notebook. Then she opens it again. She wants to know what happened to the woman with whom she has

97

two big things in common. They are pregnant. They live in this house. Surely that counts for something. Emma will never tell anyone what she reads, not even Ben. She'll keep this woman's secrets.

Dear Diary,
Sorry I haven't written. I haven't been feeling well. I've been reluctant — afraid — to complain. That's why I'm glad I have you. Someone to talk to, even if I'm talking to myself.

You're talking to me, thinks Emma. She pities her. Abandoned by her lover, surrounded by cranky actors, a shady doctor (if he even *was* a doctor), and his creepy wife. How lucky it makes Emma feel, a nice husband, enough money, a house that's going to be gorgeous. A baby she can love — and keep.

She reads on:

Morning sickness is now all-day sickness. Every day is like having the same bad dream. I wake up to find Mrs. Fogel standing by my bed, with crackers to help the nausea.
One morning she said, "I'm trying to find out if that's your real voice. If someone

98

wakes you from a deep sleep, if you'd still sound like bad-imitation Marilyn Monroe."

"That's my voice," I said.

"You're good at this," said Mrs. Fogel. "You should have been an actress."

Her dry soda crackers don't help. They make it worse, and I practically knock Mrs. Fogel over as I race to the bathroom. She has no sympathy. She doesn't try to hide it.

The Fogels seem to know I'm an orphan.

Tears spring to Emma's eyes. She and the mysterious diarist — Rapunzel — have that in common, too. They're orphans. Did she also lose both her parents at once in a car wreck?

I don't remember telling Mr. H. about my family. I don't remember him asking. I don't remember him asking one thing about me, except whether whatever he was doing felt good. I always lied and said yes. I wasn't going to tell him I was thinking of my high school boyfriend, who was cute, but who is married and laying wall-to-wall carpet in our old neighborhood. My first week in New York, I got drunk and called him, but his wife hung up on me.

The Fogels must know I have no one to

stick up for me, no one to help me.

I sing to the baby. "Wouldn't It Be Loverly." As far as the baby knows, I *am* Julie Andrews.

Mrs. Fogel cooks for me. She's a . . . passable cook. The others eat fairly well, since Dr. Fogel always says that nourishment is essential to the recovering body. Many people who come here have been living on a liquid diet. Hardly any meat is served. Supposedly for health reasons, but probably because they're cheap.

I eat what I want. The problem is figuring out what I want. Lamb chops used to be a treat. That's what I ordered the first (and last) time Mr. H. took me out to dinner. After that, we dined on sleazy hotel room service. Now the smell of lamb makes me sick.

I've been craving oranges. Mrs. Fogel makes sure I get them. She says, "The baby knows what the baby needs. Vitamin C."

The other day, I ate seven oranges. But it's hard to fill up on oranges. So, Mrs. Fogel serves me soggy fried chicken, lumpy mashed potatoes, chalky creamed spinach.

I like wandering through the narrow halls and huge public spaces, into the theater where they stage those ghastly talent shows every other week. Someone plays the piano badly, someone else croaks out a mediocre song from the mediocre musical that "made" their career. It's eerie, like watching a talent show staged by ghosts.

The average age of the residents is about two hundred. My fellow guests have been drinking hard for years. Maybe they handled it better when they were young. Or maybe they got away with it because . . . they're actors! They played sober until they aged out of the part.

It's like boot camp. Even in the snow, Dr. and Mrs. Fogel lead us all — I'd say there are twenty residents here — on marches through the forest. The doctor is right about one thing: The forest in winter is a tonic, good for our bodies and souls. When I breathe in that crisp cold air, I forget Mr. H. and my worries about the baby. I feel glad to be alive.

I hate the counseling sessions with Dr. Fogel. All the residents have them. Mostly they talk about their careers, the standing ovations, the flops that drove them to drink. Dr. Fogel asks them about their childhoods and (the women, anyway) about their sex lives.

It's different with me. Dr Fogel wants to

know what Mr. H. is like in bed. Perverted personal questions. Did he do *this* to you? Did he do *that* to you? Very specific. I can sense him getting excited under his (probably phony) white medical coat. At least he doesn't "examine" me. Maybe he knows I wouldn't put up with it.

Emma turns the page.

Three reasons not to run away from Hideaway Home:

1. Pregnant and no money.
2. No friends.
3. No family.

One plus one plus one equals three equals no place to go.

One morning, in the breakfast room, two old guys — Mr. Bergen and Mr. Leath — asked to sit at my table. They told me they wound up in Hideaway Home because they played Macbeth. The bad-luck role. They were drinking smuggled vodka in their fruit juice.

Another bad thing about this place is the Cold Spa, which I'm spared. I can hear them yelling when they're plunged into a bathtub of ice. I can look out my window at ice dumped on the lawn at the end of Cold Spa day.

No one's saying what will happen to the baby. If they know, they're not telling me.

Sometimes I'm afraid they'll steal the baby, and my child will grow up in a home full of Broadway drunks. If I have to, I'll sneak the baby out. I'll kidnap my own child.

Emma puts down the notebook. There's only so much she can take. And there's something about it that feels — superstitiously, she knows — unhealthy. Who was this unlucky young woman? There must be plenty of stories like hers. But this one happened here.

One afternoon Emma picks up the black-and-white composition book and a pamphlet falls out, an eggshell-blue examination book. She'd found books like that among her mother's possessions when she died. She still has them somewhere, in storage. Maybe now that they have this big house, she can retrieve them. But why?

Her mother's papers were mostly session notes in the neat script that grew smaller and shakier as she grew older. That was how Emma and her dad first knew something was wrong. Emma's dad was driving her mom for a second opinion when their car got totaled.

Emma wishes she'd appreciated her mother more, even if her mother wasn't always . . . maternal. Emma would give anything to have her here now, to talk about being pregnant. As a mental health professional (it always annoyed Emma when her mother called herself that), Mom might have something to say about a time when Hideaway Home was a treatment center for actors with substance problems. Her mother was never all that nice to her. Mom did nothing to build up her confidence. Her parents thought she was weak, and she's never stopped showing them that they were wrong.

The writing in the exam book is the same as in the composition book, the same elaborate penmanship, the same overly bright peacock-blue ink.

Emma reads:

It's crazy how humans are born. Crazy that a man and a woman can . . . do that . . . and then the woman builds a body out of her body and maybe a little of his. The first person who made the connection between sex and having a baby nine months later was a genius.

■ ■ ■ ■

Emma pages through the book with growing excitement. She's read plenty of baby books: informative, reassuring, sometimes maddening, but this . . . this is what *she* thinks.

Emma could have written it. She's pretty sure she's said something more or less like this to Ben. It's no accident that they bought this house, that she came up to this attic and found the journal.

It could have been written for her.

By her.

She's reading the little blue book when she feels the baby stir inside her, a flutter so light that she can't be sure if she imagined it. Then she feels it again. The baby is moving.

She edges closer to the dusty window, for light and air, though the window is curtained with spiderwebs and dead flies.

She looks out at the field behind the house.

She sees them again.

The girl and the baby. Standing in the field.

CHAPTER FIVE:
A DINNER PARTY

How strange that the only friend she's made here is a woman whose name she doesn't know, who lived in this house more than sixty years ago.

How *do* people make friends? Some of her city friends are from art school, some from work. People ask how couples first met, but they hardly ever ask how you became friends.

Emma goes to a tag sale at the local firehouse. There are a few shoppers, mostly moms with preschool kids. A couple of the kids seem slightly feral, ready to tear the place up if their moms weren't holding them back. The women have no energy or attention left for Emma. They're not looking to make new friends. The merchandise — lamps with frayed cords, coffee mugs featuring cartoon characters she doesn't recognize, a box of bloated cookbooks — is set out on long tables, and the older women sitting behind the tables are talking. They don't even glance at her. She finds some baby clothes that look practically new, and though they smell a little funny, they can be washed. A friendly woman takes Emma's money, looks at the pile of neatly folded unisex yellow onesies, and says, "You can't have too many of these."

"No," says Emma. "You can't."

The supermarket is ten miles away. Maybe because it serves such a large area, she never sees the same person twice. She could shop here for the rest of her life and never feel like a regular. Maybe no one does. In the city, she knew everybody: the dry cleaner, the newspaper guy, the butchers, the two Jordanian brothers who run the tiny corner grocery.

Fifteen miles past the market is the local public library, but it keeps erratic hours. Every time Emma goes there, it's closed. How can the library not have a website? If it does, she can't find it.

She still has friends in the city she can talk to on the phone, but now either they have kids and no time to talk, or jobs and no time to talk. How did they find time before? They used to meet every couple of weeks for drinks, but Emma couldn't do that now, even if she lived there. Nothing's worse than sipping ginger ale while your friends get hammered.

At the end of the week, JD shows her a list of what he's done, an accounting of materials, a sum of hours the boys put in. She zones out while he goes through it, item by item, but she's aware of how near he's standing as he reads the list of expenses and costs. She fights the desire to run her hand along his arm. Another unruly hormonal impulse. It's too bad Ben doesn't seem to share the same urges. Last weekend, when she and Ben had sex, she had to ask him to turn off the TV.

She needs to focus on the total: what they owe JD. She agrees to whatever he says. She has things she wants to ask — he grew up near here, after all, he knows the area — but she can never figure out how to begin, how to move their conversation away from the cost of nails and two-by-fours. She's never asked him one personal question. Not one.

She finds him more attractive than she wants to admit. So what? She likes him. If there's only one other person around, it's lucky that one person is nice — and nice to look at.

The work is going quickly. Record-breakingly fast. She has no complaints other than being — occasionally — lonely.

And apparently hallucinating a girl and a baby.

One afternoon she decides to take a walk. On instinct she heads in the direction where, from the attic window, she saw the girl and the child.

The wild grasses have grown past her knees. She's slathered herself with insect repellent, not the poisonous stuff, but something that works reasonably well. After she gets back she'll take a long bath and check her skin for ticks.

A few hundred yards from the house, she crosses an area that's overgrown but still partly paved. Maybe it was a patio once. Some of the stones are a few inches above the ground, while others lie flat.

A graveyard. It's a graveyard.

None of the stones are marked.

Part of her wants to poke around. Explore. It's her land. The cemetery is a chapter in the house's history. And part of her wants to be anywhere but here. That's the part that wins. The dry grasses scratch at her legs as she hurries back to the house. She's out of breath by the time she gets to the door.

JD comes over.

"Are you okay? You look like you saw a

ghost. Two ghosts."

Emma stares at him. Does he know about the girl and the baby?

Then she says, "A snake. I saw a snake." Why is she lying? Something keeps her from asking him about the graveyard. It would be such a simple question. He grew up around here. Doesn't she trust him?

"Striped or black?"

"Huh?"

"The snake." He knows she's lying.

"Uh . . . black," she says.

"Black snakes are nothing to worry about. Unless you happen to be a field mouse."

Given Emma's failure to make friends, she's more agreeable than she would have been when Ben tells her, on the phone, that they're invited to Lindsay's house for dinner on Saturday night.

"Lindsay?"

"Earth to Emma," says Ben. "Our Realtor. You *do* remember our real estate broker?"

Of course Emma remembers. She'd just gone fuzzy for a moment.

"I think it's a friendly follow-up thing. She wants to see how we're doing. And she's inviting people from around here, people she thinks we'll get along with."

110

Emma likes the sound of that.

Ben says, "What I really think is she wants to find out if we have rich city friends looking to relocate."

"I wish we did have friends moving up here," says Emma. "Sometimes I can't help wishing we weren't such pioneers."

"Don't worry. Once our friends see our house, we'll have crowds of new neighbors."

That Saturday morning they drive across the river and north to an art fair near Hudson. Ben's heard about it from an actor friend. He thinks it might be fun. The show is in a barn attached to a café with a hip young chef and a stylish brunch menu.

Attractive young couples lean back in their chairs and chat over blueberry pancakes while their children roam the fields (treated to keep away ticks) and climb on the sculptures. Why didn't Emma and Ben move *here*? Why aren't *these* people their friends? Then Emma remembers that she and Ben wanted to get away from all that. All this. Why move this far to become another city-stroller mom, with acreage and a massive renovation project? And what *has* she become? A pregnant woman with no friends, acreage, and a massive renovation project.

Her bad mood shadows the not-so-great art event. She's forgotten the art she's seen by the time they're back on the road.

Lately she's been loving that moment when they drive around the giant scary oak tree and see the house. The truth still takes a few seconds to sink in: The house is theirs. This is their home. And she's been feeling all the warm, cozy emotions that go with that idea. That word. *Home*.

But this afternoon she feels overwhelmed. The house still needs so much work.

Emma goes upstairs and takes a long nap. She wakes up thick-headed and grumpy. Then it's time to get up and dress and leave for Lindsay's.

Who's going to be there? People they'll get along with. It's these mystery guests for whom Emma dresses up, not too much but just enough so that when she looks in the mirror, she doesn't groan. If she weren't pregnant, she'd feel self-conscious about having no waist, but now it seems like a sign of progress.

Little Person is moving more often now, but whenever she tells Ben, "Put your hand here, you can feel it!," the baby stops moving.

Ben says, "Mama's boy's not performing for Daddy. Say hi to Daddy, buddy."

Emma hates it when he calls the baby "buddy."

"Maybe it's a girl," she says. "Are you going to call her 'buddy'?" They still haven't decided if they want to know. The last time she visited Dr. Snyder, he'd almost slipped and told her, but she reminded him: They want it to be a surprise.

The appointment went well. Everything's fine: blood work fine, blood pressure and weight fine, check check check. The baby's growing nicely, not too fast, not too slow. Whatever she's doing is right.

She and her doctor have decided she'll have a natural, drug-free birth, unless the pain becomes unbearable, and then she and Ben can change their minds. At her last visit he suggested that she might want to search out a pregnancy group in the country. A Lamaze class or something. It sounded like a good idea, but she couldn't find one. Fine, said Dr. Snyder. When she goes into labor, she just has to remember to keep breathing and not panic.

Ben says, "Maybe it's a little early. Maybe you're imagining that the baby's moving."

"I'm not," says Emma.

She decides not to tell him about seeing the girl and the baby on the lawn — or about the cemetery behind the house.

113

■ ■ ■ ■

Lindsay's house — a tiny, vinyl-sided cabin painted barn red and surrounded by a ragged lawn — has the same unlived-in, uncared-for feeling as her office. After an awkward stall at the door — handshakes? Kisses? They opt for friendly hellos — Lindsay shows them into a room that could have been furnished yesterday from Craigslist. A hard plaid couch from the eighties is separated from the huge TV by a scratched, glass-topped coffee table. A wedged-shaped knickknack shelf occupies one corner without even one knickknack on display.

Lindsay says, "We've only been here two months, and we've both been working . . . Before that — full confession — I was living with my parents, and Beth . . . well, that's her story to tell. We were together — but not together. I mean, not living together? This was the first place we could afford? You'd think a Realtor would get a special break, but not when the Realtor is working for her dad."

That leaves a silence that Emma feels obliged to fill by saying, "Too bad!"

"What's too bad?" says Lindsay.

"Not getting a break," says Emma.

"Yeah, well, I've had a lot of showings, so we've mostly left the home decorating to Beth."

As if on cue, a young woman — Beth — emerges from the kitchen, wearing a black chef's apron that says, in red and black letters, *This is what a freakin' awesome Grill Master looks like.*

Beth is the one with the sense of humor. The apron is like armor, and you have to deal with it before you deal with Beth.

Ben cocks his finger like a gun, points it at the apron, and says, "That's funny."

Emma has never seen him do that. It's an LA thing. Early in the spring he spent four days on the West Coast. Maybe he picked it up there. Obviously, Ben feels as awkward as she does, but it's his fault. He made her accept Lindsay's invitation. If they'd said no, it would have looked like Emma's decision. And Emma would have been annoyed if he'd decided without asking her. Poor Ben was in a lose-lose situation.

Under the apron Beth wears tight black jeans, black work boots, and a stretched-out white T-shirt. Her hair is dyed shoe-polish black. Everything about her says toughness and fight, and yet she seems furtive, hunted, like a kid who expects to be caught doing something wrong.

Emma is getting a sinking feeling about the evening ahead.

In an alcove, the table is set for four. Oh, no!

Lindsay says, "We were expecting a crowd. I've lived here most of my life, and I know everyone in town. I invited the coolest people. But everyone canceled at the last minute. Or else they were *out of town.*" She speaks in a funny mimicking voice. "Or their kid got sick, or they got a better invitation."

She rolls her clear blue doll's eyes to show that no one could possibly get a better invitation.

"So it's just us four? Well, fine, it's a beginning. You guys are here now. There will be a whole summer of parties. If the weather was better we'd be grilling? By *we* I mean Beth . . . ?"

When Lindsay gets nervous, more sentences come out as questions.

She gestures at Beth's apron. "Beth's the cook."

"So I gather," says Ben.

Lindsay says, "I was a vegan until I got together with Beth."

Beth grins. "She only eats meat to please me. I'll make a carnivore out of her yet."

I'll bet she's a carnivore already, thinks

116

Emma. Where did *that* thought come from? She should feel grateful for the hospitality, not disappointed by the lack of other guests. No one else has invited them over since they moved here.

"That's what true love will do," says Ben.

"Neither of us drink," says Lindsay.

"We met in AA," says Beth.

"Well . . . we knew each other in high school. And we met up again in AA."

"That's what I meant," says Beth.

"That's great." Ben casts a panicky look at the bottle of red wine they brought. He'll drink it himself if he has to.

Emma says, "I'm not drinking."

"Of course not, *Mom,*" says Lindsay.

Emma remembers Lindsay's dad calling his wife "Mother." She remembers thinking that if Ben ever did that, the marriage would be over. She'd meant to tell Ben that. It would have amused him. But she forgot.

Ben looks like he's ready to open a vein if he doesn't get some wine.

"Do you want a glass?" Beth asks Ben, not a moment too soon.

"I'm sure we have a corkscrew somewhere," says Lindsay. "For guests. I'm not sure we have any wineglasses. Will a water glass do?"

Emma can practically see Ben praying for

117

a corkscrew. At last a corkscrew and a water glass appear. Emma can't help staring every time Ben takes a sip. She has never wanted a drink so much. Without alcohol, there's nothing to oil the social wheels. Their attempts to talk start and stop like an engine stalling out on a cold winter morning. *Cough, cough.* Nothing.

Lindsay notices that everyone is still standing.

"Have a seat," she says. Emma and Ben fall into the plaid couch that's harder than it looks.

"It's a foldout," says Lindsay. "In case we ever have guests. Which we don't."

"TMI," warns Beth.

Lindsay says, "I don't know why it bothers Beth, but it does. Why she thinks that wanting privacy is something to be ashamed of. I think it's romantic living like two hermits. Don't you agree?"

"I wouldn't know," says Emma. "I mostly live like one hermit."

"Ha ha. Emma's alone for three days a week tops," says Ben. "I'm up here the rest of the week."

"More like five days apart," says Emma.

"What's a number?" says Lindsay. "As they say about age." Is Lindsay referring to how much younger than Emma she is?

Where is Emma getting that? Lindsay doesn't seem competitive or mean. She has nothing to gain from making Emma feel old.

"So . . . how's the house coming along?" Lindsay says.

Does Lindsay talk to JD? He's never mentioned her after that first conversation when he said she was a piece of work.

Here's something strange: Emma didn't tell Ben about the night the bat got into her room and JD saved her. It seems like something she'd want him to know. But she doesn't. She can think of all the teasing remarks he might make, and she doesn't want to hear any of them.

"The house is a big subject," says Beth. "Let's continue this at the table, Baby Girl." She's quoting Ted, obviously. Is she affectionate or mocking? Emma can't tell.

"I wish my dad wouldn't call me that," says Lindsay. "It makes him sound like a pervert."

Ben reaches out to help Emma up from the couch, a thoughtful gesture that Emma would normally appreciate. But she makes a point of getting up on her own. She's not that pregnant yet, and she certainly isn't weak. As Lindsay waits for them to come to the table, she's bouncing on her toes, as if to demonstrate how youthful, thin, and

119

energetic she is.

"Sit wherever you want," Lindsay says. "We're very informal here."

There isn't much choice among the four seats. Ben and Emma sit across from each other. Lindsay goes to help Beth in the kitchen.

Emma unfolds the rough, dark red napkin in her lap. It still has a store label attached.

She says, "This is weird. It's like a stage set. For a play called *Dinner.*"

"*Dinner Party,*" corrects Ben. "That's the title of half the off-off-Broadway plays ever written."

Beth comes in with a platter that Lindsay takes from her and places on the table. Lindsay is wearing a very short skirt that rides up as she bends over, exposing childish white cotton underwear decorated with floral sprigs. Why is she flashing Emma and Ben? Because she can. Emma no longer can, if she'd ever wanted to. Lindsay's showing off is not about sex so much as about power — the power of the young over the old, the power of the pretty over the less pretty.

"A composed salad," Beth announces.

Is Emma being snobbish to think that a composed salad means that you arrange the ingredients with some care and attention to

120

presentation? Beth seems to think that *composed* means one thing on top of another. Sliced beets have stained the crumbled egg yolks pink, among the roughly torn lettuce leaves and chunks of tomato.

"Shoot! I almost forgot the asparagus." Beth hurries back into the kitchen and reappears with a giant platter of thick asparagus.

"She outdoes herself," boasts Lindsay. "She's a magician."

Beth says, "Some people like skinny asparagus. But we like them . . . meaty."

How could anyone cook asparagus so badly? It's woody on the outside, mushy in the middle.

"This is . . ." Emma can't bring herself to say *delicious*. "Amazing."

Ben says, "This is delicious." Ben has gulped down three glasses of wine and is speaking at the slightly slowed-down rhythm he falls into when he's on his way to being drunk. He's sailed off and left Emma alone on shore.

Beth smiles proudly.

That settles it, thinks Emma. Ben is a better person than she is.

"When's the blessed event?" says Beth.

"January," says Emma, before she has time to speculate about Beth's tone: *the blessed event.*

121

"A New Year's baby," Lindsay says. "New baby, new year. So how *is* the house?"

"Coming along," says Ben.

Beth says, "Now that they've bought the place, Lindsay, you can tell them all the weird stuff you didn't mention before."

"Shut up, sweetheart," says Lindsay. "Withholding information from a client would have been technically illegal. But that doesn't mean the creepy backstories, just structural stuff and —"

"Oh, please," says Ben. "We're fine with it all. We've gone this far, and . . . anyway, I don't think there's much Lindsay could tell us that would turn things around at this point. Is there? Emma?"

Emma nods. Well, is there? What if someone was murdered in the house? What if something awful happened to a child? She pictures the marbled composition book. Maybe she shouldn't have read it, invaded Rapunzel's privacy. What if someone did that to *her*? There's no chance of that. She doesn't keep a journal.

"Glad to hear it," says Lindsay. "Because the story gets hairier. Dr. Fogel didn't exactly die and leave the place to his estranged crazy niece and nephews. He went to jail, and they got it."

"What did he go to jail for?" Emma isn't

122

sure she wants to know.

"Manslaughter, I think. There were some suspicious deaths at the clinic . . ."

"How many?" says Emma.

"I don't know," says Lindsay irritably. "More than three. Less than fifty."

"Jesus Christ," says Ben.

"Hate to tell you," Lindsay says. "But they might be buried in your backyard. Hideaway Home had its own graveyard that saw more business than you might think. There was an ex-actor named Bobo who earned his keep working as their part-time gravedigger. Bobo? Can you believe it? Hello, Central Casting? Can you get us a gravedigger named Bobo? Broadway stars check in and they don't check out."

"Roach Motel," Beth says.

"You got it!" Lindsay says.

Was that the graveyard Emma found? But why were the tombstones so small, and why were none of them marked with a name? Emma shivers, then catches Ben watching her. How is she supposed to react to the fact that their home might be a crime scene?

"I wouldn't go digging them up," Lindsay says. "But hey, it's your land and —"

"Was there ever an investigation?" asks Emma.

"The clinic did what it wanted," says

123

Lindsay. "That's what I heard. This isn't the city, you know. It's the Wild West up here. And those three old crazies, the heirs . . . After they took over, no one went anywhere near the place."

For just a moment Emma feels slightly woozy.

"Emma?" says Ben. "Are you okay?"

"Oh, I'm fine," she lies.

"People *have* dug around in there," Beth says. "Just a heads-up in case —"

"Who would excavate someone else's yard?" says Ben.

"Freaks," says Beth. "Ghouls. History buffs. Metal detectorists thinking Grandma must have been buried with her diamond ring. There's a lot more metal-detectoring than people imagine. I work part-time for the county historical society. We have a ton of crap about local history. I've been digitizing it, but it's slow. You wouldn't believe the junk we've got in shoeboxes and storage bins."

Emma thinks of her attic. Those journals and papers, shoes and coats . . .

Just then the door slams open and JD walks into the room. Maybe it's just the noise of the door, but Emma notices that her heart is beating faster.

"Hi," Beth says coldly.

Lindsay watches him without speaking as he pulls a chair up to the table without being invited.

"How've you been, sis?" JD asks her.

"Okay," says Lindsay.

It's not that Emma doesn't recognize JD. Of course she does. What's confusing is more like that feeling, in a dream, when a person appears in a wholly new context. What is he doing here? Why can he just breeze in as if he has every right? And why did he call Lindsay "sis"? JD and Lindsay had said they'd known each other, but . . .

Emma looks at Ben, who's as mystified as she is.

"Wait a second," Ben says. "Are you two . . . related?"

"Brother and sister," says JD.

"*Half* brother and sister," says Lindsay.

Emma's trying to remember what they said about each other. *Piece of work.* And didn't Lindsay tell them that the contractor she had in mind was a friend from high school?

Does Ben remember? He does. "How come we didn't know this? Lindsay, didn't you say that our contractor was a high school *friend?*"

"That's my business partner," says JD. "Luke. He's been in Toronto taking care of his sick mom. It's a long story. I lived in Florida when I was a kid. My dad left my mom to marry Lindsay's mom and move up here. Then my mom died, and Lindsay's mom died, and I came up here to live with my dad and Lindsay."

It's way more than Emma has ever heard JD say about himself. But now, only now, she realizes where she saw him before. It wasn't at the gas station or on the road. He was the scowling blond kid, his face mostly turned away, in some of the family photos in Lindsay's office.

"Then who's Sally?"

JD hesitates for a moment, a long moment. Do JD and Sally have some unpleasant history he doesn't want to discuss? Lindsay is staring at JD. What does — or doesn't — she want him to say?

"Sally was Lindsay's mom's best friend." There's more to this, but no one's saying.

Why did Emma assume Sally was Lindsay's biological mother? Why did she assume anything at all? It feels strange, not knowing these basic facts about JD. But all they ever talked about was the cost of building materials . . . and getting rid of a bat.

"So now you know the whole sordid family history," says Lindsay.

"It's not that sordid," says Beth. "It's

pretty ordinary."

Silence.

"Anyway, awkward," says JD.

"Seriously," says Ben.

It's almost as if the two men are ganging up on the women.

Lindsay shoots Beth a freighted look that Emma can't read.

"Right. So now everybody knows everything." JD smiles at Emma, who can't help smiling back. Everyone sees. Do they think it means more than it does? No one else is smiling. Someone has to be nice to JD, someone has to welcome him, and it's Emma's impulse, even if it's not her house. Lindsay has made it obvious he's not welcome. What's the truth about their half-sibling relationship? Emma wishes she knew. She certainly likes him better than Lindsay. And she's grateful for how much work he's done — so rapidly — on the house. She's glad he's not sitting next to her. Everyone would notice her uneasiness and make too much of it.

"What's for dinner?" asks JD.

Lindsay glares at him.

"Fee-fi-fo-fum," chants JD, in a giant's deep voice. "I smell . . . asparagus."

"Sorry," says Beth. "There's none left."

"I could have some of Emma's," JD says,

calling attention to how much she hasn't eaten and suggesting they're more intimate than they are. There's a funny slur, or lag, to JD's speech. He's tipsy or high or both. Emma feels Ben watching her. Are she and JD so close that he can eat off her plate? She shakes her head at Ben, just slightly, so (she hopes) only he can see.

"You *could* have mine," Emma says. "My appetite's gotten all weird." She's thinking quickly now. "I can't eat like I used to —"

"That's all right," says JD. "I wouldn't dream of stealing a pregnant lady's asparagus."

He goes to the kitchen. They watch him return with a plate of something buried under red sauce and a tangle of wilted salad.

"You cut into the eggplant parm," says Beth. "I mean . . . you could have waited."

"I love eggplant parm!" says Emma. Why does she feel that she has to disarm every conflict, smooth out every rough spot? Beth turns to her, clearly grateful.

"It's a company dish," she says. "You can never be sure if your guests eat meat, so I always cook something vegetarian, just in case."

What company is Beth talking about? Lindsay has already said they live like hermits.

"I've changed," says Lindsay. "I eat meat now. For her."

It's the second time she's told them this, but Emma tries to look as if she's just hearing it now.

"Awesome," JD says.

The tension is too thick to ignore. Some sibling problem, obviously. Why should Emma care? The truth is, everything's gotten more interesting since JD got here. If only he was less handsome. Something about his looks makes Emma feel as if saying anything would put her at the end of a long line of women who've tried to impress him. So she's glad for whatever problem he has with Lindsay. No one's paying attention to Emma.

"Your wife's amazing," JD tells Ben. "The other day I was nailing up some Sheetrock, and she looked at it and said one edge was crooked by a half inch. I thought she was bullshitting me, excuse my language. But I got out my level, and guess what? She was right."

Emma feels herself blushing. At the time her whole body had gone warm when JD complimented her: another hormone rush.

"I'm not surprised. Emma's an artist." Ben has said that before, but never with less enthusiasm.

"She's got an eye," says JD.

Emma pretends to cough so she can hide how pleased she is.

The conversation stops.

The only sound is JD, slurping eggplant.

"Dude, leave some for someone else," says Lindsay.

"Brothers and sisters," Emma says. "It's always complicated. Even when they're close." Could she possibly say anything more banal?

"Brothers and sisters! That sounds like the start of a sermon," says Ben.

Nervous laughter. Emma shoots Ben a look, but she isn't sure what she means it to express.

More silence.

Finally, Beth says, "Can I ask what you guys are doing with the theater?"

For an instant Emma feels weirdly territorial. How does she know about their theater? But of course Beth's seen it. Lindsay would have shown her the house before it sold.

Ben says, "Emma and I haven't really discussed it. For now, we've decided to clean it up and leave it be for a while, maybe with some minimal improvements, just enough so it's safe."

"The reason I ask is . . . our town puts on a Nativity play," Beth says. "We've been doing it for ages. The historical society has a giant file of pictures taken over the years. Since the Baptist church burned down, we've been doing it in the grade-school auditorium, over in West Covington. But it's sort of grody. Wouldn't it be cool to do it in the Hideaway Home theater once it gets renoed?"

Lindsay and JD both look like they've been thrown a curveball. Clearly, Beth hasn't mentioned this to Lindsay. And JD is obviously out of the loop. Emma wonders if the town is going to flock to a Christmas play in a former dry-out clinic and haunted house. Maybe Halloween would be a more suitable occasion for their first community gathering.

Lindsay says, "Sure . . . I guess. And with Ben being in the theater, he could give us pointers."

"Emma and I would need to talk it over." Bless Ben's sweet heart.

JD says, "There's a ton of work to be done between now and then. A ton."

Emma does the math in her head. "I'd be nine months pregnant by then." She sounds like some annoying mom-to-be who can't think of anything beyond her pregnancy. But it's true. By the holiday season, she might be back in the city. Having a baby.

"You wouldn't need to be up here," says Beth. "We'd take care of the house. We'd be careful when we rehearsed. And you could come up to see the play."

"I don't know," says JD. "Do we really want the preschool angels toddling after the angel Gabriel in a place where Broadway drunks got sober?"

Emma wishes he hadn't said that. Rapunzel's story wasn't that simple. It wasn't a joke. Emma feels protective of the diary writer whose name she doesn't even know.

JD says, "If I say something here, will you promise to forget it by tomorrow morning when everyone's sober?"

Could there be a better way of putting everyone *more* on edge?

"Everyone's already sober," Lindsay says icily. "Except you."

"And me. I'm a little *not sober,*" says Ben. "I mean, I'm trying not to be sober."

Emma is the only one who smiles.

"Emma's driving," Ben says.

JD says, "I've been having this weird dream since I started working on the house."

Lindsay looks anxious. On guard.

Is there something else — something worse — that Lindsay hasn't told them?

Lindsay's watching, trying to figure out

132

how to intervene, if she needs to.

Lindsay says, "Don't you love listening to other people's dreams?"

JD shoots her a dark look. But she's not going to shut him up.

"Emma makes me listen to her dreams," Ben says. "I have no choice." Emma can't remember one dream she's told Ben. She makes a point of not boring him with her dreams. So why is Ben throwing her under the bus? Social discomfort makes people say strange things.

JD says, "I keep dreaming that I'm looking out the window of the house . . . and I see this girl with blond hair. She's carrying a baby on her hip. They look like they come from another century. She doesn't look happy. Then I look again, and she's gone. It gives me the creeps. I wake up in a cold sweat."

Emma tries to speak and can't. She doesn't know what she'd say. How can JD be dreaming about the girl she saw out the window? She hasn't told anyone about it, not even Ben. Not since that first time they came down the driveway.

Wait. She did tell Lindsay. That day they came to look at the house. She told her she'd seen the girl and the baby and asked if Lindsay knew who they were.

133

Emma doesn't believe in ghosts. She doesn't believe in ghosts. She doesn't believe in ghosts.

Words take shape in her head. She knows what she wants to say: *How weird is this? I've seen a girl like that. A girl with a baby. I've seen her twice. JD's dreamed about her, and I've seen her and . . .*

Emma says nothing. How would she begin?

"Emma, are you *sure* you're okay?" Ben gets points for noticing. The mere fact of his attention calms Emma, pulls her back from the edge of . . . what?

"I'm fine," she says. "It's just . . . the baby kicked."

"Ooh," say the two women, in the voices they'd use for a supercute puppy. "Amazing!"

JD returns to his eggplant parm.

"Why can't I feel the baby move?" says Ben. "It's the strangest thing."

"Maybe it doesn't like you," says JD.

"What's that supposed to mean?" Does Ben realize that JD is joking? *If* JD is joking.

"It means JD's drunk," says Lindsay.

"Right," says Beth. "Sober, he's the nicest guy in the world."

"The nicest brother in the world," says JD.

134

"The nicest half brother in the world," says Lindsay.

"Also the nicest brother-in-law in the world," JD says, leaning toward Beth. "Don't forget."

Beth sings, "How can I forget you if you don't go away?" It's hard to tell if she's imitating someone with a good country voice, or if she just has a good country voice.

"I guess that's my cue to be pushing off." JD rises to leave.

"Are you okay to drive?" Ben's right to ask. So why does Emma wish he hadn't? It's made him sound sort of stodgy, like somebody's dad. Well, soon he *is* going to be somebody's dad.

She likes the sweet JD who works on her house better than the slightly aggressive, slightly pushy person he is around his sister. Family often brings out the worst in people. Not her family, she promises herself.

JD leans down and kisses her cheek, right in front of everyone. He's never done anything even remotely like that before. But there's no way to say that. Emma touches her cheek where his lips have been. She wishes she didn't feel that jittery buzz.

"Bye, boss lady. Bye, boss. See you Monday morning, bright and early."

Then he's gone, and Ben is still looking at

135

her. Why does *she* feel guilty? She didn't do anything wrong! She didn't do anything wrong!

"Beth, can I help?" Emma gestures weakly at the dishes on the table.

"Stay where you are," says Lindsay. "You're pregnant."

"I can carry a dish to the sink." Emma's trying to make a joke of it. It falls flat. Why did she and Ben move here? She misses her friends. She misses her old life.

Lindsay slumps in her chair, like a moody teenager. Beth rises to clear the table. Beth doesn't protest when Emma picks up a stack of dishes and brings them into the cramped, messy kitchen. Hadn't Lindsay said that Beth is a cook? In Emma's experience, cooks are neat. She and Ben are.

Beth dries her hands on her grill master apron and turns to look at Emma, the first time she's looked directly at her all night.

She says, "I'll bet there's some stuff about your house in the historical society archives. Records and ledgers from when it was a rest home. Patient charts, deeds of sale, stuff like that. Probably newspaper clippings. You'd be amazed how much crap there is. I think the local paper reported every time somebody took a dump."

Emma says, "Text me the hours you're open."

"It's pretty fluid. Text me when you want to come. It's not like there's a line out the door."

"When JD's using some toxic substance, it would be great to get away from the house."

Oh, why had she made it sound like the only reason she was accepting was to escape a toxic event? She's curious about the house, the doctor, his wife, and the woman who wrote the diary.

On Wednesday she drives into the city for a sonogram. Ben was supposed to come with her, but a last-minute meeting was called, and she has to go alone. Today is just a routine test, nothing important — she hopes. There will be more doctor's appointments. It's okay if Ben skips this one.

But she wishes Ben were here when Dr. Snyder glides the mouse across the slippery blue gel on her belly. If only doctors would learn to say *Excellent, Great, Looking good,* to keep up a constant stream of encouraging patter. She stares at the screen, at the marbleized patches of black and white, stretching and contracting. She turns away. She's too anxious to look.

Finally, the doctor says what Emma has been praying to hear: Everything's fine.

137

"Look," he says. "You can see it."

The blue cartoon arrow on the screen points at a shivering peanut.

"Wow," says Emma.

"Country life must be agreeing with you. Keep it up. See you in a month."

She'd planned to have dinner with Ben, but when she calls to tell him the good news, he says he doesn't know how long his meeting will last. It's about financing. Ben plans to float the names of actors who might be able to get them money if they are attached to the project.

Emma thinks of calling her friends, and going out for . . . a ginger ale? Her finger hovers over the phone. She doesn't want to call them. She thinks of various crowded places she could have dinner by herself, restaurants she could order from. She used to like take-out Chinese food, even if it wasn't all that great, but that taste has worn off with pregnancy. She could drive upstate and be home in time to make herself something delicious on her beautiful stove.

She leaves a message for Ben so he won't worry if he tries to reach her while she's driving through a dead zone.

How can he not take her call? Right. He's in a meeting.

Emma likes the feeling of leaving the city

138

without telling anyone. It feels like running away from home. It's five o'clock when she gets to the house upstate, and the golden afternoon light shines down through the trees. She slows down, passes the giant oak, and she's there.

Home.

There are no vehicles in the driveway. The front door is open.

JD always makes sure the house is closed tight when he leaves. She knows he was working today. Maybe one of the high school kids came back for something and forgot.

It makes her nervous, which isn't what she'd expected. The door's blown open. That's all. She needs to tell JD to make sure it's shut. The last thing she needs is raccoons in the kitchen.

Once more she feels that Little Person is protecting her. There's nothing to worry about. She walks up the front steps.

On the porch, in front of the door, is a heap of orange peels. Someone sat here and ate orange after orange.

The journal. The woman who wrote it said she ate seven oranges in a day. A coincidence, obviously. Emma's being silly. One of the kids must have brought oranges, and they had a little after-work party on her porch. That's all. Better oranges than boxed wine, weed, and oxy.

Still, she feels ill at ease. She checks out every room. She even looks behind the moldy drapes that JD hasn't gotten around to disposing of yet. Just as well, since she and Ben haven't gotten around to replacing them. Nothing jumps out and says *Boo!*

Years ago she was house-sitting for a friend in Brooklyn. One morning she woke up and found the screen had fallen out of the door. Convinced that someone had cut it, she called the police. The cop who came was polite, but he obviously thought she was neurotic. How young she'd been, how alone, how anxious. She was a different person then, bouncing from job to job, wanting to feel secure. Pretending to be tough. The brave girl her parents didn't believe in.

Ben likes her nerve, her independence. He doesn't want someone weak and clingy.

She's older. About to become a mother. But still, an open door and a pile of orange peels is . . . unnerving.

That night she hears noises, footsteps in the attic that make her tense until she convinces herself she's imagining things. Maybe it's squirrels: almost but not quite as bad as a person. She gets the knife and puts

140

it under her pillow. Anyone would. It doesn't mean she's a coward.

She lies in bed for a long time until she stops feeling anxious. An owl moans in the distance. She can relax, let her mind drift toward something that happened not that long ago, something pleasant, what was it, something she means to do . . .

She's startled awake by the sound of JD's truck pulling up.

It's morning.

She dresses quickly and meets JD on the porch.

They've never mentioned that evening at Lindsay's. The more time passes, the more awkward it would be. *How come you didn't mention that you and Lindsay are related?* Emma and JD don't have that kind of relationship. She still knows nothing — besides what she learned that night — about his life. It doesn't seem like he's hiding anything. Lindsay's hooking them up with her half-brother contractor, and not telling Ben and Emma they were connected, was maybe a shady thing for a Realtor to do. But so what? It's worked out really well. She just wishes she could forget that JD kissed her at Lindsay's. It meant nothing. He was drunk.

Emma says, "The door was open when I got here last night. I found all these orange peels on the porch."

JD looks horrified. "But you're okay?"

"I'm fine," says Emma. "I mean —"

"Orange peels?"

Emma nods.

"I think I know who it was. Some of my guys have pretty chaotic home lives. They're in no rush to go home. I'll have a talk with them. I'm sorry. I'll tell them again. Usually I lock up myself, but I had an appointment for a friend to look at my truck, which has been running a little funny."

"Funny?"

"Funny terrifying."

They laugh. JD says, "I promise it won't happen again. I'm really sorry."

"That's okay," says Emma. "I survived." She sounds more pitiful than she'd intended.

JD rests a comforting hand on her shoulder.

"Are you cold?" He must have felt her shiver.

"I'm fine, thank you." How sad to feel thankful because a guy notices she shivered. Ben used to give her his jacket. He hasn't, not for a while. She misses that kindness, that thoughtfulness. The worst thing she can

142

do is feel sorry for herself.

Sometimes, lately, Emma imagines she is involved in a love triangle: herself, Ben, the house. When Ben's up from the city, he spends less time with her than he does roaming from room to room, pausing to gaze out each window. He can't seem to stop running his hand over the surfaces that JD and his guys have brought down to burnished wood.

Ben often seems to be in a kind of trance, a sort of dream as he floats along the halls, looking in the bedrooms JD has repaired, averting his eyes from the ones that are still in rough shape. She thinks of Cocteau's *Beauty and the Beast,* of Beauty wandering through the Beast's palace.

Even on the most gorgeous summer afternoons, Emma has to beg Ben to join her out on the porch. He sits beside her for a few minutes, but his mind is elsewhere. She has to repeat everything, and it makes her realize how little she has to say. No wonder he isn't listening. After a while Ben says he needs to go inside and get something, he'll just be a minute. But when he doesn't return, she knows where to find him.

He'll be sitting in the theater staring at the stage. Transfixed. It's as if he's watching a play only he can see.

Maybe it's the musical he's working on, *Peter Pan and the Lost Girls.*

Or maybe it's a play that doesn't exist, a play that's still being written.

A play about the house.

CHAPTER SIX:
DEAR DIARY

June 15, 1957

Dear Diary,
Actors — even washed-up drunks — are *so* status conscious. Who's more famous, who gets better reviews, star billing. Even at Hideaway Home, the saddest corner of the barnyard, there's a pecking order.

I'm the alpha hen. Though I never tell anyone, everyone seems to know that my baby's father is a star. Also, I'm the youngest. I have a future. Maybe.

Dr. and Mrs. Fogel favor the ones with money. Lorna Florian-Beck — a stylish older lady who wears diamonds and furs to breakfast — runs ahead of the pack. She sits with her friends at meals. She talks nonstop, and the others listen.

One day at lunch she paused by my table. I was alone. I always eat alone. She leaned down. She smelled of French tobacco.

She whispered in my ear. She said, or I thought she said, "I'd be careful if I was you. I'd get the hell out of here while you can. Because . . . you know why. I don't have to tell you."

Then one of her friends whisked her away, leaving me shaken.

The next morning Lorna Florian-Beck didn't show up for breakfast, which was very unlike her.

She'd never missed a meal.

Mrs. Fogel checked her room. Suddenly people were rushing around, shouting and making phone calls. We were all ordered back to our rooms.

I'm scared of dead bodies. I'm superstitious.

I spent all day by the window, watching for them to wheel her out. They didn't, unless it was in the middle of the night. I never saw her again.

In the afternoon, I went for a walk in the field. I saw what looked like a fresh grave.

Emma puts down the journal.

The graveyard. No wonder there are no names on the stones. The people who died there disappeared. Didn't they have fami-

146

lies? Emma tries to think of the name of the horror film about the hotel where the guests keep disappearing, but the hotel can prove they never checked in.

Why did they even bother with stones? Bobo the gravedigger . . .

That day, lunch — cold cuts, bread, oranges for me — was quiet. All the residents seemed subdued. Mrs. Florian-Beck had already changed from a rich old pain in the butt to everyone's dead best friend.

Just before dinner, the doctor called us into the theater. He was sorry to announce that Mrs. Florian-Beck had passed. A heart attack. But as always with a sudden death there would be an inquest. A purely routine procedure.

Pretty soon we heard rumors about Mrs. Florian-Beck's will. She'd left a third of her estate to her two Persian cats, and the rest to Dr. and Mrs. Fogel.

Two long-haired gray cats with undershot jaws moved into Hideaway Home. They were beautiful but furtive. They ran when they saw me coming.

The coroner found no evidence of wrongdoing.

No one had seen anything. Well, I had. I'd seen Mrs. Beck's diamond ring on Mrs.

Fogel's finger one morning when she brought me crackers in bed. She must have slept with it on and forgotten. Is there anything tackier than sleeping in a dead woman's diamond ring? The only thing worse would be killing her for her money. And burying her in the field.

The next day, Emma decides to take another walk in the field. This time she avoids the area where she found the little graveyard. The place where she saw the girl and the baby.

JD needs to get someone to mow the grass in back. It's like summer wheat, golden and high, with sharp edges that scratch her legs. No matter how many layers Emma puts on, seals her cuffs and wrists with rubber bands, and tucks her hair up under her hat, she still feels ticks swarming her.

Back inside, she rips off her clothes and throws them in the laundry. She fills the tub and stays there, reading, adding more hot water when it gets cold. She's ordered, from her bookstore in the city, a stack of British mysteries: Agatha Christie, Dorothy L. Sayers, Margery Allingham. One thing she likes about them is that the husband didn't always do it. She's careful not to get the books wet, but still the pages pucker in the steamy air.

At four she stops reading, gets dressed, and goes outside.

JD and the boys are splayed around the porch, sitting on the floor, leaning against the columns. JD sits in one of the rockers. Emma eases into the other.

JD says, "Is it okay if we hang out here?"

Emma says, "Please stay. I'm glad for the company." She hopes she doesn't sound pathetic. They already know she never sees anyone but them, and Ben on weekends.

It's nice, being there with them. They're talking about a friend of one guy's dad and what a jerk he is. The drone of their voices, their laughter, is comforting. Nothing's expected of her. She can sit there, staring at nothing. She's allowed. She's a pregnant lady. The boss. The baby kicks and snoozes, kicks and snoozes. Sweet.

JD's drinking a beer, as are the two older guys. The rest, Emma's glad to see, are drinking some kind of energy drink.

JD says, "It's all going great. It's as if the house *wants* to be fixed," and one of the older guys says, "Really, it's awesome."

"Thank you all," Emma says.

"You're welcome," JD says. "No problem." And then they all fall silent and listen to the crickets.

After a while, JD says, "Is it okay if we get started?"

He means they're going to talk about parts and labor, but it's the most interesting thing Emma will do all week. Of course. Of course it's okay.

JD takes a paper from his briefcase and reads out figures. Emma can't listen, and neither do the kids. Emma closes her eyes, listening to JD's calm deep voice. The insects, the birds, the breeze. Nature is buzzing. It's peaceful.

Emma says, "Can I ask you guys a weird question?"

She senses JD getting tense.

"You guys know there's a graveyard out back, right?"

"Every house in this county has dead bodies buried somewhere," says one of the kids, and everybody laughs. "Usually in the cellar. People are too lazy to dig up the fields." The boy's skin is mottled with scaly patches, and Emma thinks of the still unidentified orange-eater, who's never done it again.

Emma says, "Do you guys know they had their own undertaker? And the three hermits, and —"

The silence is sudden, deep, and uncomfortable. Everyone feels the temperature drop.

Finally, JD says, "People had different ideas. Different laws. Who knows what's six feet under?" He includes the yard with a sweep of his arm. "A septic system that needs work."

One of the younger kids says, "It's *that* horror movie. The city couple comes up and zombies climb out of the swimming pool."

Emma laughs. They all laugh. The moment is over.

The next day Emma goes back to the attic and begins to read from where she left off.

Either Mrs. Beck gave Mrs. Fogel the ring or she stole it. I don't feel like playing detective. I'm not here to see justice done, but to wait for the baby.

I appreciate Mrs. Florian-Beck's warning. But I've begun to think it wasn't the first time she'd said that. At the end of her career she'd specialized in evil housekeeper roles. At least she can still spook people, she still has her acting chops. In the days since she'd said it, I'd convinced myself that she just liked scaring people. That's all it was. The Fogels are unappealing, but I don't think they're killers. Mr. H. wouldn't have sent me here.

If the Fogels kill me, it might mean real

trouble for his career.

Or would it? Nobody knows I'm here.

Emma looks up from the book. *Acting chops.* How modern Rapunzel sounds.

Dr. Fogel's lectures can be strange, but today's seemed a little . . . unhinged. This one was called "Home Burial; or, Keep the Living Close and the Dead Closer." Some of it was hard to understand. I focused when he began to talk about having the spirits of the dead near enough to exert their influence on their loved ones. Public cemeteries were inhuman, he said.

We held Mrs. Florian-Beck's memorial service in the theater. They covered the painted backdrop in black, though Lorna Florian-Beck might have preferred the mural of the palace garden.

Emma shuts the notebook. She can picture it. The mural in the theater. She and Ben decided to leave it there because it was so beautiful. They couldn't take it down.

She imagines creepy Dr. Fogel, standing in front of the mural. A framed photo of the dead actress, draped in black.

Once she would have been eager to tell Ben, but now she doesn't want to. He'll tell her the diary isn't good for her. He'll say, *You're the one who worries about scaring the baby.*

She and Ben used to tell each other everything. She can't recall when that ended. Maybe when she got pregnant. She's become another person. But these aren't really important secrets to keep from him. A journal in the attic. Something that may or may not have happened at the house.

On an easel, surrounded by lilies, an enlarged head shot of Mrs. Lorna Florian-Beck — young and gorgeous, covered in jewels and furs, styled and made up, starring in a Broadway musical — dominated the stage. She looked happy to be there. Happier than in life.

Residents took turns speaking about what a great actress and friend she was. They were actors playing the part of dry-out-clinic mourners. A few people talked about how great she was as the evil housekeeper.

I'd hardly spoken to her. She'd warned me to be careful. She'd scared me, and she'd meant to.

I didn't tell anyone that I'd seen Mrs. Fogel wearing Mrs. Beck's ring.

After the service we went out on the

153

lawn and posed for a group photo. Dr. and Mrs. Fogel were always taking pictures of the guests and staff. We had to smile and say "Cheerful!"

I don't know what they used the pictures for, probably advertising. Look at all the happy, recovered Broadway stars! It made me uneasy. That and the dead woman's warning.

I've begun to think about leaving before the baby is born.

Emma looks out the attic window, braced to see the girl and the baby. There's no one on the lawn. The emptiness is almost as scary.

CHAPTER SEVEN:
THE PHOTO

As promised, Beth texts Emma about when the historical society will be open. They arrange to meet there on Wednesday at two.

Emma asks JD if he needs anything from town. He gives her a list of plumbing supplies from the hardware store where Ben has opened a charge account.

The historical society is one of the only functioning establishments on Main Street in Luxor, an avenue lined on both sides with empty storefronts, their windows swirled with soapy white circles and graffiti. It's in a two-story building behind an arcaded facade that runs the length of the block. It looks like the Wild West or a Wild West theme park.

Emma parks in front of the museum. As she gets out of her car, she hears music blasting, coming from the museum's second floor. Presumably, it's Beth.

The first surprise is the volume: Beth must

assume it's okay, the town is not just asleep but dead. No one will hear or mind, and the motorists driving through aren't here long enough to care.

The second surprise is the music itself.

Édith Piaf singing "Non, Je Ne Regrette Rien."

The song that ends Ben's play.

She pushes open the unlocked door and finds herself in a sort of museum, set up like an old-fashioned one-room school-house, with a dusty blackboard, a desk, and two pull-down charts, one of the alphabet and the other an anatomical chart of the human body. There are rows of wooden half desks into which children carved their initials. The classroom smells of sour milk, stale air, dust, and neglect. Cobwebs stick in the corners of windows so dirty they seem to be made of gray-tinted glass. Someone has gone for historical interest, but the effect is creepy, gloomy, and depressing. Ghost children, ghost teachers.

At the top of the stairs is a loft-like space filled with shelves of boxes and cartons and bins, separated by narrow aisles. Emma thinks of *Hoarders,* the reality show about the houses of people who have never thrown out anything. So many smells — mildew, paper, ink, old photo albums. It's like her attic, but larger and more densely packed. Emma admires Beth for trying to put the chaos into some kind of order.

Beth is sitting at a desk covered with stacks of documents and photos. She's reading a yellowed newspaper, and the music's so loud she doesn't hear Emma. She startles when she looks up and sees her. She comes around the desk to greet her. Her smile is friendly and genuine. She gives Emma a brief, warm hug. She's dressed like she was at her house, minus the grill master apron.

"Welcome. Is this place crazy or what? I call it the Museum of the *Children of the Corn*. But it's cool. I like it. I'd like to write about it someday."

"Piaf?" Emma says.

Beth gives her a funny look. "Love her. Always have."

"That's amazing," says Emma. "You do know Ben's show is about Piaf?"

"Of course I know," says Beth. "Your husband and I talked about it at dinner when you were in the john."

Did Emma go to the bathroom at Lindsay and Beth's? A memory swims into focus, a ceramic toothbrush holder in the shape of a whale, across which was written: *Have a whale of a great day.*

"Right," Emma says.

Beth says, "I'd forgotten about Piaf, so I downloaded a bunch of her songs, and something came over me, I kept turning the volume higher."

It's hotter up here than it is downstairs. Emma wishes Beth would offer her a chair, but she doesn't. Maybe she doesn't expect her to stay long.

She says, "I tried to excavate this mess to find what I could about Hideaway Home, but it turns out there isn't much. A bank book under the name of Heinrich Fogel that kept growing and growing and then emptied out in one day."

"Intriguing," Emma says.

"Maybe," says Beth. "If we were private detectives."

"Forensic historians," Emma says.

"I did find a ledger from the fifties, with a list of residents."

"Wow," says Emma. "That would be great. Could I see it?"

Beth opens a large account book and shows Emma a list of names scrawled in a barely legible hand and black ink that's bled into the paper. The names mean nothing to Emma. Mr. This, Mrs. That. What was the name of the rich woman who died? Mrs. Beck. Lorna Florian-Beck. Her name isn't on the list, though some names have been crossed out. Why?

"Oh, wait. One more thing. There's this. A group photo of the staff and residents. Taken, I'd guess from the hair and clothes, sometime in the 1950s."

"Are you kidding?" says Emma. It's exactly what she wanted. Maybe she'll recognize the people in the composition book, or figure out who the writer of the journal was, or . . .

"I was saving the best for last. Plus, I thought I'd misplaced it. Isn't that always the way? Whenever you put something in a special place, that's when you can't find it."

She gives Emma a framed photo. The backing and glass feel slightly greasy. It's shocking to see her house in this image, cracked and faded but clear enough.

Three rows, men and women, stand in front of the porch.

One row sits stiffly in chairs on the lawn, the second stands stiffly behind them. And the third stands stiffly on the steps behind the second row. On the far right, also standing, is a man in a long white lab coat. With swept-back salt-and-pepper hair and a distinguished, well-tended mustache, he looks like someone playing a mad doctor in a horror film.

The photo is labeled on the bottom: *Hideaway Home, Dr. Fogel, guests and staff. 1957.*

Emma is searching for Mrs. Fogel when her attention is caught by something else. Standing in the center of the second row, turned slightly to one side, is the thin blond girl Emma saw in the field.

The girl with the baby.

There's no baby in the photo, but it's the same young woman. Emma has no doubt. But how could the person in the picture be the same age as the girl she saw? Did she write the journal? Is she pregnant? Her body is hidden by the head of an elderly man seated in front of her.

Nineteen fifty-seven. The year the journal was written.

In a heartbeat Emma goes from feeling normal to feeling lightheaded and unsteady. She fainted once, during a high school trip to Washington, D.C., on a terribly hot spring day. By the time she'd woken up, she was stretched out on a park bench, with her teachers' huge worried faces looming above her.

It was more embarrassing than frightening. But fainting now, in the stifling historical society, would be more scary than embarrassing. A shut-off of oxygen to her brain would not be great for the baby.

160

Emma hears a voice from her childhood, the voice of a kindly teacher: Put your head between your knees. Emma grabs her knees and bends over.

"Are you okay?" says Beth.

"Dizzy spell. Goes with the territory. I'll be fine. It's happened before," she lies.

In a short time — it *seems* like a short time — she's recovered enough to ask, "Do you know who this is? This blond girl."

"She looks more like a resident than staff," Beth says. "Though if I had to guess, I'd say she seems a little young to need a dry-out clinic. But come to think of it, there was a kid around that age, at the meeting where Lindsay and I met. He'd talk about how he'd finish what was left in the glasses after his parents' parties . . . Also, I think they did a side business sheltering unwed mothers . . ."

Beth brings Emma a glass of water and shows her to an old-fashioned couch. A cloud of dust puffs up when she sits, but Emma no longer feels faint.

There must be a logical explanation. She'll figure out how the girl in the photo from the 1950s could possibly be the one she saw. Maybe the woman in the portrait had a daughter who looks like her and lives around here, with a baby. A daughter? A granddaughter? Emma can't do the math.

She needs to go home.

The relief she feels when she reaches the end of her driveway is mixed with a new worry: Maybe she should stop driving. It isn't *safe;* it's a danger to herself and others to drive twenty miles from town to home and have no idea how she got there. She must have been paying attention to steer around the oak. She can never admit her lapse to Ben. He'd take away her car keys. If she wants to stay up here, she has to be cool and pay attention.

The last thing she wants Ben to think is that he has a crazy pregnant wife stashed away in the country. He'd have even less of a reason to rush upstate to hear her deranged fantasies about dead girls and old photos. She used to be smart and independent and fun. And no matter what her parents said, brave. She hasn't stopped being that person.

"How are you, babe?"

"Fine."

"You sound a little . . . tired."

"No, Ben, really. I'm fine."

"Are you eating well? Getting enough sleep?"

"Totally."

"So . . . what did you do today?"

"Nothing, really."

"Nothing? You did *nothing* all day?"

"You sound annoyed, Ben."

"I'm not annoyed. I just can't believe you spent an entire day doing nothing. Are you painting?"

"A little."

"And?"

"Well, okay, I went to the historical society."

"That's not exactly nothing."

"Well, it was. Sort of."

"Did you find out anything about the house?"

"No, not really."

"I guess I'm not surprised."

"Why not?'

"I'll bet that all the cool stuff is still up in our attic. No one there ever threw anything away."

He's told her a million times not to go in the attic. And now he's saying that all the cool stuff is up there? Does he want her to explore the attic? Is he testing her, tempting her? Is this another dare he knows she has to take?

"Don't go up there without me. We're not even sure if the floor is solid . . ."

163

He's just trying to keep her safe. But it pisses her off. Doesn't he know that the best way to make someone do something is to tell them not to do it?

"Don't worry, Ben. I won't."

"Promise?"

"I promise." Now she's made it impossible to tell him anything.

JULY 4, 1957

The worst Fourth of July ever. Sad little barbecue. Cheap, thin, charred hamburgers and hot dogs. Where's the beer? Where's the gin and tonic? I'd hoped Mr. H. would come see me. The theater was dark for the holiday. I was kidding myself. He hasn't been here for months. I wasn't allowed to call him at home, and he doesn't call back when I leave messages at the theater — under an assumed name, as we'd agreed. He's forgotten me, except that I guess he's paying the bills at this house of horrors.

I catch the Fogels staring at me, and when I ask them about the baby — where I'll deliver and what will happen after that — they never give me an answer.

Like a pair of robots, they say, "You're looking very well."

I had a hot dog and a hamburger and waited around for the fireworks, which Bobo the gravedigger set off. The perfect guy for the job. The fireworks fizzled and died.

I caught Mrs. Fogel drinking from a hip flask, breaking the rules of the house, but so what? It was a holiday. Maybe it would turn her into a human being whom I could ask a few questions.

A mosquito landed on my forehead, and when I slapped it, Mrs. Fogel said, "I assume you've been feeling well?"

"I'm fine. I've been wanting to ask you again what we're doing about the baby."

"We've found a lovely family. Very stable, well-off. Very loving and able to provide the child with all the creature comforts. And very generous about our fees and expenses."

"Expenses? Are you *selling* my baby?"

"I'm telling you we've found it a good home," she said. She turned and started to walk away. I thought of poor dead Lorna Florian-Beck. Now it was Mrs. Fogel playing the evil housekeeper.

I grabbed her shoulder and pulled her around. Her furious face said: *Straitjacket.* It said: *Call whoever's working security on the holiday.*

In my most reasonable voice, I said, "I need to talk to Mr. H. I might want to keep the baby."

It was only when I said that that I thought it might be true.

"You do realize the home we've found is better than any you could provide?"

"Mr. H. will help," I said.

"I assumed you knew that Mr. H. has taken himself out of the picture."

I got the strangest feeling, as if the baby was talking to me, warning me, telling me I had to get out of there right now.

Mrs. Florian-Beck had been serious.

"I need to leave," I said.

"I'm sure you're tired. You need to rest."

"No. I need to leave this place."

Mrs. Fogel glowered at me. Then, shockingly, she said, "Fine."

Was she letting me go? Just like that? Where would I go? I'd solve that problem later. After I escaped.

Don't think. Just leave. We need to get out.

"Don't be hasty. Sleep on it," said Mrs. Fogel. "You need your rest."

It was true. The hot sun and the fizzled fireworks and watching the unhappy elderly alcoholics try to get through the Fourth without drinking had been exhausting. In the morning I'd wake up fresh and figure out my exit plan.

I was extremely tired.

In the morning, I woke up to find that someone had put a chamber pot in my room, beside my bed.

Did they think that as my pregnancy advanced, I'd have to pee so often I couldn't make it down the hall to the bathroom.

It didn't matter. I was leaving. This morning.

I needed to go to the bathroom. I got my robe and walked to the door.

Which was locked.

From the outside.

What are they doing? What's going to happen to me? But I don't feel alone. The baby is here with me. Together we'll figure it out.

I feel like the baby is communicating with its kicks, its naps.

Sometimes I think it's a boy. Sometimes a girl.

For now, I call it "Little Person."

Emma takes a deep breath. Then another. Then she realizes with horror what she's probably inhaling up here. Anyway, it's distracted her from the shock of learning that the woman who wrote the diary thought of her baby the same way — in the exact same words — Emma thinks of hers.

Maybe it's common. Maybe lots of women do. Otherwise it's just too weird. A pregnant woman in this house thinking the same words about her baby.

Still a little shaky, Emma turns to the next page. It's blank. Then another. Blank.

Is this where the diary ends?

Emma riffles through the last pages. Nothing. Nothing.

And then, on one page, a few pages from the end, is one huge word in that brilliant peacock-blue ink:

HELP

What happened to her?

In the movies, this is where Emma brings it to the dedicated detective who opens the cold case file. But this isn't a movie. It's real life, and Emma hates thinking that anything like this happened in her house.

Emma puts the book on top of the cardboard box where she always leaves it. She rushes across the attic, careful not to trip. She nearly misses the bottom rung of the pull-down staircase.

She needs to talk to Ben.

She can't explain on the phone. She has to wait for his next visit.

CHAPTER EIGHT:
PETER PAN

It's a balmy July evening. JD and his crew have accomplished so much that Emma and Ben can sit on the rocking chairs on the porch and feel that they have come home. Ben's sipping contentedly from a glass of red wine. He's chattier and more forthcoming than he's been for a while.

He's been reluctant to talk about *Peter Pan and the Lost Girls.* Actually, he hardly mentions it. When she's asked, he says he doesn't want to jinx anything by talking about something that's still up in the air, and his mood plummets so sharply that she's learned not to bring it up.

In theory, it's opening sometime in the spring. Emma suspects that things are going badly, that there are delays. But now he seems positively genial as he tells her — he knocks on wood — that they've finally put the cast together. They've decided they want a beginner to play Peter Pan, because what's

170

the point of boasting that you'll never grow up if you are obviously thirty, and already a star, like so many of the actresses who have played Peter? Ben thinks they've found someone, an unknown. Avery and Rebecca are sold on her. Ben thinks she can do it, but he's not sure.

It's cutting it close for rehearsals, but he's beginning to think that the production might shape up in time, and that it might actually be good. Emma's just happy that he's talking to her about it. Lately he's gone so quiet, she's started to take his silences for granted.

She just wishes that his vague air of distraction didn't make her wonder what a man with a glamorous life in the city has in common with his pregnant country-mouse wife. Well, their baby, for one thing. Not hers. *Theirs.*

There's so much she wants to tell Ben. She wants to line all the uncanny events up in a steady narrative that began the first time they came here, when she saw the girl and the baby. She fears he'll get the wrong idea about her life, and about what she's been thinking. If he thinks she's going a little crazy, that will not be helpful, since sometimes she thinks that too. So many things that have been happening to her have no logical explanation.

Little Person. The woman who wrote the journal called her baby Little Person.

Emma goes into the house and starts cooking. She's decided to make duck breasts — Ben's favorite — even though the sight of the purplish hunks of meat nearly makes her sick. They look like some small, dead, skinned creatures, more like bunny than duck. They look better when she slices them so thin they curl under her knife. She makes a perfect green salad with miso dressing, slices tomatoes, and puts a peach crumble in the oven.

She loves looking at the plates and platters that she's so tenderly culled and cleaned and stacked, choosing which ones to use. She loves thinking about how their food will look on this or that color or pattern — she has so many to choose from — and how pleased Ben will be to eat something not only delicious but beautiful too.

She sets the kitchen table with candles and cloth napkins, and arranges the large, round, pale blue plates. Ben takes the first few bites of duck and makes those contented purrs he makes.

Emma takes a deep breath. "You bought that stove, didn't you? To help convince me to move into the house. You knew I wanted a stove like that."

Ben's smile is broad and innocent. Open. Loving.

"Busted," he says. "Well, it worked. You'd said it was something you'd always wanted. I knew exactly what you were describing. It wasn't that hard to find. Bonus: The stove cooks like a dream."

"Why didn't you tell me?"

"You never asked."

It's true. She didn't.

"Besides," Ben says, "I thought it was a nice thing to do. Fun. Was I wrong?"

"No. You were right. It was sweet. Thank you."

"You're welcome. I'm glad it all worked out."

They finish their duck — it seems like an accomplishment for Emma not to get queasy — and the peach cobbler with heavy cream that Emma whips as Ben watches.

"I'll never get tired of watching you do that," he says. "It's like a magic trick."

The good feeling between them lingers through the evening. That night, they have sex for the first time in a while. It's good, but not great. Emma remembers when it was great. She doesn't want to think that Ben is remembering that too. Comparing. Emma feels Ben holding back. Or worse:

He's trying. Making an effort. Maybe he's worried about harming the baby. She understands. She'd like to feel free, unconstrained, less like a third person's in bed with them, watching. Still, she loves the intimacy, the warmth. It's just hard to lose yourself in sex with other things on your mind.

Afterward, he says, "Want to watch a movie?"

"Sure." She'd rather just sleep. But saying that would be even worse than the less-than-amazing sex. "You choose." She can't think of anything to watch because there's nothing she wants to watch.

"What about *Juliet of the Spirits*?"

It's an odd choice. Ben's not a big Fellini fan, and they mostly avoid foreign-language films, because it's hard to read subtitles on the laptop between them.

"Great idea," says Emma.

And, at first, it is. The film is beautiful, and the star, Giulietta Masina, has the most expressive face Emma has ever seen. But it would be better if Emma wasn't fading out. A wife whose husband is cheating on her, hears voices, and sees things that aren't there . . .

It's like her situation, only the wife is older, not pregnant, and . . .

When she wakes up, the movie is over, the

room is dark, and Ben is gone.

After a while Ben comes back and slips under the covers.

"Emma! You're awake?"

"Where were you?"

"Walking around the house. Everything looks so beautiful in the moonlight."

"How did the movie end?"

"It doesn't matter. Let's go to sleep."

The next morning, lying in bed with Ben, sipping herbal tea while he drinks coffee, Emma feels confident enough to say, "Ben, listen. The weirdest thing happened. I know you asked me not to go up in the attic. But I did. Just once." She crosses her fingers under the covers. "I was reading this old journal by a young woman who'd had an affair with a big Broadway star and she got pregnant and he sent her here to have the baby."

"Sounds interesting." Ben doesn't sound interested. At least he's not annoyed at her for exploring the attic when he told her not to.

"I'm sure there was a lot of that here," he says. "Unwed moms were probably as common as Broadway drunks."

"But listen. Here's the strange part. One of the strange parts. She called her baby

175

'Little Person.' Like I do."

"Weird," says Ben. "But still. I don't mean to be insulting, babe, but it's not the most original name. If you were to take a survey of the funny little names pregnant women call their babies whose gender they don't know, Little Person would probably be in the top five."

Emma *is* insulted. Ben probably thinks that lots of things about her aren't especially original, even a little banal. Having a baby, for example. He seems to be moving further away, the nearer the baby gets to arriving. It would be so much easier if they felt close.

"I'll go get it. I'll bring it. I'll show you."

"Let's go together," he says. "Just in case."

Emma's sorry she mentioned it. Sorry she offered. She doesn't want Ben reading the journal. She still feels as if the book is full of secrets. She knows it's ridiculous. But she can't shake the feeling.

Emma has gotten so used to pulling down the ladder, she knows exactly how to do it — what angle to come at it from, how much force to exert. But like a good wife, she steps back and watches Ben struggle to get it right.

Ben turns back to help her up the ladder. She can't refuse his hand.

She knows exactly where the book is. On

top of which cardboard carton, in the space she's cleared so that she can sit on a little stool by the light of the window. She leads him toward the window and tells him to sit on the stool while she looks for it. The box is where it always was.

But the black-and-white book is gone. It isn't anywhere. And she hasn't taken it, hasn't misplaced it. She paws through the papers in the box, raising a cloud of powdery debris.

"Jesus Christ," says Ben. "Don't breathe."

"Sorry. It was right here."

"Where?" Ben sounds impatient. "Where is this great book you've been telling me so much about?"

"It was right here."

"It's a big attic. A big mess. It could be anywhere."

"It couldn't. It's always here. And it's gone."

Ben lets a silence pass. "Listen, sweetheart. The next time you see Dr. Snyder, maybe you could talk to him about these . . . weird thoughts you've been having. Maybe there's something he can give you, something to calm you down without hurting the baby."

I don't need it, Emma thinks. *I don't* think *these things happened. They happened.*

Ben takes her by the elbows, gently pushing her away from him, looking at her hard. "Ben, strange things have been happening." She's fighting tears. "Stuff I don't understand, coincidences, seeing things that might not be there and . . ."

"Are you serious? Emma, sweetheart, darling, tell me you're not serious. I mean, Jesus . . . is this some kind of *Rosemary's Baby* shit?"

He's never called her *sweetheart* before. He's never called her *darling*. That's how theater people talk. He's always been so proud of not being like that.

This is a very bad time for Ben to have become someone else.

"I mean . . . tell me you don't think you're carrying the spawn of Satan." Ben's laughing, but it's not funny. Emma fakes a smile.

They're both acting.

Emma has a morning appointment with Dr. Snyder, so she decides to stay over in the city. Maybe she'll spend two nights, maybe go out to dinner and a movie with Ben.

At first Emma hoped Ben would be going to Dr. Snyder's with her. She wants him to see Little Person on the sonogram screen. She wants him to be as excited as she is.

But when she decides that she might want to tell her doctor about all the strange . . .

emotional problems she seems to be having, she's relieved when Ben says there's a rehearsal he can't miss. The director needs him to tell the cast something they need to hear.

The hormones are messing with her again, because what she wants to tell Ben is *Maybe the doctor will tell you something* you *need to hear. Something more important than whatever you have to tell the cast.* But it would be a mistake to set up a competition between Ben's domestic life and his work. Besides, she doesn't *want* Ben coming to the doctor with her, so what's her problem?

She gets to the apartment around five. Ben is still at the theater, and he doesn't pick up his phone. That is not a good sign: not taking your pregnant wife's calls. But work makes him absentminded, narrowly focused. She's known that from the start. That intensity is one of the things she'd admired about him. Admired and loved.

The refrigerator is empty. What has Ben been eating and why isn't he thinking she might want something to eat when she gets here? That's unlike him. He's always been so thoughtful. And he can cook. She'd assumed he'd been cooking for himself, as she had.

In fact, she isn't hungry. But the baby

needs a snack.

She can go get something from the Jordanian grocery on the corner. The two brothers who own the grocery, Salim and Joe, know her. She'd told them she was leaving the city and why, and they'd broken into big grins. "Congratulations!" Their kids' photos are all over the wall behind the cash register.

The brothers ask how she's feeling and beam at her when she says "Good!" She buys Swiss cheese, fresh pita bread that Joe's wife makes and you have to know to ask for, and a ripe avocado. Back home, she makes a grilled cheese sandwich and tops it with slices of avocado.

There is never any question of her meeting Ben at the theater, watching him work. She's asked a few times, and he has always said no. Maybe later, but he's under pressure. Emma's presence would be a distraction.

She's asleep when he comes in, and she wakes up just long enough for one sleepy kiss.

In the morning, they eat the pita bread and cheese.

Ben says, "Call me as soon as you're done with the doctor."

"I will," says Emma.

"Promise you'll tell him about all this stuff that's been bothering you?"

It always takes a while to realize she's actually listening to the baby's heartbeat. At first, she thinks it's just the thrum of the machine, running beneath the beeps. It takes a while to get up the nerve to look . . . and there it is, pulsing and dancing, swimming and dreaming. Does the baby recognize her voice?

"Look," Dr. Snyder says, "there's the heart. And there's the foot. And there — Oops. Sorry. We're keeping that a secret. Still?"

Emma nods.

She senses that he doesn't entirely approve of their not wanting to know the baby's sex. But lots of couples must feel the same way. Maybe he thinks it's unscientific. Science is wanting to know the facts. There is always a beat where the doctor almost says "girl" or "boy," or uses a revealing pronoun, but he catches himself. Maybe he's teasing her. Or maybe Emma is imagining it, the way she's been imagining so much.

"Good, good, good," the doctor says.

She thinks about an afternoon not long ago. They were in the country, taking a nap. Ben finally felt the baby turn over. His smile was so radiant, so amazed, Emma knew everything would be fine.

Nothing is easy, Emma tells herself. She never believed it would be.

"Emma?" Someone is calling her. "Emma?"

The doctor is saying her name. Oops. She needs to prove she's right here, right now. Fully present and aware.

"Okay, Mom," the doctor says. She wishes he wouldn't call her "Mom." It seems like bad luck. He probably calls all his obstetrical patients "Mom," but it's annoying. Does he call the dads "Dad"? Probably. Ben is never here with her, so she doesn't know. If Ben calls her "Mother," the marriage will be over.

Who called his wife "Mother"? That's right. Ted. Lindsay's dad. He called Lindsay "Baby Girl." Emma does little memory tests on herself, to make sure her brain is still working.

The doctor hands her a paper towel to wipe the gel off her belly.

"You can get dressed. Take your time. Then let's chat in my office."

The sonogram screen goes blank. The heartbeat stops. Goodbye, Little Person. Be good. Be safe. But why say goodbye? They're leaving the room together.

"So?" The doctor's desk is cluttered with charts and medical journals. "How's everything going?"

"Fine," she says. "Really really great."

"Really really? Two 'really's worry me. Is something bothering you, Emma?"

"No." She wants to say yes.

"I've been doing this for a long time." He has four kids of his own, all very tall and athletic, in photos on his desk. He was her mother's doctor. He'll be retiring soon. She wishes he wouldn't.

Was Dr. Fogel a real doctor? Emma shudders. Best not to think of the journal now. It's uncomfortable when one part of her life seeps into the others.

"It's normal to worry. Sometimes it helps to talk about it."

Emma says, "I don't know . . . it's probably nothing . . ."

"What is?"

"The house . . . it's a lot of work. Ben's in the city a lot. And our contractor is a great guy, I trust him completely, the work's going well, but . . ."

"But . . . ?"

"I don't know . . ."

"Emma, do you know how often you've said 'I don't know'?"

"It's just that . . . sometimes, it's like I

183

have these . . . hallucinations. I see something out of the corner of my eye and then it's gone."

She'll stop there. No need to tell him about the journal. Or the graveyard.

"What are you seeing?" He leans forward. Is he curious or concerned?

"A woman with a baby."

He smiles. "You're seeing your future."

He seems oddly okay with a patient saying she's hallucinating. Maybe he thinks she's exaggerating, or that it's a metaphor, or — She hopes *that's* not her future. The girl looked half-starved and unhappy.

"Emma." The doctor's voice couldn't be kinder. "Hormones are rampaging through you. Some you'll need later, some you'll never have to deal with unless you have another baby. Your sensors are on high alert, instincts you never needed. Try and stay as calm as you can, but look around. There isn't one human being born whose mother wasn't worried."

He makes it sound so simple. So normal and healthy. He makes her doubts and fears sound . . . *necessary.* Except that he hasn't, not really. She talked about hallucinations, and he talked about hormones.

"Think of this as the calm before the storm." Dr. Snyder chuckles at yet another

184

remark he's probably made a thousand times. Well, fine. "The second trimester. This is the easy part." He knocks on his massive wooden desk. "Enjoy it."

CHAPTER NINE:
THE EASY PART

The second trimester. The easy part.

Emma keeps searching for the black-and-white composition book. Wearing masks and gloves, she works outward from where she put it. She searches through cartons of ancient account books, boxes of moth-eaten blankets.

The book isn't there. It isn't anywhere. There has to be some explanation. It must have fallen under something or through a crack between the floor and the wall.

The real question is: What happened to the woman who wrote it? Poor Rapunzel. Emma knew from the start that Mr. H. would desert her. There was no way she was going to have a baby and then go back to the chorus in *My Fair Lady*.

What happened to the baby?

Emma makes rules for herself:

No more frantic searching for the notebook.

If something bothers you, don't dwell.

Don't go back to the little graveyard.

Paint whenever you can.

Ben isn't there when he *is* there. You hear stories about men who have affairs when their wives get pregnant. Once her friend Mattie's husband came on to Emma at a bar, the day before Mattie went into labor. Men are scared of the baby. Of change. They need to think they're still hot guys and not just dads, that they will be the same person they were before.

Is Ben having an affair? The idea floats in and out of her mind. She can't afford to give it safe harbor.

In September JD's workers go back to school and are replaced by local guys who must be finished with their summer jobs and who are even faster and more skilled than the kids — and who also look up to JD. Ben says that this should go in the *Guinness World Records* for speedy, problem-free renovations, and JD says, Thanks, maybe they could just post about him on Angie's List or Yelp.

Most people count the days until work on their house is over, but Emma doesn't like to think about the work ending, and not seeing JD anymore. Whenever they talk, even if it's about tile grout or floor sanding, she replays their conversation in her head and always feels a little embarrassed by whatever she said. Well, who can blame her? He's handsome, and sweet, and he is the only man who talks to her, who looks at her, for most of the week. The only one who seems to *like* her. Of course she feels affection for him — trust and gratitude. It seems awful to have a crush on one man while you're pregnant with another man's baby, but it probably happens all the time. Besides, a crush is nothing.

Among her second-trimester resolutions is to make friends, to force herself out into the world. Several times she texts Beth and even stops by the historical society. But the place is always closed, and Beth doesn't answer Emma's texts. Emma hopes she hasn't offended her. Their last conversation was pleasant, though Emma wonders if Beth thought Emma was asking how someone like Beth could know about Édith Piaf.

It's a beautiful fall. Emma falls in love with each tree, as she watches them turn, leaf by leaf, from red to orange to yellow to brown. She loves the flat, perfect blue of the sky against the brilliant leaves. She wishes she had someone to talk to, just to say,

"Look at that!" She says it to the baby, but that feels silly and sad.

One afternoon, in the supermarket, a middle-aged woman with curly gray hair tucked under a bright blue baseball cap accidentally crashes her cart into Emma's, and when she stops apologizing, the woman does a double take and says, "Emma! How are you?"

Emma has no idea who she is, but it's pleasant hearing someone say her name, meeting a friendly face. She plays along. The woman's name — or who she is — will come to her sooner or later.

As soon as the woman says, "How are you and your handsome husband enjoying Hideaway Home?" Emma puts the pieces together. It's Sally, Lindsay's mother. *Stepmother.* Emma hasn't seen her since she and Ben went to the office to talk about buying the house. It seems like a hundred years ago. How does Sally remember her? Emma recalls thinking the office didn't see much business.

"It's . . . great," Emma says. "We've done a lot of work and —"

"Can I tell you a secret?" Sally says.

Emma's startled. How often does a near stranger you meet in the supermarket lead with a question like that? There's no way she can say no.

"I saw you from across the market, and . . . I kind of purposely ran into you." She giggles. A sweet laugh. "The thing is, I know how hard it is to make friends in this town. I grew up here, I lived here for years with my first husband, and everything was fine. But then I lost him, and Ted lost his wife, and no one's forgiven me for replacing her. His *second* wife. Lindsay's mom died of heart failure, but people seem to think I caused it. Which I did not. He and I didn't get involved until after she died. But people believe I stole him. Now they make these nasty hints, meant for me to hear, hinting that Ted's going to dump me for a new wife. That seems unlikely. It seems a little late in the day for Ted, don't you think?" Another little giggle.

Emma smiles again. How is she supposed to know if Ted is capable of getting rid of Sally and finding someone else? She only met him once.

"So I just wanted to say hi and let you know . . . well, whatever." Sally frowns briefly, but her face brightens as she says, "I've got an idea! Are you busy? Can I take you out to lunch?"

Of course Emma isn't busy. Of course she'd be happy to have lunch with Sally.

She nods, trying not to seem as pitifully grateful as she feels. "That would be lovely."

"Just one thing, Emma. I need to stop by the office. There's something I need to pick up. And I always check . . . if you don't jiggle the toilet handle, it runs all day. It's terrible for the environment, but Ted always forgets. This will take all of five seconds, and then we can be on our way."

When Emma hesitates, Sally says, "Lindsay and Ted went to show some land up in Livingston Manor. To practically give away some land, if you want my opinion. They won't be back till much later."

Sally isn't stupid. She's sensed Emma's reluctance. Emma hasn't seen Lindsay since that awkward dinner. She'd sent her an email to thank her and got no reply. She doesn't feel like seeing her, though not for any particular reason. Lindsay just puts her on edge.

Emma says, "Great. Let's do it," though she would have agreed regardless.

She follows Sally's fire-engine-red Kia back to the office. She thinks of waiting in her car, but Sally stands there, outside, beckoning, inviting Emma in. Sally has taken charge.

Sally opens the door, and the smell of mildewed carpet reminds Emma of what now seems like the distant past. Before they had the house.

"Sit down." Sally motions at the chair behind the reception desk. "It's the most comfortable chair in the place. Take a load off your feet while I get my things together."

"I'm fine standing."

"No, please. Sit. My God. You're pregnant." There's something oddly fierce about Sally's insistence that Emma sit behind the desk. Does she want Emma to feel what it's like to be her, every day, inhaling mildew and dust? It's hard to refuse. Emma obediently goes around the desk and sits in Sally's chair.

It's not all that comfortable, but there's plenty to look at. On a shelf are bobble-head Beatles dolls, a small vase with a single pink tulip, a gilded baby shoe, a coffee cup that says *World's Best Mom*. A scatter of framed photos. It occurs to Emma that this is why Sally insisted she sit here. She wants Emma to see the pictures. There's something she needs Emma to see — to know — before they continue with this lunch, or friendship, or whatever.

Several photos are like the ones she remembers on Lindsay's shelf. Ted, Lindsay, JD looking away from the camera. There are none of Lindsay and Beth together.

And there's one that Emma hasn't seen.

The girl in the field. The girl with the baby. But there's no baby in the picture. The girl is young — maybe twelve. But it's the same girl, only younger. Emma would know her anywhere.

When Sally comes back in, Emma says, "Who's this?"

Sally's lips begin to work strangely, but no sound comes out. Tears well up in her eyes. She takes off her glasses and wipes her cheek with her sleeve.

"I should take that photo down. I don't know why I keep it here. It's like how I never know what to say when people ask how many kids I have. I have a stepdaughter and a stepson. I used to have a daughter. That's Evangeline. My daughter. From my first marriage. She died the year after that photo was taken. It seemed like nothing — a flu — but it got worse. We finally took her to the hospital in Ellenville. She was dead the next day."

"I'm so sorry." Emma can't think of anything else to say. She can't imagine the shock, the pain, the grief. She regrets having asked, unless it helps Sally to talk about it. Maybe Sally wanted Emma to know. Maybe that's why she made her sit here.

What if the girl in the photo is the girl in

the field? The ghost girl. The ghost of Sally's daughter.

"Let's go, shall we?" Sally says. "There's no point ruining a gorgeous afternoon with sad memories." Sally has put on a heavy raincoat and a wool hat, though it's warm out, with no sign of rain. "Better safe than sorry. That's what I always say since . . ." Sally looks about ready to cry again.

"I understand," says Emma. But she doesn't. She can't. She hopes she never has to.

"Let's go. I've made reservations at the Nibble Nook."

It's a joke. The Nibble Nook is the local lunch spot. The point is: They live here. They know it's a joke to talk about making Nibble Nook reservations.

"Hi, Virginia," says Sally, as they walk into the steamy luncheonette.

"Hi, Sally." The waitress turns toward Emma.

"I'm Emma." Emma isn't a local. She's never eaten here, just driven past and counted the cars — the lack of cars — in the near-empty parking lot.

Sally sits down at a table and motions for Emma to sit across. The table is too low for her belly to fit comfortably underneath, so Emma pushes away from the edge. She's

194

sorry she'd made Sally think about her lost daughter, but maybe Sally would have told her sooner or later.

"My daughter was beautiful," says Sally.

"I'm sure she was," says Emma. They fall silent. The waitress comes over. Sally orders a tuna sandwich — something Emma never would order in a low-turnover place like this. She orders chicken barley soup, then worries that it will be too salty. Better salt than salmonella. What a citified snob she is! No one's getting poisoned here. She doesn't deserve to make friends.

"Their tuna salad is world-famous." Is Sally joking? Emma can't tell.

"Soup is warming." Emma sounds apologetic. "I've been a little chilly all day." That makes no more sense than Sally putting on a raincoat on this beautiful day. But it's the only thing Emma can think of to say. "How's the real estate business?"

"Picking up. It's just a matter of time till this area takes off. Dutchess and Columbia Counties are already priced out of reach, Ulster's getting there. Kingston is turning into the new Williamsburg. That's what I heard at the real estate conference last month, at the Loring. Or what used to be the Loring."

The Loring was a grand hotel during the

glory days of the Catskills. Emma isn't sure what it is now. An events space, apparently.

The waitress brings their food. The soup isn't terribly salty. But it's gluey, and the effort of swallowing and acting like she enjoys it takes so much energy that Emma feels too depleted to talk.

Sally says, "There's something I've been wanting to tell you and your husband ever since you came to look at the house. I guess I wasn't ready. I guess it's why we sent Lindsay to show Hideaway Home to you, and why we were so happy when you bought it."

For some reason, Emma has a queasy feeling about what Sally is about to say next.

"I was born there," says Sally.

"Where?" Emma knows what Sally means. She's stalling.

"In Hideaway Home, as they called it back then. A creepy name, am I right?"

Emma smiles. Sally would never have said that before she and Ben bought the house.

"My mother gave birth to me there. She'd been sent away to have the baby. The baby? I mean . . . me. There were a lot of girls. I think the home for unwed mothers was a sideline that they ran along with the rehab clinic."

Could Sally's mother have been Rapunzel? Emma feels an onset of brain fog. A lot of girls, Sally said. It could have been anyone.

"Did you know her? Your mother?"

"No. I was adopted right after I was born. For all I know, they sold me. A local family took me in. My adoptive dad was a lawyer in Ellenville, and my mom came from local money. Lovely people, really. I've been downwardly mobile ever since, but I don't mind. Life gives you what it gives you. Lemons or lemonade or . . ."

"Did you ever try to find your mom?"

"A few times. When Beth joined our little family, she researched it at the historical society. But the trail ran cold at the edge of town. At the door to Hideaway Home. Several inmates wrote memoirs, but they left out their time at Hideaway Home. I can't imagine why."

Sally laughs, and so does Emma.

"And your biological father?" It's unlike Emma to ask such personal questions when she hardly knows Sally. But Sally wants her to ask. Emma senses it.

"I always imagined that he was a Broadway star who sent my mom up here to have his baby. I did one of those DNA tests, and they said my dad was either British or Scottish, but that was all they could tell me."

197

Henry Higgins. *My Fair Lady.*

Emma *sees him.* She sees Eliza Doolittle. Julie Andrews.

All I want is a room somewhere . . .

Emma's breathing gets ragged. She tries and fails to put down her spoon before the alarmingly neon-yellow soup spatters the plastic tablecloth.

Sally says, "I guess I want you to know that some good things — my birth, for example — happened in your house. It wasn't all Broadway washouts trying to get sober."

Emma hardly hears her.

Could Sally be Rapunzel's baby? Emma can't do the math.

She knows better than to say, *I found a diary that might have been written by your mother.* She needs to think. What if the dates are wrong? Whatever fragile peace Sally has made with her past might be destroyed. Her hopes raised and dashed again. Anyway, there *is* no diary. Emma has nothing to show her, no way to prove it existed. No way to prove she hasn't imagined it, which is what Ben seemed to be implying. He must think she's gone crazy. Maybe she has.

No. The book was there. The book is gone. She doesn't know how it happened. But it did. She hasn't completely lost her mind. Not yet.

"You're not eating your soup," Sally says. "I hope I haven't upset you. That was the last thing I wanted —"

"No, not at all. I like knowing that babies were born there. You're going to have to come visit and see all the work JD's done."

Sally's face clouds, just a little, when Emma mentions JD.

Something's going on there.

"Oh, we will. We'll be there for the Christmas pageant," says Sally. "Beth and Lindsay are very closely involved. They've been begging me to take a little part, play one of Mary's handmaidens or something, except that I'm too shy. I can sing, I used to sing in the church choir, but I can't see getting up onstage . . . Anyway, it's a nice thing to do. It brings the community together."

"Oh right," says Emma. "The Christmas pageant. How could I forget?"

How could she forget? Because she'd only heard about it twice, first at that dinner at Lindsay's house, and about a month ago when Ben said he'd run into Beth at the gas station and she'd mentioned doing the Christmas pageant in the Hideaway Home theater. If JD gets it fixed up. Which he has.

Emma had said, "Are we doing this?"

And Ben said, "We'll figure it out."

It never sounded like something Ben would go for. Strangers in his house acting out the birth of Jesus.

But now it seems as if Ben has decided. Without consulting Emma. How bizarre is that? Did Emma sleep through that, too?

"I assume it's okay with you," Sally says. "Lindsay and Beth were thinking that if it didn't work out with you guys, maybe we start a GoFundMe or something and really do an upgrade and have the show at the Loring. We could take up a collection —"

Emma doesn't want them to do the play at the Loring. She wants it at her house. Why have a theater if no one is going to use it? Anyway, Ben has decided. If she objected, it would be on her.

"We'd love it," she says.

"I'm so glad," says Sally.

Well, fine. It could be fun, a good way of being welcomed by the neighborhood, even if they are the ones doing the welcoming. Like having a giant block party without having to provide food or entertainment. But she'll do something. Candy canes for the kids, vats of hot cider, and those yummy doughnuts they make at the farm stand down the road.

"That auditorium was so dismal," Sally is

saying. "It will be great to have a new venue, and a storied one, at that."

What does Sally think are the stories that Hideaway Home has to tell? Stories of the drunks singing Broadway hits and trying not to relapse? But Emma hopes that, if they do it, she and Ben will be accepted faster. The community will know what Ben does, how useful he can be. They'll owe them.

"We're honored that Ben's directing. Your husband has so much Broadway experience to bring to our teeny-tiny little town and our even teenier Christmas pageant."

"He mostly produces," says Emma. Maybe that's it: Ben has always wanted to direct, even if it's just local folks acting out the Christmas story. He used to say that he was only producing so he could direct. He hasn't said it in a while. But now he is directing.

Why hasn't he told her? Because when he's here, he'll only talk about the house. Which wall he wants to knock down, the brickwork that needs to be fixed. Of course he would want to do something in the theater. He still spends so much time there, staring at the stage.

"I hope we won't be inconveniencing you. Especially with you expecting. There're just two Saturday rehearsals, when folks don't

201

have work. A lot of folks have been playing the same roles for years, so there's not much work for your husband. He must be a busy man. Maybe you could be in the play, if you want to and still can . . ."

Sally looks over the table as if to check out Emma's belly. If they're worried about when the baby's due, and the chance that Ben and Emma might busy, they should have thought of that before.

"I'll still have another week or two," says Emma.

"First babies are always late," Sally says. "My daughter was . . ."

There's a silence.

Finally, Sally says, "Well, we're all dying to see how you've fixed up the place. JD's not a big talker, but he really seems proud."

"He should be. He's done wonders."

Sally calls for the check.

"Can I take you out?" asks Emma. "This one should be on me."

"No way in hell," says Sally. "My idea, my treat."

Emma drives home over the speed limit, rehearsing what she'll say to the cop who stops her — I'm pregnant, I have to go to the bathroom. She's a hazard to herself, to the baby, to everyone on the road.

JD is sitting on the porch, smoking a cigarette. When he sees Emma, he stubs it out and fans the air.

Emma's more tongue-tied than usual because what she really wants to say is: *Did you know that your stepmother was born in this house? How come you didn't mention it? Or the fact that you're Lindsay's half brother? Is everybody around here related like some bad joke about rural intermarriage?*

"JD . . . can I ask you something? Did Sally ever mention that she was . . . born in this house?"

JD flinches. "Sally? To be honest, I don't know that much about her early life. We're not that kind of family. I was born in Florida. That's where my dad married my mom, and then left her to come up here to marry Lindsay's mom. They met when he came up here on vacation. Then Lindsay's mom died and he married Sally. Sally could have been found in a cabbage patch for all I care. I was twelve when I came up here. I was almost on my own already. We thought, Hey, let *Ted* pay for my sneakers."

He'd come to live here at twelve. That explained his absence from the earlier family photos in Lindsay's and Sally's offices, and his surliness in the ones in which he appears. Also, maybe that explains the tension in the family that was hard to miss.

"Sally and I don't have deep conversations about her childhood. And God only knows what went on in this place. I don't want to think about it, and neither should you."

JD pats Emma's shoulder, then goes back into the house and calls to one of his workers.

Her shoulder tingles where he touched it.

Things are strained enough between Emma and Ben. She doesn't want to start an argument on the phone. So her anger at being left out of the decision about whether to have the Christmas pageant in their house has the rest of the week to simmer before Ben comes back upstate.

Still in the doorway, he hugs her and fondly pats her belly. She wishes she didn't feel as if he's just going through the motions.

It's five on a Friday evening. He offers to cook even though he's just driven up from the city. He makes a brick chicken, crispy, juicy, and delicious.

Let them enjoy the meal before she says what she has to say. "Why didn't you tell me that we're doing the Christmas pageant in the house?"

She's been rehearsing this in her head.

She couldn't ask any more clearly.

Ben seems genuinely surprised. "I thought we'd talked about it that night at Lindsay's house. And then I asked you again. Here. In bed. I remember your saying it was okay."

Emma doesn't remember. She gets up and starts to clear the dishes, mostly to hide her confusion. Could she have forgotten something like that? Ben said they'd been in bed. Maybe she was half-asleep, or asleep and Ben didn't know it. He was talking to an unconscious person. It's not hard to imagine.

Ben says, "I don't know why I thought you'd said it was okay. I am so sorry, Emma. I would never have said yes if I didn't think you were on board. I didn't realize you hadn't made up your mind. I wished I'd known, I really would —"

Ben's apologies, if that's what they are, follow her in and out of the kitchen. If Emma doesn't say something, he'll go on forever.

"If you want, we can still cancel. We can say your due date's been moved up, we won't be here, we'll be in the city with a new baby. It might be hard for them to find a place at short notice. I'd rather the whole town be unhappy than you be."

"In other words, the town will never

205

forgive us."

"Joking," says Ben. "Where's your sense of humor? They'll forget the whole thing by New Year's."

If there's one thing Emma hates more than being told to relax, it's being asked, *Where's your sense of humor?* "That's all right. It's fine. I just wish . . ."

"Well, then. All's well that ends well," says Ben. "Isn't this chicken amazing? Everything tastes better up here."

As it turns out, Dr. Snyder was right about the second trimester. By late September, Emma feels a greater sense of peace. Her fears and worries — or anyway, most of them — seem to subside, or at least become manageable. She's looking forward to the birth, to the future. The baby will enter their lives, and she and Ben will fall madly in love with their child. They'll be a family. On her computer she plays, on repeat, the Sister Sledge song, and she sings along: *We are family. Ben, Little Person, and me.* The rhythm is off, she knows, but it makes her happy.

After the baby is born, Ben will spend more time in the country. The midnight feedings and diaper changes will be nothing compared to the bliss of having the baby —

real and present and, she knocks on wood, healthy — in their lives.

Emma and JD have worked out a plan. Since it's clearly impossible to finish the entire house, and since, even with all the insulation JD is putting in and the wood-stoves he and the chimney guy he brought in are installing, it will be ridiculously expensive to heat the entire place this winter, they'll shut off parts of the house. She asks JD to check the theater again, especially for safety issues, since they'll be using it for the Christmas pageant.

Emma likes to imagine the baby growing up into a child that feels at home all over the house, in all the unoccupied rooms, the uninhabited nooks and crannies. She imagines her child taking its little friends to whatever room he — or she — picks as a playroom. Her fantasies are like a child-friendly version of *The Shining,* without the horror, the dark visions, and the walls dripping blood. She'd rather not think about *The Shining,* its terrors augmented by her memory of how disappointed Ben was when she didn't want to watch it.

They hardly watch movies anymore, but still, the time Ben spends upstate is enjoyable enough. They eat well, and she likes the comfort of someone sleeping beside her.

She does wish Ben talked more about the baby, and less about the house, but it makes sense: the house is here and very real, the baby still abstract and in the future.

She's also fine when Ben's in the city. Lately she's been drawing again. Little watercolors, nature sketches. She'd forgotten how much she loves seeing an object — a living thing — slowly appear on the page. And she loves how it makes her like and admire herself for being someone who can do that.

On warm autumn days she sets up a little desk on the porch and brings out her watercolors and paper, just to get her hand doing some quick landscapes in which she tries to capture the moment when the colors begin to change. The orange maple, ahead of the rest, the red Virginia creeper climbing the trunk and losing itself in the still-green oak leaves.

Ben is gone more and more, yet Emma feels hopeful. Eventually, *Peter Pan and the Lost Girls* will open, and his constant presence at rehearsals and meetings will no longer be required. They've found a theater — not Broadway, as Ben had hoped, but close enough: one of the prestigious little theaters on far West Forty-Second Street.

Emma can't wait. But waiting is what

she's doing now. It's her job.
Ben waits.
The baby waits.

CHAPTER TEN:
THE THEATER

October passes in a kind of dream, a good dream. Dr. Snyder compliments her on how much stronger and less worried she looks, how much more content. The baby is growing nicely. Emma's weight is staying where it should.

Ben rarely arrives later than Friday night, and sometimes they spend all evening snuggling in front of the woodstove that JD installed. Mostly Ben sits in the theater, where he's set up a light by which he reads manuscripts from hopeful playwrights. On a sofa by the living room window, Emma reads Jane Austen, so funny and whipsmart. All those heroines trying to find husbands in the British countryside: the perfect place for her mind to go, as she rests and builds up her strength in her own lovely autumn countryside.

Emma can see, really see, the life they could live here.

Sometimes, during the week, she sits in the theater. Partly to feel what Ben feels. Partly just to be there. JD has repaired the chairs and blasted the cobwebs out of the curtains. He's left the painted backdrop of the French garden untouched. The radiators work. She imagines how impressed her neighbors will be. She tries to see it through their eyes. She likes sitting in the third row and letting her mind drift. She loves watching the dust motes play in the aisles, in the light from the tall windows.

No wonder Ben spends so much time here.

She's stopped going up to the attic. She's determined to stay focused on the present and the future. She's outgrown her unhealthy fascination with the past and the space stuffed with junk. That's how she thinks of it now. At some point, when she and Ben and the baby are in the city, she'll ask JD and his guys to get a big dumpster and clean out the attic. She'll tell him to save anything that seems interesting or (Emma doubts it) valuable, and to put aside anything they can donate to the historical society. JD's smart; she can trust him to save the notebook if it turns up. She doesn't necessarily want to keep it. Should she have given it to Sally? Or to Beth for the archives?

Too bad it was lost before she decided.

By early November things seem so stable and calm that Emma and Ben decide to invite a few friends to a country Thanksgiving.

Can Emma handle it? She's eight months pregnant.

Ben promises she won't have much to do. He laughs, even as he says it. She'll have plenty to do.

He'll cook the dinner, like he used to before this crazy business of the musical and the house renovation and their leading semi-separate lives. It would be nice to have friends bring kids, but that would mean more work and chaos. Much of the house is still a construction site, mined with dangers that might not be obvious until a kid gets hurt.

Once Emma and Ben have kids of their own, their holidays will include lots of children. For all they know, this will be their last all-grown-up Thanksgiving. They should enjoy it with their (so far) childless friends.

Emma loves the new tenderness in Ben's voice, and his taking on responsibility for her, for their house. For the family they'll have. She feels taken care of. This is Ben's home. Her home. Their home. She'd known this would happen — and now it has.

One reason she agreed to Thanksgiving was that she doesn't believe anyone will want to come all this way for the holiday. The first three couples they invite text them instantly. *Definitely! See you soon!* Why is Emma surprised? People fantasize about an old-fashioned country Thanksgiving.

Rebecca and Avery, Charlene and Jeb, Brock and Mel — they're all coming. Ben's friends. Emma called three of her friends in the city, but they have plans for Thanksgiving. They are all going to their husband's parents' houses.

The guests are so excited! What can they bring? Emma asked JD to fix up some of the rooms they'd closed off and make sure they have heat. She asks him to paint them right away, so the fumes will be gone by the time the guests arrive.

Ben says she needn't worry. The paint they use now doesn't smell. They just need to keep the windows open for a few hours. Emma wishes Ben wasn't correcting her — especially since she's the one who's been going to the grocery to avoid the fumes Ben claims don't exist.

JD understands. He says, "Sure." That's the difference between him and Ben. She pushes that thought away as fast as she can.

When she tells JD that friends are coming for Thanksgiving, he looks a little sad. As if he wishes he'd been invited. She doesn't ask what he's doing for the holiday. Not going to Lindsay's, she bets. Emma wishes she could invite him. She likes him better than anyone who's coming. But it would be weird. She knows better than to ask Ben.

Ben takes Thanksgiving week off. He and Emma shop for a turkey and drive all the way to Kingston to buy expensive wines she can't drink. But she is determined not to be the kind of pregnant woman who makes everyone feel guilty for drinking when she can't. She and Ben plan the menu, work out the details of cooking and cleaning and preparation, scheduling everything around the pleasant naps that she requires, more and more often.

It's going to be a slow week for Ben. *No Regrets* is sold-out. Tourists have bought every ticket. There's nothing Ben needs to do about it, and rehearsals for the new play are on hold.

Their friends go crazy for the house. They can't believe how enormous and beautiful it is, all that light and air and space. All those gorgeous vintage details. They ooh and aah. They aren't just being polite. Emma and

214

Ben feel proud, encouraged by this evidence they aren't crazy, that they're creating a beautiful, magnificently eccentric work in progress.

Or, apparently, Ben is. At least that's how he tells it. Emma's surprised and a little annoyed to hear him say "I" all the time. Never "we."

"For a while *I* thought about that perfect Monet-kitchen blue," he says. "*I* got them to restore the pegboard in the downstairs bathroom and bring it around all four walls."

Even *we* would be an exaggeration. The truth is that Emma and JD made those decisions. But she's not going to correct Ben in front of his friends. She's not going to be the cranky pregnant lady making things awkward for everyone.

She's also a little irritated that Ben is so forthcoming about exactly how much they paid for the house and how much they're spending on the renovation. Boastful, almost. She reminds herself: It's his money. That must be how he sees it.

Avery and Rebecca are Ben's producing partners, so they must realize how much time he's been spending in the city. How few days he's spent here with Emma. All those decisions he claims to have made —

215

did he make them long distance?

Avery has known Ben since college. They're in business together. *No Regrets* is their joint project. And Rebecca, Avery's wife, works with them in some capacity Emma doesn't quite understand, overseeing the accountants and publicists they hire. Emma's never trusted Rebecca, who has long red hair and a great body and is sexy in a way Emma doesn't find attractive but she knows men do.

Rebecca has never been all that nice to Emma. Sometimes Emma thinks that Rebecca believes Ben should have married someone smarter and prettier. Why Emma? A little sparrow with no career. An art teacher. How sweet. And now Emma's gotten herself pregnant. Sometimes Emma thinks that Rebecca wishes she'd married Ben instead of Avery.

It's hard not to compare herself and Ben to perfect Rebecca and Avery. Avery's expensive haircut and stylish facial hair, frat-boy handsomeness, Rebecca's tastefully showy clothes, bought — she'll tell you if you ask and even if you don't — in Tokyo.

Rebecca is the sort of woman who thinks you need a signature scent, so that even your nose registers her presence when she walks into the room. A dusky mix of ambergris and night-blooming jasmine. Emma knows, because she asked, as she was meant to.

Alone with Ben, Emma mostly forgets that he's a "theater person." But around his friends, she remembers.

Emma keeps looking at them to find out what they know about Ben — and her marriage. Is he really working that hard or just avoiding being with her? Maybe it's too much pressure to put on Thanksgiving guests. Maybe Avery and Rebecca sense her curiosity. Maybe that's why they look away whenever she looks at them.

Everything Emma says not only falls flat but stops the conversation until someone awkwardly restarts it.

The last thing she wants is for Ben to notice how out of it she is. She doesn't want him to pity her — or resent her. She tries hard to act more engaged. More engaging. She promises herself not to let hormones and pregnancy chemicals ruin their first holiday with friends in their new home.

Their friends love the kitchen. Ben tells the story of the stove — how he bought it and had it installed before they even made an offer on the place. Already it's become a charming anecdote about their marriage, about a trick Ben played on Emma, a clever stunt that worked out for the best. How funny. How cool and loving. What a fabulous couple!

Their friends love the staircase, the pantry, the view onto the back field.

Ben and Emma save the best for last.

"The showstopper," Ben says, ushering them into the theater.

Emma wonders how many times he'll say that in their lives here.

All six go into ecstasy. What a magical place, how special, they've never seen anything like it. And when Ben mentions that they're planning to hold the community Christmas pageant there, anyone would think that Ben and Emma (mostly Ben) have found a way to span and heal the differences between city and country, rich and poor, between the lifetime locals and the newly ex-urban pioneers.

"Can we come up and see it?" Rebecca asks.

Emma sees Ben give Rebecca a puzzled look. Almost like: *Why are you acting surprised?* But he'd thought Emma knew they were hosting the pageant when she didn't. So there's that. He doesn't answer Rebecca.

"That is awesome," says Jeb, Ben's lawyer, who handled the closing. "Do we have a director?"

"Yours truly," says Ben.

"Genius," says Mel.

"It's what you always wanted," says Brock.

"Start small," says Ben.

Rebecca and Avery say nothing. They don't look at Emma. What are they hiding? Is Ben seeing someone in the city? Is that why he's not here more often? Do they know about it? Is he having an affair? Is he having an affair with . . . Rebecca?

All these thoughts cross Emma's mind, but she trusts Ben. He loves her. It's their first Thanksgiving in their new home. Their friends are here. The baby is on the way. They're happy.

Someone is talking to Emma. It's Jeb. "Have you met people around here? Made friends?"

"Slowly," lies Emma.

She can feel Ben looking at her. Why doesn't she tell the truth? He's as frustrated as she is by how few friends she's made. But where is she supposed to meet them? Ben should meet some new people if he thinks it's so easy. Ben has plenty of friends in the city. What happened to Emma's old life? Why have her friends stopped calling? She's moved on to another life, and they've moved on without her. Are they all really celebrating the holiday with their husband's families? Maybe they're spending the day together and didn't invite her.

The dinner is spectacular, the spatchcocked turkey perfectly crisp-skinned, moist, juicy, cooked through. There are all the great classic sides — buttery mashed potatoes, bread-and-sausage stuffing, sweet potato casserole, gravy, cranberry sauce from the can, which everybody secretly prefers — and Ben's innovations: porcinis in the stuffing, chestnuts in the brussels sprouts.

Emma helped him peel the chestnuts, which was hard but rewarding. Cooking together was one of the nicest times they've had in a while. She felt close to Ben when it was just the two of them at the kitchen table. But now he's a million miles away.

The guests have brought pumpkin and pecan pies, cheeses from Murray's, bagels, all kinds of goodies that you can only get in the city, and that Emma has convinced herself she doesn't miss.

She can't get into the fun. Sometimes she isn't sure what everybody's talking about, and Ben doesn't explain, which would only make her feel worse. The news, the gossip — how has she gotten so out of it? Or maybe it's just that she's pregnant, sleepy, preoccupied, tired from eating an enormous meal and carrying all that weight in her belly. None of them have been pregnant. Let them see how it feels.

When she catches Ben looking at her, she practically jumps to attention.

As if from a distance, she hears Avery say, "That stove works better than we ever expected when we were looking for one."

So Avery helped Ben buy the stove? It makes Emma feel even more left out. As if they plotted against her. Plotted? Ben arranged a sweet surprise. But why did it take him so long to admit it?

Emma looks at Avery so fiercely he can't look away. "Did you help Ben buy the stove?"

"Your husband and I drove all over New York, New Jersey, and Connecticut. It was like a location shoot. I can't remember where we finally found it."

"Kingston." There must be an edge in Emma's voice. Everyone looks at her.

Silence.

Rebecca says, "The guy really must love you to go through all that." She's talking straight to Emma for the first time since she got there. Is she reassuring her? No, she's correcting her. Giving her instructions.

"Which I really do." Ben blows Emma a kiss down the table. She pretends to catch his kiss in her hand, puts it to her lips, and laughs.

They're acting. All of them. Why spoil it? Why be angry at Ben? Next year at this time they'll have a baby. A new life.

"Anyway," says Ben. "Let's not give the stove all the credit. Even with a stove that awesome, you could screw up a meal. A toast to me and Emma! And our beautiful new house."

Everyone raises their wineglasses. Emma raises her water glass.

"Don't toast with water!" says Rebecca. "Unless you want to be poor for the rest of your life."

Emma puts down her glass.

Ben says, "I don't think that, at this point, the baby would mind a sip of white wine." He gets a clean class, pours an inch of wine, and gives it to Emma. Everyone toasts Ben and Emma.

The wine is delicious.

"Names," says Jeb. "Have we decided?"

"Not yet," says Ben. "Emma and I can't agree."

There's a rough moment. A beat.

"Laurel and Hardy," Avery says.

"Brad and Angelina," Rebecca says.

Everyone laughs except Emma, who's watching how Ben and Rebecca watch each other when they think no one is looking.

That night, in bed, Ben puts his arm around Emma and tenderly pulls her head onto his chest. The physical warmth melts away the unpleasant ice of the evening.

"I'm sorry," he says. "I'm so sorry."

There are so many things that Emma doesn't want to hear next. "For what?"

"For taking all the credit. For acting like I put the house together when we both know it was you. I don't know why I did that. I was being an asshole. Everybody knew. I'll never ever do it again. Can you forgive me? Emma, please?"

Emma breathes again. She's imagined so much worse. Of course she forgives him. Most men don't apologize, ever. They always take the credit for everything and they don't even notice. Ben gets points just for saying it. He knows the evening was hard for her, and he's sorry for that too. He cares about how she feels.

They sound like a happy couple as they discuss how great the dinner was, how much their friends love their house. But something's bothering Emma.

She says, "I need to ask you something."

"My life is an open book," says Ben. "Ask me anything. Go ahead."

"Is there something like . . . something . . .

going on between you and Rebecca?"

The silence lasts less than five seconds before Ben bursts out laughing.

"You're kidding," he says. "If there were, you'd smell it all over me. My god, that hideous perfume. I had to ignore it so I could taste the food."

Emma finds it comforting. She knows him. He's telling the truth.

"Don't be like that, Emma," says Ben.

"Like what?"

"Please don't ruin the weekend."

Emma hadn't known she could. She feels the happiness trickling out of her like sand from an hourglass.

"Good night, sweetheart," Ben says.

"Good night, darling," says Emma.

They don't even sound like themselves.

Lindsay and Beth are in charge of casting the Christmas pageant, or, as Beth puts it, rounding up the usual suspects.

On the morning of the first Saturday in December, around thirty people show up at the front door, awkwardly wiping their feet on the doormat, offering to take off their boots, acting as if they're auditioning for a professional production, as if they'd never done this before, though many of them have been doing it for years. For the first time since Ben and Emma moved here, cars and trucks fill the semicircular drive and are parked along the road farther than Emma can see.

Welcome welcome welcome, Emma keeps saying, we're so happy you're here.

It's true. She's glad her neighbors have come. She hopes some will want to come back. She doesn't want anyone to feel intimidated by the house or think it's weird that they'd want to live in a former rehab clinic, a former haunted house with crazy hermits.

It's neither of those things now. It's a family home, and the neighbors are welcome.

Several guests tell Emma how they've been doing the pageant in the auditorium since the stupid public school outlawed religious observances. The pageant isn't religious. It's a play. The rec center is "a real pit," they say. It reeks, just *reeks.*

The neighbors fall silent when they walk into the theater. As if they're entering a church. A cathedral.

Emma overhears a woman say, "I can't believe this is part of someone's house."

So much for no one feeling intimidated by Hideaway Home.

When JD arrives, he stands at the back of the theater, looking uncomfortable in a way that Emma finds touching, especially considering that, for months, he's worked here five days a week. At first, he'd refused to be in the play. But then he changed his mind. He told Emma he thought he'd better be onstage, just in case.

"Just in case what?" Ben asks Emma, when she tells him. "In case someone falls through the stage?"

"I don't think he meant that," Emma says. But what did he mean? Is Ben jealous of JD? The idea makes Emma feel guilty, partly because she likes it that Ben cares.

JD will play one of the shepherds. He's made it clear he won't wear a head cloth and a rope around his head. Beth promised he won't have to.

Emma recognizes people from the supermarket, the post office. The guys from the gas station and the tire place. The girl from the convenience store. And the women at that charity sale she'd gone to early in her time here, the women who had made her feel so excluded. Now they couldn't be nicer, asking when the baby is due, is it a girl or boy, do they have a name picked out?

When she says that they don't know, the neighbors scrutinize her belly and predict the baby's sex. So what if she doesn't want to know? They're going to tell her.

A few moms ask if their kids can touch Emma's belly. The kids don't want to touch her any more than she wants to be touched. Emma hardly feels their little hands through her thick jacket. JD's been working on the heat, but the theater still isn't warm.

Emma has come to greet people and guide them to the cider and doughnuts, and now as the chat dies down and they take their seats in the first rows and start getting serious about assigning roles, she finds a seat in the third row. It's where she sits when she comes in here alone. But it feels so different with people here. She thinks of the journal in the attic. That poor woman came to talent shows here. What happened to her book?

The seats on both sides of Emma stay empty. Emma tries not to feel hurt because no one wants to sit beside her. She tries not to look around or seem desperate. Everyone knows everyone else, but no one knows her.

Finally someone sits next to her.

Sally!

How happy Emma is to see her! How glad they had that lunch. Sally will be her guide. Sally will explain who everyone is, what they're saying, what they're *really* saying. She'll help Emma understand their community.

"Good to see you!" Emma says.

"Good to be here," says Sally. "It's so nice of you, opening your house like this." Then she puts her finger to her lips. Hush. The rehearsal's beginning.

Lindsay, Beth, and Ben take the stage. Lindsay thanks everyone for coming.

Beth says, "Mostly we'll do what some of you have been doing for decades. I'll narrate. Lindsay will stage-manage. Stage-micromanage, I should say."

Everyone laughs politely.

"And this year we have a director." People clap, uncertainly. Ben bows. He looks out over the audience, and Emma wonders if he was imagining anything like this when he sat in the theater.

Earlier that week, Lindsay and Beth came over to work out some ideas for the play. Ben invited Emma to join them, but she could tell Lindsay and Beth didn't want her. She was puzzled by Beth's coldness. But Emma knows Lindsay never liked her. Emma has decided that she's the type of woman who doesn't like other women and doesn't care if other women dislike her.

Emma had been asleep by the time Ben came upstairs and kissed her on the forehead.

"And a star shone over Bethlehem," he said.

"Just in time," said Emma.

Now Beth has a list in front of her, but Lindsay seems to know it by heart.

Joe from the pizza place will play Joseph. Mr. Aiello from the school board will play Pontius Pilate, which everyone thinks is hilarious. She lists the kids who will play shepherds and reminds them to sign their lambs out of the prop room.

Lindsay calls on a very old man who has raised his hand. He volunteers some lambs from his farm to be in the play.

Sally whispers, "He does this every year. Those so-called lambs of his are eight months old by now. Smelly and disgusting."

Lindsay thanks him, but they're trying to keep it simple. She flashes a toothy smile at the farmer, and they move on to asking the high school art teacher if she can paint another cardboard camel, because last year's succumbed to a leak in the auditorium prop room.

Then Lindsay says, "You know what? We have an actual pregnant woman in the house! Wouldn't it be awesome if Emma played the Virgin Mary being visited by the angel? And then we could get someone else — maybe someone with a baby — to play Mary, holding the infant Jesus as she greets the kings and shepherds."

"And the shepherds' wives," a woman pipes up.

"Of course," Lindsay says. "The shepherds' wives. Emma, would you consider it? I know it's a lot to ask —"

She's half shouting down to Emma, and Emma has to half shout back as everybody watches.

"I don't know . . ." says Emma. It seems like the worst bad luck, pretending she's pregnant with the Baby Jesus.

"I know it's probably a hardship in your condition —"

It's that "in your condition" that annoys Emma into saying, "Let me think about it."

"Do that." Emma can't read Lindsay's tone. "That would be great."

"So," Lindsay goes on, "who is going to play the Madonna in the manger? Who's got a baby old enough not to puke and scream but not old enough to jump off her lap and wreck the place?"

There are some small children in the audience, but no babies, and no one wants to cast an angry wriggling two-year-old as the Christ child.

"Who used to play the Madonna?" Emma asks Sally.

"For years, it was the high school princi-

230

pal's daughter. She got married and stayed around here and always seemed to have a new baby. Then her husband got into drugs, and she took the kids and moved to New Jersey."

Lindsay seems to have said something that's gotten everybody excited, and when the buzz dies down, even an outsider can feel the tension in the air.

Lindsay says, "Let's ask Heather."

Emma looks at Ben, but he's looking at Lindsay. Who is Heather?

Sally leans toward Emma. "Lindsay is a genius."

It's not how Emma would describe Lindsay, but she gets it: Sally is trying to be a supportive stepmother.

"Poor Heather," Sally says. "Nobody knows who the baby's father is, and she's never told. Probably because this is the only place north of the Bible Belt where anyone still cares about unmarried girls having babies. But now, if they listen to Lindsay, they can feel good about themselves for letting a single mom play the Blessed Virgin. They can feel big-hearted and forgiving and Christian."

Lindsay beams at the audience. "Is anyone not okay with that?"

Not one hand goes up.

"Bingo!" Sally tells Emma, and Lindsay leads the audience in a round of applause for their own forgiving hearts.

"Who wants to ask Heather?" asks Lindsay.

A woman says, "I babysit for baby Barry, so I know her schedule. She's taking classes at the community college. One of her classes is on Saturday morning. I usually stay with Barry, but Heather's mom is visiting from California. That's why I can be here now. I don't know how many Saturday rehearsals Heather can make."

"That could be a problem," says Ben.

Lindsay won't let it go. Not after the whole neighborhood has applauded her generosity and goodness.

"I've got an idea," she says. "I'll sit in for Heather. And then when Sullivan Community College goes on holiday break, she can attend the second rehearsal."

"I don't know," says Ben.

"Come on," says Beth. "This isn't a Broadway spectacular, Be—en." The way Beth says Ben's name makes Emma think that Beth has been resenting the attention Ben and Lindsay have been getting. Beth must think they've been hogging the spotlight. Beth wants some light too.

"Beth's right," says Lindsay. "Mary is an

important part. But all she has to do is sit there and smile while everyone worships her baby."

There's some uneasy chuckling from these kindly, hard-working people. Many of them have known each other since childhood. This town is their home. Now it's Ben and Emma's home. Maybe it will take time for the newcomers to be accepted. Hosting this play is a step in the right direction.

Sally says, "The town has been using the same costumes forever. One of the women who plays a shepherd's wife runs the dry cleaning and alteration shop. So we can keep the costumes shipshape all year long for free."

Ben has downloaded some beautiful medieval and Renaissance church music, which he plays full volume on his speakers. Beth is the narrator. She'll read the Nativity story from the Gospels. No one else wants the part, and Beth has a pretty voice, melodious and mellow.

Lindsay doesn't want to be in the play. She says she prefers to work behind the scenes.

In the beautiful old theater, *her* theater, Emma loves watching people figure out how to put on a play in which no one will speak except Beth. The music — Gregorian chants, Pergolesi's *Stabat Mater* — is powerful and stirring. Emma makes a mental note to download Ben's playlist onto her phone.

A tall, pretty high school girl named Karen will play the angel Gabriel. How funny, that was the part Emma played in school, and now she's the one being visited by the angel.

"Okay," says Emma. "I'll do it."

No one hears her.

"Okay," she repeats, louder this time. "I'm in."

"Excellent!" says Lindsay.

Ben looks at Emma, looks at Lindsay. He's frowning, but he doesn't object. Maybe he's the only sensible person, wondering what will happen if Emma delivers early.

So it's decided. When it's Emma's turn to take the stage and sit quietly, everyone understands that if she kneels, like the Virgin in an Old Masters painting, it will take two strong people to help her stand up again.

Fear not.

"Fear not, Mary," Beth reads, "for thou hast found favor with God." Emma is shocked to feel tears spring into her eyes. It's miraculous, the wonder of birth, of new life. Okay. She's emotional. Pregnant. People will understand. Anyway, no one's

234

paying any attention to her. Not even Ben.

"Fine," says Lindsay. "Let's let everyone get back to their busy Saturday morning lives. See you all here next week. Same time, same place."

Emma is looking forward to the second and final rehearsal. The dress rehearsal. She likes the idea of hearing that beautiful music and being around so much faith and community spirit.

She's a little anxious about her costume. She imagines her robes smelling like a year in storage. Or like dry-cleaning chemicals. But the costume department has done a great job. The blue gabardine robe fits perfectly, and the white cloth that Emma wears over her head smells like lemon detergent and lavender water.

My signature scent. Emma wishes she hadn't thought that. She hates thinking about Rebecca and how uneasy she'd felt at Thanksgiving. Since then Ben's given her no further reason for suspicion, but then again, he hasn't been around much. Maybe that's reason enough for suspicion.

Like any production, even the homegrown Christmas play has problems. The biggest one is the town's insistence that the pageant

235

be immediately followed by a local talent show. The grade-school pianists, the preteen gymnasts, the ancient violinists. They've been doing it this way for generations, and no one has ever objected. It makes everyone feel more involved, closer to their neighbors. It gives everyone a chance to shine. Displaying their skills and talents is like giving one another Christmas presents.

"I hate talent shows," Ben tells Emma. "I was always the guy who dropped the pins I was supposed to be juggling, the kid who forgot the lyrics to the duet I was singing with the prettiest girl in eighth grade."

"Who was she?" asks Emma.

"I don't remember." Ben gives Emma a kiss meant to say that Emma is the only pretty girl he remembers.

He tells Emma that Lindsay and Beth ignored his suggestion that they have a separate talent night. "Go ahead," Lindsay apparently told him. "If you want to alienate the entire community. If you want everyone to, like, totally hate you?"

Ben imitates Lindsay for Emma's benefit, and Emma giggles obligingly.

What makes it even worse, in Ben's opinion, is that the talent segment won't be rehearsed. No one can agree on a convenient rehearsal time, and no one is even sure

236

they *want* to perform until they see how they feel that day. Either folks will feel moved to sing and dance and do whatever they do . . . or they won't.

Emma thinks it sounds like a mess. But if that's how they do it here, who is she to object? She and Ben are the outsiders. If not for the theater, they probably wouldn't even know about the pageant, let alone be invited to participate.

To minimize the chaos, Lindsay will stand at the back of the theater with a clipboard, and the would-be performers will go on-stage in the order they register with Lindsay.

It's way outside Ben's comfort zone. He's a professional. This is too loose for him. Emma feels at once proud and sourly triumphant when Ben gives in. The town will do it the way they've always done it.

The other problem is that Heather still hasn't shown up. Community college went on break, then she got a cold, then the baby got a cold.

But Heather keeps sending messages through her babysitter. Don't worry. She'll be there.

Fear not.

Emma's blood pressure is up. It's nowhere near the red zone, but still Dr. Snyder says they'll keep an eye on it. It scares Emma more than it should, and when she tells herself that fear is bad for the baby, she gets even more upset. Lying on the doctor's table, she breathes deeply until she calms down.

Maybe it would be good to spend some time in the city. Just to be safe. She'll stay in the country for the pageant, and then she'll go back to the city with Ben. They can leave one car upstate.

After that she'll pretty much stay in the city until the baby is born. JD is still working on the house, so he'll watch it for them. He'll be there all week and check it on weekends.

Emma will miss the country. She'll miss JD. But there are some things she won't miss. Despite all JD's best efforts, a draft rips through the house when the wind blows from a certain direction. She looks forward to cocooning in the overheated city apartment, to seeing Ben every night, even if he comes home late. The play is in its final weeks of rehearsal. He's at work a lot, but he'll be nearby when she needs him. He'll pick up his phone, no matter what.

He's promised.

Ben tries to talk Emma out of being in the

pageant. The stress of being onstage, being in a crowd, performing — it could raise her blood pressure. Emma says that sitting there while a high school girl in a long white dress and a tinsel halo raises her arm and tells her to fear not will not be stressful. She's looking forward to it. She'll like being told to fear not.

She's glad Ben is being so thoughtful. And yet she can't help feeling that he just doesn't want her to be in the play, there's something he doesn't want her to see. Is he worried that the pageant will be bad? Does he really have such a personal investment in this little community performance? Poor Ben. He just wants things to go well. Why is Emma being so mistrustful?

Everything will be fine. The baby isn't due for another month or so. First babies are always late.

The Nativity play and the talent show will mark Emma's temporary goodbye to the house. When the baby is a few months old — in early spring — they'll return.

Emma and Ben and the baby.

The week before the Nativity pageant is one of the busiest in Emma's life. All day long, neighbors are delivering bits of scenery they made in the high school art classes, cardboard camels, straw for the manger, brooms and containers to get the straw off the stage. One kid drops off a tuba, another a drum set, another a small trampoline, all of which gives Emma a sinking feeling about the talent show. Well, maybe it will be charming.

It's amazing how smoothly everything runs, though Heather still hasn't shown up, which makes Ben uneasy. How can they do a manger scene without the Madonna?

Two sweet, responsible high school girls, Denver and Maren, are assigned to take care of Emma and help her down from the stage and out into the audience into her reserved seat, from which she can watch the rest of the play and then the talent show.

Denver and Maren are friends with Karen, who's playing the angel Gabriel. They're Emma's personal guardian angels, making sure she's comfortable and hydrated. Secure.

There is no dressing room. Backstage is stuffy, small, and cramped, but the girls find an armchair for Emma so she can wait for her cue.

CHAPTER ELEVEN:
ONSTAGE

All that Saturday — the day of the performance — the house buzzes with people coming and going. Emma sleeps away much of the afternoon so she can be rested. She wakes up just before four thirty, when the cast is scheduled to start assembling in the theater.

By now she recognizes everyone. It seems like a sign of progress: her neighbors, whom she hadn't known until the rehearsals started.

Emma's feeling calm, centered, looking forward to the evening ahead. The baby is squirming, thrusting out a foot or an elbow every so often as if to reassure Emma of its presence and good health.

A blond girl with a baby is standing uncertainly in the door of the theater. Emma sees her from where she's standing, up front, near the stage.

It's the girl from the field. The girl who

was there and then wasn't.

For a moment, Emma feels breathless, unsteady on her feet. She feels as if she's having another hallucination. But this time she's not imagining it. A few people go over and greet the girl. They're not hugging Emma's fantasy or stroking the hair of an imaginary baby.

It's the same girl. There's no mistake. And the baby is the same baby — older since the first day Emma and Ben came to look at the house. But still . . . the baby.

The girl — Heather — wears a pink jacket and purple leggings that she manages to make look old-fashioned, like something a medieval page might wear. She's small and thin, and her face has that hollowed-out, Depression-era hunger that Emma saw from the road and the window.

She's the girl who turned up in the photo at the historical society and then again in the photo in Sally's office. How could the same girl be alive — at the same age, at different times?

There's a logical explanation: small-town DNA. Sally comes from here. Her daughter looked like Sally. A female relative, generations back, worked at Hideaway Home. But what was Heather doing, standing in the field?

Everything has a reasonable explanation. Doesn't it?

This is good news. The girl was not a hallucination. She hiked to the field, she hiked behind their house. But still the memory delivers an unpleasant jolt.

Lindsay leads Heather to the front of the theater. "Emma, this is Heather, Heather, this is Emma, our hostess."

Heather looks puzzled.

"This is her house," explains Lindsay.

"Pleased to meet you," they both say at once. Heather sounds like a normal young woman, and her smile suggests she's eager to please. The baby, in a furry blue snowsuit, sits on her hip and watches.

"Have we met?" asks Emma. "I don't know why I have the feeling I've seen you before."

A flash of unease blazes in the girl's sleepy eyes. Emma's hit on something. The girl knows something she's not saying.

"Nice house," says Heather.

"Thanks. What a beautiful baby." Is it? Emma's too distracted to tell.

"Have you been here before?" Emma says. "Do you . . . hike around here?"

"No," says Heather. "Gosh, I've got enough to do with school and the baby and —"

243

The baby has seen Emma before. But Emma knows that's impossible. The baby would have had to see her from a distance, farther than babies can see. Emma's imagining things again.

"When are you due?" asks Heather.

Lindsay's tapping her foot. Emma feels an edge of guilty triumph at excluding Lindsay from the world of moms and moms-to-be.

"A couple of weeks or so," Emma says.

"Wow," says Heather. "Get ready. You do have a lovely house. I guess I already said that."

"Thank you again," Emma says.

Lindsay says, "We assume our audience won't care that the Madonna is like twenty years younger than the Virgin Mother getting the good news from the angel." She waits for them to laugh, but Heather looks blank. Emma's slightly dazed by the shock of meeting the girl in the field, but not so out of it that she doesn't notice: Lindsay's calling attention to Emma's age is not especially nice. Lindsay must think it's funny. Has Emma lost her sense of humor, as Ben has been suggesting lately?

"Nice to finally meet you," Emma says. It *is* a relief to find out that her hallucination is a real person. Then why does she feel so unsettled? Something's still bothering her

— but what?

As Heather moves away, the baby looks over her shoulder at Emma.

The play is scheduled for six in the evening, and by five thirty every seat in the theater is filled. Everyone seems slightly high on frayed nerves and goodwill. The audience has lots to say, but everyone gets very quiet the instant the lights go down and Ben's music comes on. Even the babies and toddlers are stunned into silence.

Rob, who owns the hardware store, is doing the lights. A spot comes up on Beth, who is dressed in a red choir robe, standing at a lectern. She begins to read from the Gospel in her low, musical voice. "Behold, the angel of the Lord appeared unto Joseph in a dream, saying, 'Joseph, thou son of David, fear not to take unto thee Mary, thy wife, for that which is conceived in her is of the Holy Ghost.' "

The Holy Ghost. Emma's not religious, but those three words bring tears to her eyes.

A bright light hits the top of the curtain. The star of Bethlehem! It's Emma's cue to let Denver and Maren guide her from the chair in the wings to the chair onstage. Diane, who runs the church thrift store, has given her some needlework in a frame as a prop, and Emma pretends to work on it.

The curtain opens, the audience applauds. It doesn't bother them that these scenes from the Bible are taking place in front of a set that shows an eighteenth-century French garden. They're just happy to be here, watching.

The needlework gives Emma something to do, something to look at until Karen, the angel Gabriel, enters stage right, followed by a dozen little girls dressed as angels, along with one little boy — a first this year, Emma has heard.

Karen raises her arm. "Fear not, Mary, for thou hast found favor with God."

Tears stream down Emma's face.

How beautiful this is. All these good-hearted people, the music, the hard work that's gone into their doing this for one another. The loveliness of the angels, the poetry of the Gospels.

The Holy Ghost.

She's aware of the audience watching her. Everyone knows this is her house. She's not only restored but redeemed it, transformed the space that has seen so much unhappiness, so many broken souls trying to heal. And now it's the center of light, of hope, occupied by saints and angels.

246

The angels file off, leaving Emma onstage. The lights go down again, and Maren and Denver reappear to help her change out of her robe, underneath which she's wearing a light sweater and jeans. She'd been barefoot — the stage floor was cold — but now the girls kneel to help her put on her boots. It reminds her of what she'd forgotten for a few moments: She's so pregnant she needs help. It reminds her that pregnancy is an inconvenience as well as a blessing.

Something brushes against her cheek as she leaves the wings. It's Ben, kissing her. Gratitude and relief flood through her.

Everything will be fine.

Fear not.

All Heather has to do is sit there and hold the baby and nod as the shepherds kneel and pay their respects to the child, little baby Barry. When the cardboard, wood, and shag-rug camels appear onstage, the audience cheers, an exultant moment in the mostly serious pageant.

The Three Kings — high school boys in fake beards and turbans — bring down the house.

Emma almost bursts out laughing when she spots JD, painfully self-conscious in his burlap shepherd's robe, tied at the waist with a rope. Emma's happy to see him. She's glad he's still working on the house, that after she returns with the baby he will still be there, and they will continue working together — planning and deciding on construction details while the baby nurses and sleeps.

Finally, Beth comes to the end of her reading. Everyone onstage — Mary and Joseph, the shepherds and kings — face the audience and bow solemnly. Wild applause rocks the theater.

Ben's mixtape switches over to Handel's *Messiah*.

For unto us a child is born, unto us a son is given.

Joy, pure joy. They've done the play. It all worked better than anyone could have imagined.

"Intermission," announces Beth. "Ten minutes, then back in your seats for the talent show."

Just when Emma's wishing she could slap Ben a high five for the success of the pageant, Ben appears out of the crowd, raises his hand, and they grin and exchange high fives. They're reading each other's minds. They're doing this together. It's their house, and in a way, their play. Maybe they'll do it every year. Maybe this is their future. Babysitters, groceries. Emma can paint when the baby naps. Ben will have another hit play.

Ben puts his arm around her and they stand like that for a while. No one comes to talk to them, but everybody is aware of them, and gives them friendly smiles. The guy from the hardware store gives them a hearty thumbs-up.

Emma turns to see people lining up and giving their names to Lindsay, who is nodding and writing everything down on a clipboard. Sally stands beside Lindsay, chatting people up. Emma can tell she's trying to make them comfortable enough to go on-stage.

The success of the Nativity play must have encouraged more people to participate in the talent segment. They can tell it's a friendly audience, an easy, generous crowd.

"That's as good as it's going to get," says Ben, too low for anyone to hear. "Don't expect much from here on."

"Come on," says Emma. "There's something so sweet about this whole thing. It could be fun."

"Let's hope," says Ben. "Meanwhile, I'm going backstage in case one of the hula-hoopers gets hurt."

Lindsay gives the clipboard to Beth, who is going to be the emcee. The first act is a middle school girl in a white dress that seems to have been stitched from shredded scraps of Kleenex and a guitar slung across her chest. She sings "Landslide," her voice a trembly octave above Stevie Nicks's. She keeps pulling and lifting the guitar strap, so maybe the instrument is too heavy for her, which is maybe why she gives the lyrics an oddly furious tone. Then a woman in a cheerleading costume does a slightly inappropriate dance to a Shakira song, swinging her long blond hair, crouching and grabbing suggestively at her crotch. It stuns the crowd into silence.

But harmony is restored when a sweet, overweight eighth-grade boy comes out and plays "The Star-Spangled Banner" on his tuba. A few kids stand, maybe wanting a better view of their friend, maybe confusing the national anthem with the Pledge of Allegiance. Other kids laugh as parents push their standing kids back into their chairs. A piano is wheeled out onstage and a woman Beth introduces as "everyone's favorite piano teacher" plays the first section of the *Moonlight* Sonata.

A little girl sings a passionate love song Emma doesn't recognize and can't pay attention to because the girl is the wrong distance from the mic, which explodes every time she sings "baby" and "please," two words she repeats a lot. Plus, the drum machine is too loud.

A cute little boy in thick glasses plays the spoons, a talent Beth introduces as a "lost art." He's Emma's favorite. A girl with two knee bandages and scraps of tulle mysteriously tucked into the waistband of her denim shorts does a melancholy gymnastic routine to Antony and the Johnsons' song about wanting to become a girl. Does the audience know what the song is saying? Would they care? Five kindergarteners sing "Do-Re-Mi."

Finally, Beth says, "And now for our last act."

The audience applauds so hard at their last chance that Emma misses the name of the final performer.

A woman tiptoes out onstage, sideways, like a crab. The audience applauds. She's wearing a funny hat shaped like a pastry tart, an old-fashioned wasp-waist jacket, a long skirt, and sensible shoes. And she's carrying an umbrella. An open umbrella indoors? Doesn't she know it's bad luck?

She closes it. Her smile is coy and flirta-

251

tious. Tendrils of gray hair peek out from the edges of her dark wig. Her heavy makeup makes her look like a clown-faced Mary Poppins.

Emma knows her from somewhere, but the wig and makeup are confusing. Who is she? The audience knows. They're laughing. They love it.

She stands at the microphone and waits, as if for an orchestra to start up. There is no orchestra. She's on her own. She frowns. She seems distracted, totters a little. Is she ill?

She begins to sing. Her voice is wobbly but clear. A good church-choir soprano, a cappella and very slow, like a record played at the wrong speed, threatening and dirge-like:

"All I want is a room somewhere."

Seven words. That's all it takes. Emma's adrenaline spikes. She lays both hands flat on her belly.

Stay calm. Stay calm. Stay calm.

It's not Mary Poppins.

It's Eliza Doolittle. Eliza Doolittle from *My Fair Lady.*

Now Emma recognizes Sally. She should have known right away. Why didn't she?

Because it's too perfect. Too strange. And Sally said she'd never dare to go onstage. But it's true. It's her. She's singing the last song Emma wants to hear, the song she heard in her head all last summer, the song Rapunzel sang in the Broadway chorus.

Why does Eliza Doolittle need an umbrella? And why is she singing so slowly?

Sally is singing the song her mother sang in the chorus on Broadway.

The song Sally's mother wrote about in her journal.

"Far away from the cold night air."

Emma scrambles to put the fragments together. She's missing the piece — the critical piece — that might solve the puzzle.

Earlier, in the Nativity pageant, there was . . . the girl and the baby. The baby looked at her. He knew he'd seen her before.

Only crazy people imagine that babies see them from a distance and remember them months later.

"With one enormous chair."

The woman reaches into an enormous carpet bag slung over one shoulder and pulls out a doll. It's a baby doll, with a frilly bonnet and a bow around its neck. A black bow. She turns it to face the audience, but the doll has no face, just a jagged wound surrounded by a stained white ruffle. Its face looks as if it's been chewed off by an animal, leaving two ragged holes, extruding stuffing where its eyes should have been.

Emma feels tiny, as if she's being pushed into a gigantic armchair. She's a child, a child's doll, drowning in the upholstery, struggling to breathe. She's Alice in Wonderland, shrunk to the size of a mouse.

The woman points the doll at Emma, then dances it in the air in time to her slow, menacing song.

Emma's having a waking nightmare. She's not herself. What does *herself* even mean?

She watches herself — watches *her* — doing things she would never do.

Interrupting the performance. Jumping up. Her chair scrapes, loud.

Everyone turns. Let them look.

She turns.

It's her house.

The theater is inside her house.

She lives there.

She faces the stage.

Eliza Doolittle is looking at her. She knows that Emma knows. She's waving the doll in Emma's direction.

Something terrible is happening. But why is it happening to *Emma*?

Someone is dead or about to be dead.

"Oh, wouldn't it be loverly?"

The woman stuffs the doll back in the bag and opens the umbrella again, raises it, and twirls around. She misses a step, almost trips, catches herself. When she stops, she's staring out at the audience. Staring at Emma.

As if from a distance Emma hears herself scream. She never screams, not even in nightmares when she so wants to scream, and she can't.

She turns. Who hears her? Who will help?

Faces float around her like headlights in the dark, like bulbs on a Christmas tree. They drift in and out of focus, a theater full of worried strangers wondering what to do about a massively pregnant woman, standing there.

Screaming and screaming.

When she tries to open her eyes everything is covered with mirrors, glittering. Too bright! Finally the light dims, and she sees people around her, above her, looking down. She's lying on the floor. She feels someone behind her, supporting her head and shoulders. She turns. It's a man. She assumes it's Ben, but it's JD. Upside down. He smiles at her, and she tries to smile back. But she can't, she just can't.

She's lost track of time. Seconds or maybe hours later, Ben pushes his way through the crowd. At first he seems to be scowling at her and JD, she can't be sure. Ben adjusts his face to look more like a guy whose beloved pregnant wife has screamed and fainted in the middle of the community talent show than a guy who . . . what? Emma's woozy again.

It's so hot in here. She claws at her sweater.

She's gone off script. Wrecked the show. That's what she sees in Ben's face. He's more annoyed than worried. She's dizzy, disoriented, but not so far gone she doesn't know she's ruined the event, ended it before they could even announce the winner of the talent show.

Through the fog, she hears Ben saying that she's been having blood pressure problems. Maybe she stood up too fast and the blood rushed to her feet and she felt off balance and screamed because she was going to faint. Suddenly lots of people are helping or trying to help. They ease her into a chair.

Beth goes up to the microphone. "Good night, everyone. Let's hear it for the performers."

There's some confused applause. It's weird to be clapping with Emma still half-conscious. Beth thanks everyone for coming and wishes them a Merry Christmas and a Happy New Year.

Once, when she was a girl, she'd turned on the light switch in her friend's house and faulty wiring blew her across the kitchen. This felt a little like that. The shock of Sally singing the song that was in the journal — the notebook that, as far as she knows, no one else has ever seen — knocked her clear off her feet.

Ben helps her stand. The dizziness is beginning to go away, and she doesn't seem to have hurt herself falling. Nothing hurts. Nothing aches. Her light-headedness is improving.

"Are you feeling better, dear?" It's Sally, with her clown makeup off and without the wig and hat. How did she change so quickly?

"Why did you pick that song?" says Emma.

"I always liked it," Sally said.

257

"And that's all?"

"What else would there be?"

Emma believes her.

All I want . . .

Then Sally comes close to Emma and whispers in her ear. "I'd be careful if I was you. I'd get the hell out of here while you can. Because . . . you know why. I don't have to tell you."

The words sound familiar. Emma feels as if she's heard them before. Or . . . read them before. Wait. It's what the old lady who got murdered said to the woman who wrote the journal. Does Sally know? Why is she warning her? Has Sally read the journal? Emma feels woozy again.

Sally's saying something. "I was forced to sing that song. It wasn't my idea. I am so sorry."

"Who did?" whispers Emma. "Who made you sing it?"

Sally is moving her mouth, but Emma can't hear her. Everything — her hearing, her vision — has gone terrifyingly fuzzy.

By the time this new spell of dizziness has passed, Sally is gone, and Ben has taken her place. Is he frowning or looking concerned? How odd that Emma can't tell.

Emma props herself up and puts her hands on her belly. The baby kicks hello.

There must be an explanation. A reason for everything. It's very simple, she just isn't seeing it. She feels stupid. But no one warned her that she was going to have to deal with this on top of being nine months pregnant. No one prepared her. No one could have imagined it. No one — including Emma — knows what's happening. A haunted house and a decades-old murder is not in any of the baby books.

She needs to be near the hospital, her doctor, just in case. What if she faints again? What if she hurts the baby?

"Let's go to the city," she tells Ben.

"We're on our way," says Ben. "We'll leave the minute we can."

The crowd has put on their coats and left. Emma seems to have lost track of time again. Two camels and a cardboard sheep are all that remain of the play. Lindsay, Beth, and JD stand around awkwardly, waiting for direction. JD offers to close up the house and look after things while they're gone. Beth and Lindsay say they'll help.

Emma's calm enough to tell Lindsay that she had an emergency bag packed and ready, in case she suddenly had to go to the hospital. It's in the bedroom closet. Lindsay skips away and returns with the bag, plus a coat, scarf, and gloves into which they bundle Emma.

Ben eases her into the front seat of his car. He's had the engine running for a while to warm it up. It's cozy and nice inside. How thoughtful everyone is. And how unhinged Emma is, to ruin everyone's evening, for which they worked so hard, just because of some coincidence, a Broadway song she read about in a book that might not even exist. A weird coincidence.

What else could it be?

In the car, all the way to the city, Emma weeps. Pregnancy is a great excuse: the discomfort, the hormonal shifts. The worry! The scariness of having fainted. The embarrassment of fainting in front of the whole town. The guilt for having ruined Ben's hard work, though she knows it's not really her fault.

She's having all the wrong emotions! The right one would be . . . anger. She needs to make Ben help her figure out what is going on.

Because the real reason for her despair is the frustration, the fact she can't ask Ben for help. She can't tell the person who is supposed to be her closest ally.

She can't begin to tell him about Sally, the song. She can't say *Explain this, please!*

He showed her that there was no journal. And now Sally has sung the song from the nonexistent journal.

Maybe the gap between them started opening a long time ago and she just didn't notice.

She's afraid to say what she wants and needs to say. She's afraid he'll think she's crazy. She's afraid he'll tell other people she's crazy, and they'll take the baby away. *Where did that thought come from?* It's impossible, unreal. But how to explain what's happened? The notebook, the song, the girl in the field . . . Maybe she *is* out of her mind. The chemicals, the hormones . . .

Sally. The journal. The song. Everything seems connected, everything makes perfect sense and no sense at all. Something keeps eluding her. It's like trying to remember a dream. If she tells Ben, it will mean talking about the journal again. Which she couldn't find when he came up to the attic. Did he think she'd made it up?

Of course he wouldn't understand why she was so shocked when Sally sang that song. Especially since Emma wonders if Sally could be the journal writer's daughter. Even so, how would Sally — given away at birth — know about the song, maybe the only song her mother ever sang on Broadway?

There is nowhere Emma can begin. No way she can unravel the knots without making Ben think she's lost it.

Ben is driving a little too fast, and every so often a sliver of ice slaps against the window. The lights of Route 17 blur into flashes of color coming at them from both sides of the slick highway.

And that's when she realizes: She's scared of Ben. Not of something he might do to her, but of how he might see her. Of whom he might think she is. A crazy woman, a lunatic.

An unfit mother.

Another nasty rogue idea has wormed its way into her brain.

No one has ever suggested she wouldn't be a good mother. But Ben has hinted that she was imagining things. It's only a few small steps from *hallucinating* to *unfit*. You don't let a person who is hallucinating take care of a baby!

Does Ben want to leave her and take the baby?

Maybe he *is* having an affair with Rebecca. Rebecca can't have kids. Maybe Ben and Rebecca are plotting to steal Little Person.

Ben looks grim. It's begun to snow, and

driving takes all his concentration. There's black ice, and an icy mist coats the asphalt.

He's a good driver. Emma trusts him.

Every so often he looks over at her, obviously worried. Her face aches, half from weeping and half from smiling to prove that she's fine.

"Please," says Ben. "Please don't cry. Everything will be okay."

But how can he say that when he has no idea?

Everything feels dizzying, confusing, and disturbing — but physically she feels fine. The baby is swimming and kicking. Emma's not queasy or light-headed. Her heart's beating calmly and steadily. If she hadn't screamed and fallen down in the middle of the community talent show, she'd never suspect anything unusual happened.

Ben says, "We need to call Snyder's office and take you to the ER."

"No," she says. "Please. Trust me on this. I think I'm okay. It just got very hot in there."

He knows that the theater was cold.

"Please. The hospital's where you *get* sick, exposed to all those ER germs. I feel fine."

"Let's just go there —"

"No!" The force of her resistance surprises them both. What shocks Emma more is how

263

angry she is. Ben is worried, he's trying to help. To keep her and the baby safe.

"If I go to the ER and get sick, it will be your fault. That will be on you."

"You make that seem like a threat," says Ben.

"It's a fact," she says. "Take it any way you want."

How unhappy they sound. They don't sound like a couple who love each other and are going to have a child.

"I'm trying to help you, Emma. To keep you and the baby safe."

"I'm sorry," says Emma, but she isn't. "I want to go to our apartment and lie down and fall asleep. Can I do that? Can I just do that?"

"Okay," Ben says. "But the minute you feel even slightly weird or uncomfortable, you'll tell me. Promise?"

Emma promises. But it's a lie. So many things feel weird and uncomfortable. If only she could tell him.

It feels good to be home in their apartment. It's way overheated, in that New York apartment winter-hothouse way. But cozy. The planet is going to have to forgive Emma and Ben for now. She'll turn the thermostat down tomorrow. For the moment all she wants is to be warm. Only now, when she's no longer there, can she admit that the house's draftiness was a problem. The furnace and the heating system are maybe eighty percent effective — a miracle, considering. But the house has cold spots, chilly winds blow through.

In time JD will fix that. But he hasn't yet. Why did she *imagine* she could stay up there with a baby during the dead of winter? She wasn't thinking. She'd wanted Ben to see her a certain way, wanted to *be* a certain way. Tough, independent. Daring. The woman he married. The girl whose parents said she wasn't brave.

And now it's backfired. Or something has. There are too many coincidences and overlaps, little warps in time. Something is wrong.

She slumps onto the couch and sits there like a blob while Ben bustles around, tidying up.

"What can I get you?" he asks. "Herbal tea?"

"Since when do you drink herbal tea?"

"I got it for you. I knew you were coming back and can't have caffeine, though at this point . . ."

"At this point what?" Emma is *so* sick of hearing him criticize her for being overcau-

265

tious, neurotic. Living alone in the middle of nowhere for most of her pregnancy — isn't that nervy enough?

"Look, Emma, I still think you should go to the ER. Want some water?"

"No thanks."

"You should hydrate." Ben fills a glass from the sink and drinks it in one long gulp. She watches his Adam's apple bob like . . . the baby's foot rippling in her belly.

"No. I'm fine." Is she? She's confused, is all.

Puzzle. The word forms in her mind before she recalls what pieces she needs to fit. The journal, Sally's song. Something about it terrifies her. She tells herself not to panic and panics all over again.

Maybe Ben is right. She needs to go to the emergency room. She needs to talk to someone who can help her sort things out. But where would she begin? The possible daughter of a possibly dead woman sang a song that is possibly the only song that the possibly dead mother sang on Broadway.

Could Sally have found the journal and guessed that her mother wrote it and sang the song as a tribute to her mother? Could JD have found it and given it to his stepmother? That seems like the last thing JD would do.

Scraps of the evening come back. The tuba player. *Fear not, Mary, for thou has found favor with God.* Maybe Emma can ask Ben to play that beautiful church music. . . . No. The last thing she wants is to revisit the play.

She wants to forget — and understand. She can't do both at once. She doesn't know what she wants. *Stay focused.*

Something is coming back to her.

Just before they got in the car to come to the city, Ben made a call on his cell. Emma only caught parts of the conversation, but she thought she heard Ben telling someone to straighten up the apartment, they were on their way.

Well, sure. He's been working constantly. Not a lot of time for housekeeping. She wonders who he called. She can't bring herself to ask. Not even to make conversation. Enough has happened tonight.

The real reason she doesn't want to know is that she's afraid he called Rebecca.

For now she just needs to stand. She can make it as far as the refrigerator. That will be her goal.

She'd like help getting off the couch, but Ben's in the bedroom. She plants both hands on the edge of the sofa and heaves herself up.

Two wineglasses are in the sink. There's lipstick on the rim of one. In a crime show, the detective would identify the woman by the shade of the lipstick. But Emma's way past noticing what color lipstick anyone wears.

Ben got water a few minutes ago. He must have seen the glasses. Why didn't he hide them? Maybe he *wants* Emma to find them. What a cowardly way to tell your wife you're having an affair: two wineglasses in the sink.

An alternate explanation is that Ben has nothing to hide.

"Ben, can you come here a minute?"

Ben arrives instantly. "Is everything okay?"

"Fine. I guess. Whose wineglasses are these?"

Ben laughs. "Oh no! The classic tell. The cheating husband. The murderer. The smart detective solves the case with the lip prints on the glass. Look, if I was either of those things, the cheating husband or the murderer, don't you think I would have washed or tossed those glasses the second we got home? I asked Avery and Rebecca to pop over here and make sure everything was in shape for when we got back. I called them as we were getting into the car. I'm pretty orderly, but still . . . I told them I had a good white wine in the fridge. I told them to help themselves, as a thank-you. I meant they could take the bottle home, but I guess they couldn't wait."

Emma thinks again of the looks she'd seen pass between Ben and Rebecca at Thanksgiving. It's like a photo she can't delete from her files. Is that what's going on here? The cheating husband making the wife think she's lost her mind?

The refrigerator is half-full of things that seem newly bought. A bag of oranges, a head of lettuce, a container of strawberries.

Are they things Ben likes? They're what he thinks Emma would like. Healthy food he told Rebecca and Avery to buy for her. Why is she suspicious?

"Rebecca did the shopping?"

"Rebecca and Avery," says Ben. "Get this. They *like* grocery shopping together. The happy couple. As they tell you a million times."

We *used to like grocery shopping,* Emma thinks. Ben's presence — his concern, or show of concern — is making her feel worse. It's a kind of pressure.

Not being able to ask about the journal and Sally's song — her silence roars in her ears, like white noise. Can there be an elephant in the room when only one person knows that the elephant exists?

She wants to be alone for a few minutes. She's nine months pregnant. She just played the Virgin Mary. Just fainted, just traveled all the way from the country to the city. Now she wants her husband gone, just for a while. She's gotten used to solitude. Not solitude, exactly. Her and the baby. Ben is right to feel left out. No wonder he doesn't love her.

JD was holding her after she fainted. She has a vague memory of him promising to watch over the house . . .

"You know what I'd really like?" Emma says.

"What?" She expects Ben to be annoyed, but there isn't a trace of irritation in his voice.

"Chocolate ice cream."

"Straight-up chocolate?"

"Dark. Chips. Cookie dough. Swirl. I don't care. No, not swirl. Anything but."

"I'm on it." Is Ben a little too eager to get out of the house? Why wouldn't he be? The car ride was difficult, not just for her but for him. They both need air and space.

"Just saying, I hate cookie dough." He kisses her goodbye, tenderly, on the forehead.

"Actually, I do too," she says.

As soon as she hears the door slam, she

does what any suspicious wife would do. She checks the bathroom for a forgotten toothbrush or cosmetics, looks for hair in the sink, some clothing item in the laundry. Nothing indicates that anyone — not Rebecca, not anyone — was here with Ben.

And what if she did find something? What would she do?

Anything can be explained away. Rebecca and Avery were here.

Ben returns from the corner store with a carton of ice cream. He looks as proud as if he'd brought back some delicacy from the ends of the earth. As if he'd made the ice cream himself.

"Thank you," Emma says.

Chocolate ice cream is just what she needs. The sweetness, the cold, the richness, the happiness of chocolate.

"Isn't there caffeine in that?" Ben's always made fun of her for worrying about such things. Is he serious now? She can't tell.

"I don't care," Emma says. "I want it." It feels good to do what she wants instead of what Ben or the baby want. One chocolate ice cream binge is not going to hurt the baby at this point. The baby stirs and goes back to sleep.

Maybe things will still work out. Maybe Emma has just been alone too long. Maybe the move was too sudden. After the baby's born they can rethink everything, adjust their plans and their lives. She'll talk to Ben, ask Sally, sort out all the confusion about Heather standing in the field —

Feeling pleasantly sleepy, she goes into the bedroom and stretches out on the bed. She buries her face in the pillows —

"Ben!"

He rushes in. "What's the matter?"

She can hardly speak. Finally she manages to say, "This pillow smells like Rebecca. Like her fucking signature scent." There's no mistaking the ambergris and jasmine.

So that's it. Game over. It *was* Rebecca. The shock of jealousy and betrayal is like a physical pain, like a skewer stuck in her heart. Yet she knows she's been bracing for it, tensing, preparing herself. Does that make the pain any less? Not really.

"Ugh, that's disgusting. Let me change the sheets. Maybe she and Avery took a nap. Maybe they had sex here. Even more disgusting. Maybe being here turned them on. Wait. Do you think I was in bed with Rebecca in our apartment? Could you *possibly* think that? She is *so* not my type. It is *so* not true. I am *so* insulted you'd think I'd do something like that to you. To anyone. With *her*?"

272

Is Ben lying? How can Emma *not know* if her husband is telling the truth? Well, she wouldn't be the first woman to have that problem . . .

"Swear it," she says.

"I swear it," Ben says.

"Swear it on our baby," she says.

Ben doesn't hesitate. "I swear it on the baby. I swear it on my life and yours. I never had sex with that woman." He laughs. "Seriously. I never had an affair with Rebecca. I swear it on you and me and Little Person and the house and my work and —"

Tears well up in Emma's eyes.

"Okay, okay," she says.

"Try and rest." How sweet and kind Ben's voice is.

She lets herself drift off . . .

Somewhere a phone is ringing.

Emerging from a fitful sleep, Emma hears Ben's ringtone.

Sometimes he gets calls in the middle of the night, from business contacts in Europe and on the West Coast, mostly people who have gotten drunk or high and forgotten the time difference.

But still, a call that wakes you always makes your heart beat faster.

Ben's lying beside her. Has he been sleeping too? He sits up on the edge of the bed, his back to Emma.

Emma hears a woman's voice. She hears a woman sobbing. She can't tell who it is or what the woman is saying.

"Who is it? What's happening?" she says. Ben switches on the light and half turns so she can see him motioning to her to be quiet.

"No, that's okay," says Ben. "Please don't worry — I mean, about me. I am so sorry for your loss."

"Who? Whose loss?" says Emma.

"My God, Lindsay, I'm so sorry. We're both so sorry. If there's anything I can do, please don't hesitate for a moment. Yes, I know we're having a baby, but we're neighbors, we're here to help in any way we can. Had she been sick before?"

Silence.

"I see."

"Who?" Emma says.

Ben just shakes his head.

"Please tell your dad how sorry I am. And let us know when the funeral is."

"Funeral?" says Emma.

Ben's still shaking his head as he gets off the phone. "It's terrible. Sally's dead."

"What happened?" For just a beat, Emma feels guilty, as if her screaming during Sally's song could have killed her.

"She had a stroke and died. My God. Two hours after the show ended. Beth and Lindsay and Ted and Sally were sitting around Lindsay's parents' house. Just chilling after the show. Sally went to the kitchen to get some tea. And when she didn't come back Lindsay went to check on her. And found her stepmom on the floor."

"Just like that? Out of the blue?" Emma reminds herself to breathe. Sally was *just alive*. How could she be dead?

"Not exactly out of nowhere. She'd had a series of small strokes, but she was on a new medication that seemed to be working. I feel so awful for Lindsay. I hardly knew Sally, really. You knew her better than I did. You had lunch with her, right?"

"Right."

Sally is dead.

Emma feels awful for Lindsay and Ted. For JD. For herself. Sally was nicer to her than anyone in town, except JD. They could have been friends. She feels guilty for thinking that now she will never find out the real reason why Sally picked that song. Or if she could have been the daughter of the woman who wrote the journal. Maybe Lindsay would know, or Ted, but she can't imagine asking.

This is when she should tell Ben the whole story. The girl in the field, the photo of the girl in the field, the one who looked like Heather, the historical society group photo, Sally's snapshot. Sally's dead daughter. Oh, Sally! The journal. The woman who'd been exiled from Broadway to have her baby. The baby would have been Sally's age. Sally singing that song — was it a coincidence?

Sally is dead. That much is real.

The next morning Emma wakes up and thinks, *Sally is dead,* even before she wonders, *Where am I?* Right. She's in their apartment. In the city.

It's almost noon. Emma hasn't slept this late since she was a teenager. She must have needed the rest. Bits of the previous day and evening come back to her. None of it is good.

She's hazy and sluggish. But she's hungry. She didn't eat dinner. And her doctor said it's important — for her and the baby — to eat small meals throughout the day.

She looks in the refrigerator at the food Rebecca and Avery bought for her return. None of it seems remotely appetizing. She'll get sick if she finishes the ice cream. What was that even about?

She wants food. Cornstarch-thickened,

salty-sweet, delicious Chinese food. Here's what she's missed about the city: takeout. Does this qualify as a craving? It does. Though it's not the best thing for her blood pressure, she decides to order lunch.

Shanghai Garden is two blocks away. Please let it still be there. Things change so fast in the city. Their soup dumplings are heavenly. So is their pork with edamame and dried bean curd. So what if it's all really salty? She'll drink more water later.

Every house has a drawer like this, a cupboard or closet. It's where you throw things. Where you stuff papers you don't want to toss and don't know what to do with. Receipts, repair bills, bank statements, addresses torn off envelopes. Take-out menus, doctor and dentist appointment cards.

That's where Emma goes to look for the Shanghai Garden takeout menu. And that's where — as if it leaps into her hand from the back of the drawer — she finds the note.

A page torn from a small spiral notebook, edged with ragged holes.

It's crumpled, but something — a sixth sense — tells her it's important.

Read me.

She smooths it out on the kitchen counter.

Darling Ben,

I have to run. Dentist appointment. Voice coach. Then meeting B for lunch. I'll catch up with you at rehearsal. This is the most fun thing I've ever done. Love you forever.

The shock of what the notes says pales compared to the shock of how it's written.
The elaborate handwriting.
The bright peacock-blue ink.
The familiar loops and curls.
It's the handwriting in the journal Emma found in the attic.

CHAPTER TWELVE:
THE NOTE

Emma stares at the note. She turns it around. She looks at it again.

Everyone who is lied to must think: *How could I have been so stupid?* That's certainly what Emma thinks as she tries to put the story together.

Of course Ben is having an affair with Rebecca. She knew it all along. But she didn't want to believe it. She should have been in the city more. But . . . they've been renovating the house! Someone had to be there. And how easily Emma complied when she asked to come to a rehearsal, and Ben convinced her not to. He's always been a little secretive about a work in progress, but this time it's almost extreme. It would be a distraction, he insisted, and besides, he was saving her opinion, her fresh eye, which he valued so much, for when things were further along. It was important to him that he not tell her as much as he wanted, and that she not ask: who they've cast, how the rehearsals are going, fun facts about the costumes, the lighting and the stage design. He wants her to see it as they get nearer opening night. He wants her to be surprised. He wants her to tell him what it might be like for an audience member who knows nothing about the play.

That he valued her opinion meant that she was more than a pregnant woman renovating a country house.

It's bad enough, his having an affair. But the ink and the handwriting take things to another level.

She ticks off the possibilities. She keeps coming back to the obvious: Whoever wrote that note for Ben either wrote the diary or knew about the diary and imitated the handwriting and the color of the ink.

Did Ben steal the diary for someone who read it and started writing like that?

That seems less likely than that the same person wrote the diary and the note.

Which doesn't seem likely, either. There's no way of thinking about this that seems clear, obvious, logical — or like good news.

Someone wrote it and left it in the attic for Emma to find. It had to be Ben. He'd placed it where she couldn't miss it. She'd tricked herself into thinking she'd excavated it from the rubble. And then he took it back after he knew she'd read it.

Ben and Rebecca. That must be Rebecca's handwriting. She's never seen Rebecca's handwriting. Nobody writes anymore. She'd thought she was reading something written by a ghost.

Why would someone do that to her? Why would Ben and Rebecca need to do that? People have affairs and leave their spouses all the time, even when the wife is pregnant. It's sad and miserable — but ultimately simple. *Sorry,* they say. *This isn't working out. I'm not happy. I want to see other people. I met someone.*

Why go to the trouble of forging a journal, leaving it for her to read, then making it vanish and waiting for the talent show to tell Emma the punch line?

Oh, wouldn't it be loverly?

Leaving the note here was a mistake. Someone slipped up.

Emma phones Ben. What will she say? What does she expect him to say?

The phone rings and rings.

Ben doesn't pick up.

He promised.

281

Emma sits there. And sits there. And sits there.

After a while she feels the lethargy leave her, muscle by muscle, cell by cell. She feels the kind of strength that lets people lift up a car to free someone trapped underneath.

She'll go to the rehearsal space and find Ben.

She'll confront him with the note. Make him tell the truth. Make him explain.

Maybe this isn't as bad as it looks. Maybe it's some theater thing he forgot to tell her about. Maybe there's some simple explanation.

It will all make sense. Ben isn't in love with someone else. No one staged this elaborate . . . what?

She feels a jutting elbow or knee.

It calms her. Okay. Hello there.

The baby is fine.

Despite everything, she's thankful for that.

Two cabs pass. The drivers take one look at how pregnant Emma is and speed off. Even under her heavy coat, her belly is obvious, and they're not going to run red lights or deliver a baby in their cab. Emma doesn't blame them, but she hates them anyway. Isn't it illegal? It's cruel. She's in no shape to write down their license plate numbers.

Or take photos on her phone.

Meanwhile, she's hungry. She'd forgotten about food, about ordering takeout, which — she remembers only now — made her open that drawer in the first place. She never found the Shanghai Garden menu. She found the note instead.

There's a bakery two blocks away that makes almond croissants. She heads toward Third Avenue. She has to walk slowly; the sidewalks are slippery. A few people — all women — ask if she's okay, and she says thanks, she's fine.

Behind the counter a girl with a nose ring flashes Emma a warm smile when she says, "Enjoy it!" Salty, buttery, ridiculously sweet, the pastry is just what Emma wants and needs.

It's a momentary distraction, and then everything comes roaring back. The note. The handwriting. The journal. Sally's death. Emma concentrates on breathing.

The third cab driver waits to know where she's going before he unlocks the door. She gives the address of Ben's rehearsal space, on West Fifty-First and Ninth. When he's sure she's not asking him to drive her to the hospital, he tells her to get in.

He drops her off in front of a big soulless office building. In the lobby, she tells the doorman that she's the producer's wife.

"Tenth floor," he says. "Follow the signs for Studio Space."

Her hand is trembling so hard she can hardly push the elevator button.

She hears music, singing. Thumping feet.

She's praying the studio door is unlocked. For once her prayers are answered.

No one notices her for a while.

She watches from a dark little vestibule just inside the door. The rehearsal hall is huge, bare, with a mirror at one end.

Everyone's gathered at the center of the loft. Emma can see them, though they can't see her beyond the light.

Three people are sitting in chairs: Avery, Rebecca, Ben. She recognizes them from the back. Avery's sitting beside Ben, who's sitting beside Rebecca. Ben and Rebecca lean their heads together.

So . . . it's true. Ben and Rebecca.

Only now Emma focuses on the cast. They have taken a break and are milling around, doing stretches, bending double, squatting on the floor.

Lindsay stands in the center of a semicircle.

Lindsay?

Emma's head swims. She thinks she might faint.

"Take it from the top," says Avery.

The rehearsal pianist (Emma can't see who it is) plays the introduction, and the cast tightens its semicircle around Lindsay, who is singing "I won't grow up."

Lindsay puts her hands on her hips in a stagy musical-comedy gesture.

Lindsay doesn't want to grow up, she doesn't want to be a man.

Lindsay is so into her part, so inside the song, she doesn't notice Emma. And Ben, Avery, and Rebecca and everyone else in the rehearsal space are so fixated on Lindsay that no one sees Emma standing there.

Lindsay is the punk Peter Pan, the non-binary Peter Pan, the hot Peter Pan, the magical creature who will always have hot sex and never grow old. She is Ben's dream. His old Twitter handle. She is the boy he'd wanted to be, the Peter Pan who wouldn't age, the boy who doesn't have a pregnant wife and an expensive renovation project in the country. She is the girl who will stay forever young and whose body won't age with childbirth and time and —

I won't grow up, I don't want to go . . .

Emma needs to sit down. She grabs a folding chair from against the wall and sets it up. She's afraid they'll hear it scrape on the floor, but they're watching Lindsay, as is Emma.

Avery calls for a break, and Lindsay walks over and twines her arms around Ben's neck. It's more than the sexy, play-pretend warmth that theater people affect.

They kiss. It's real. They're not acting.

It's only through sheer force of will that Emma makes herself breathe. She can't believe what she's seeing. But whether she believes it or not, that's what she's seeing. How can it be true? It can't be. Ben would never do this. He loves her. They're having a baby. Which is precisely when men cheat. Why had she thought it couldn't happen to her? Why had she been so trusting? She's always laughed at women who spent days each week away from their husbands and then were shocked when the guys found someone else. But Ben? Yes, Ben. Why not? Did she think he was better than that? Well, she did. But, apparently, she thought wrong.

Rebecca says, more bitter than joking, "Okay, you guys, get a room."

No wonder Avery and Rebecca couldn't look at Emma at Thanksgiving. They knew who had been cast in the musical. They knew about Ben and Lindsay.

Staring into his eyes, Lindsay gently lays the palm of her hand alongside Ben's face, and it's only because Emma's looking so closely, staring so hard, that she sees the stains on Lindsay's fingers.

Peacock-blue ink.

It's her. Lindsay wrote the journal. The note.

Why hadn't Emma seen the ink on Lindsay's fingers before? Maybe Lindsay's gotten sloppy. And why does this shock and sicken Emma more than anything, more than Lindsay being in the musical, more even than Ben sleeping with Lindsay? Unknowns get cast in Broadway shows, men cheat on their pregnant wives. It happens all the time. Even with Ben, even to Emma. But who writes a long, complicated journal, supposedly by someone who lived in the past, and leaves it to seriously mess with the head of the person she knows will find it?

Diabolical is the word that runs through Emma's mind. She tells herself she's exaggerating. Lindsay isn't demonic, just ruthless and ambitious, and maybe a little crazy.

Emma stands. The weight pressing down on her feels heavier than the weight of her body. Something is pulling her, pulling her down.

The contractions begin, first slow, then faster. Like someone tightening a belt around her, not too tight, then very tight, spitefully letting her know how bad it's going to get.

Emma needs a doctor.

Now.

CHAPTER THIRTEEN: LINDSAY

When Lindsay's dad gives her the Hideaway Home listing, she posts it as a joke. Let's see what crawls out from under a rock to take a look at this one. Some ancient long-hair hippie ghost hunter, some secret cult with twelve half-starved kids. There's a bit of that around here, but no one's got the cash or the time or interest to take on the renovation of a semi-ruined dry-out clinic in the middle of nowhere. Not one Williamsburg hipster, not one ex-urban pioneer shows up. No one emails or texts or calls. No one spends more than fifteen seconds on the listing.

Maybe some rich cutting-edge hotelier, your Andre or Ian or whoever, will renovate the place and make this the new celebrity luxury destination. Sullivan County, the new Hamptons? Lindsay seriously doubts it. But it gives her a reason to bother, and it's sort of fun, exploring the crazy wrecked house with Beth, snapping pictures on their phones while Beth, who's better with words, comes up with the text of the listing. They even have sex on the cleanest-looking bed in the least disgusting bedroom. It's creepy but weirdly hot.

Poor Beth has done nothing to deserve whatever Lindsay is going to do. Beth is a deeply good person who has no idea where any of this will be going. And what her role in it will be. All Beth wants is to settle down and have a nice life with Lindsay and find work she likes, maybe something to do with writing. Beth told Lindsay the joke about the lesbian bringing the moving van on the second date. Beth says she basically brought the van years *before* their first date. She'd had a crush on Lindsay in high school, but Lindsay hadn't noticed.

Beth self-identifies as a gay woman, but Lindsay doesn't. She doesn't self-identify as a straight woman. She doesn't self-identify as bisexual. She doesn't self-identify as anyone but herself.

Lindsay had been living in New York, sharing a crappy apartment with a stoner trust-fund-baby roommate, waitressing at a sports bar in Chelsea, hefting trays of beer mugs through crowds of frat bros who grabbed her ass but tipped really well if they were drunk enough. She took acting classes she couldn't afford and went out on auditions, and looked around the classes and auditions and thought, *Not one of us is ever going to get an acting job.* Now she thinks: Maybe her negativity was the problem. People smell it. She never got one callback. Not one. Most of the men she met were gay or married or both. Some of the more powerful guys had creepy sexual kinks, and that was a real acting challenge: getting out of the room without turning them against you forever.

If only to fight the boredom, she had two affairs. One, that lasted almost six weeks, was with a woman, supposedly some second-string producer's PA. The woman was a redhead, pretty, and the sex was hot, but when it became clear that the woman, Rachel, wasn't going to do any of the things she'd promised to do, things that would have helped Lindsay in her acting career, Lindsay broke it off. Rachel's guilty quality made for great sex, but she was jealous and neurotic, and finally the sex wasn't worth it.

Once, when they were showering together, Lindsay noticed that Rachel, who was always suntanned, had been covering the bare white band of skin around her left ring finger with makeup that washed off in the water. As if Lindsay didn't know she was married.

The second affair was with a good-looking stagehand she met when she tried out for one of the parts she didn't get. When she got pregnant, he ghosted her. Things did not go well. There was an injury, an infection. She terminated what was left of her pregnancy in a clinic in Murray Hill, walking past demonstrators who shoved posters of bloodied babies at her and tried to make her cry. They succeeded, but that was the last time she cried. She promised herself: No more tears. Not ever. The doctors told her she couldn't have children. They told her that in no uncertain terms. The less she remembers about all that, the better.

That was when she began trawling AA meetings. It was where you could meet rich needy guys. They would take you out to good dinners, and when they started drinking again, which they often did, they even gave Lindsay cash. None of this was supposed to happen. She wasn't even supposed to hang out with them outside the meetings, but once you started breaking the AA rules, anything was possible.

She'd been surprised to see Beth, whom she knew from high school, at one of the AA meetings. That night they went back to

Beth's tiny East Village apartment. The sex was amazing.

Lindsay has never told anyone how she feels about sex. Basically, it goes like this: You do things to a person that feel good, and then the person does things to you that feel good, and, as if that wasn't enough, you get that great toe-curling electrical buzz and the little aftershocks. You're grateful to the person who made that happen, but that isn't love. Not that Lindsay has any idea what love is. She lets others assume she does. She even says "I love you." It doesn't matter who she says it to, if it isn't true.

After a few months together, Lindsay and Beth admitted they were poor and unemployed and should probably move back upstate until they figured out something better. Beth got a job making pocket change at the historical society. When Ted took Lindsay into his real estate business — he was so nice about it — she couldn't let him see how miserable it made her. She convinced herself that working for her dad wasn't the end of the world, not the dead end of her acting dream or even a serious defeat, but just a stage she was going through. A time-out. A process.

Living with Beth is okay for now. Lindsay pretends to have been a vegetarian and gone back to being a carnivore to make Beth happy. Beth likes that, and Lindsay lets her think it. So what if it isn't true? Lindsay has always loved a fat juicy burger.

The town is backward, but not so old-fashioned that anyone has a problem with Lindsay and Beth being a couple. Though Virginia, the Nibble Nook waitress and Lindsay's second cousin, keeps asking Lindsay, right in front of Beth, when she's going to find a nice guy and settle down and get married.

None of this is Lindsay's destiny.

Something else will happen.

If there's such a thing as destiny, and Lindsay believes there is, destiny chooses Ben to be the first and only sucker who calls about the house.

First she thinks of him as The Client, then as The Husband, and after a while it's Ben. First it's The Client's Wife, then The Wife, then Emma. That's what it means to get to know someone. Names are hard, though she likes her own name. *Lindsay* could be a girl or a boy. She understands perfectly when — later — Ben tells her that he and Emma can't agree on a name for the baby.

It's not a good sign about the marriage, which is just what Lindsay wants to hear.

During that first phone conversation with Ben, Lindsay gives the house the best possible spin. She plays the not-too-bright novice country real estate broker, which in a way she is, except for the not-too-bright part. She's a trained actress, but you don't need much training to know that if you put a question mark at the end of every sentence, guys will think you're dumb.

Anyway, Ben will find out the truth about the house soon enough. One showing will do it.

She says, "Can I ask what you do for a living?"

He says, "I'm a producer."

Her heart does a little trippy dance. "Can I ask what you produce?"

He says, "Why don't you google me?"

Lindsay thinks that anyone obnoxious enough to say "google me" deserves everything he gets. Ben's still on the phone when she searches him on her laptop, and when his bio comes up, she realizes this isn't just a half-assed real estate inquiry.

This is destiny calling.

Lindsay says, "Can I tell you the truth? It's a major reno project? But it's the craziest, most beautiful house you will ever see in your life?"

She's betting a lot on this one.

"When can I come see it?"

Bingo. She used to play baseball as a kid, before the idiot Little League coach told her that girls didn't do that. Hearing the client rise to the bait feels like that fabulous *thump* when the ball lands square in your mitt.

This guy could be an end run around everything she has ever tried and failed at. All that time and money she wasted taking drama lessons and auditioning when all she had to do was sell a house to the right producer.

Ben tells Lindsay that the first time he comes up to see the house, he'll come alone. He isn't sure his wife will like it, and he doesn't want to waste her time.

Something in his tone tells Lindsay that she should wear something . . . minimal . . . to the showing. Her flimsiest, shortest summer dress, though it's still chilly. A leather biker jacket for warmth.

Ben drives a Volvo. A good sign. And he seems charmed by her sad little Prius, not that he'd want to drive one.

He notices and appreciates how she's dressed. She's shivering for his benefit. Does she want to borrow his scarf?

He's not bad-looking, not good-looking.

A little nerdy for her taste, but fine. He's not repellent. Not an obvious pervert or creep. Basically, he's not a bad guy. A potential cheating husband, but whatever. She can work with what's here. Right now she doesn't want a man who's smarter or thinks faster than she does.

From the moment he drapes his deliciously soft cashmere scarf around her neck, it's more up close and personal than your typical house tour. He trails behind Lindsay through the wreck of the house. He looks at her. He looks at the house. He looks at her. He looks at her ass. He looks at the house.

He likes what he sees.

The noises he makes from the moment they enter the hall — little grunts and moans of pleasure — make Lindsay wonder if those are the sounds he makes during sex. She doesn't want to find out, but she senses that if she wants things to go her way, she may have to. It's positively orgasmic, his reaction to the house, and — just as she expected — when she brings him into the theater, that does it.

He basically comes.

"A theater! And old-fashioned theater, in a private house. You do know I'm a theater person?"

Has he forgotten that he told her to google him?

"Sure! Congratulations. On your big Broadway hit."

"It wasn't an overnight success," he says. "First came years of work, years of failure."

He thinks *he* knows about failure? Lindsay could teach him a thing or two, and maybe she will, before this is over.

"It's just so romantic," he keeps saying, as they drift from room to room. Did he mean the house or Lindsay? He goes on about how amazing the house could be with just a little work. She lets him talk. She listens. She smiles. He's doing her job for her. Personally, she thinks it's bad luck for a guy in the theater to buy a place that's soaked up years of the bad vibes of Broadway burnouts. But she's not going to say that.

Lindsay says, "I always tell clients that the renovation is going to take three times as long and cost five times as much as they imagine." She's never told any clients any such thing. She's never actually had any clients.

"So I hear," says Ben.

So it must be something Realtors say. Lindsay's thinking of all the acting classes she took. She's playing the good-girl country Realtor.

And soon she'll play the bad-girl country Realtor.

"Oh . . . and one more thing." Lindsay's operating on pure instinct now.

"What's that?"

"If you buy this place, you're probably going to want to get a pickup truck."

He lights up, his face just lights up. Lindsay thinks he's going to grab her and kiss her right then and there. Okay, that might be a bit premature. But the thought is in his mind.

"I've always wanted a pickup." Of course he has.

"If not now, when?" Lindsay's smile beams freedom, promise, and the assurance that he's the macho pickup-truck guy he's always dreamed of being. His dumb grin makes Lindsay realize how easy this will be.

"You mentioned . . . you're married," she says.

Is he hesitating? Does he think this is that scene where the husband stashes his wedding ring in his pocket and picks her up in a bar? *No* married guy buys a house without consulting the wife.

"Actually . . . she's pregnant. She's been kind of busy with that."

"Busy?" says Lindsay.

"Preoccupied."

"That's too bad," Lindsay says.

The next day Ben calls to ask if Lindsay can have lunch in the city. Sure, sure she can. No one comes into the city to talk about a house upstate. She dresses up, puts on makeup, wears hot underwear. Just in case. There is no just in case.

It's on.

Driving into the city, Lindsay thinks she should feel guilty about sleeping with a married man with a pregnant wife. Not that she's slept with him yet. She means in theory. But thinking you should feel guilty isn't the same as feeling guilty. Lindsay tries, but she can't.

They meet in a hotel restaurant on the far West Side. Dark. The kind of place where nobody Ben knows would ever have lunch.

She orders a burger. They split two bottles of wine and don't finish their food. He talks about his musical. She tells him she read the awesome reviews. He says she'll have to come see it. He'll get her a ticket. Tickets?

"One ticket's good for now." She smiles. That settles it. The waiter sees Ben's hands shake as he signs the credit card receipt. The waiter's seen lots of shaking hands. That's the kind of place this is.

Lindsay and Ben make out in the eleva-

for the first time.

They say it simultaneously.

Ben says, "We're reading each other's minds."

Lindsay smiles. She doesn't want Ben reading hers.

This is just what she's hoped for. It's like an amazing real-life, break-the-fourth-wall audition, a chance to show a Broadway producer what a good actress she is. She's talented, she knows she is. She's a trained actress. Another first-rate actress with a run of third-rate luck.

He says, "About Emma and the house . . . I'm trying to keep things simple."

"Sure," Lindsay says. They're way beyond simple already.

"It'll be fun," she tells Ben. "Harmless fun. Sort of like experimental theater. A cross between an immersive performance, like *Sleep No More,* and reality TV without an audience. *House Hunters* meets *Real Housewives* meets —"

"Okay," says Ben. "Okay."

To complicate things just a little — and mostly for the optics — Lindsay decides she needs a mom for her mom-and-pop real estate firm, and, with a minimal loan from Ben, though she doesn't tell him what it's

tor, and her hands are all over him as he finds his key card. He pushes her lightly onto the bed, pulls down her sexy underwear.

"Wow," he says. He enters her from behind. He holds the back of her neck, not hard enough to hurt her at all, but so she knows he's in charge. He's better than she expected. This could be not just financially and professionally helpful. It could be fun.

The room faces a courtyard. They lie there in the dim light from the window. Ben asks if she has to be back home soon. She has no plans. He doesn't either. They don't have a lot to say, but it doesn't matter.

When Ben goes to take a shower, Lindsay checks his laptop. He's visited the Hideaway Home listing *many times.* He's also been watching old horror films in which houses drip blood and the walls heave with spirits. He's watched *The Shining* twice. If Lindsay were his wife, she'd think a million times before she moved to the country with a guy who's been doing that.

She closes the laptop before he returns to bed where they lie, pressed close. Neither makes a move to get up. After a while Lindsay grabs the remote and flips through the cable channels on the TV till she finds TCM.

Luck is on her side.

It's *The Masque of the Red Death.*

They watch a man in a gorilla suit climb a chandelier made of burning candles and catch fire as the gorilla and the guests scream and Vincent Price cackles hysterically.

"I miss this," says Ben.

"Huh?"

"Lying in bed watching movies. Emma and I used to do it all the time, but now she's so tired from being pregnant, she just drops off to sleep, and I'm left all alone."

That's the first time he's said her name. Emma. Until then it was *my wife.*

His wife is pregnant with his kid, and he's blaming the wife for being sleepy. He deserves what he gets.

"Poor baby," says Lindsay. "You poor thing."

This is going to be easy.

By the time Ben brings Emma to see the house, he and Lindsay have spent three long afternoons in bed at the hotel. They never talk about what they're doing. Ben prefers that, obviously. And what would Lindsay say?

On the third afternoon he says he's worried that Emma won't like the house. It needs so much work, and she's pregnant and . . . He's silent for a long time. Then he says, "Has it ever happened that someone installed a stove before they know they're going to buy the house, before they've even made an offer?"

How would Lindsay know? But what she says is, "Just because something hasn't happened doesn't mean it can't. As long as it's legal, and you can pay for it . . . and we're all consenting adults."

The main thing Lindsay needs to do is make him think he's the director. He's said to her, a few times, that he's always wanted to direct. But really, it's Lindsay who is the director. Every actress secretly wants to direct, right? And she's got her own play in mind. A cross between performance art, *Macbeth, Real Housewives,* and *Candid Camera.* Lindsay watches a lot of TV, reality shows and dramas, and her ultimate dream is to star in a series that gets renewed forever, like *ER,* until the stars age out. She'd be happy with her own reality TV series, but what would it be called? *Million Dollar Listing Sullivan County?*

Ben and Lindsay are in bed when they agree that it would be simpler to pretend they've never met, and that Ben is seeing the house

for, she hires Sally, a friend of Lindsay's dead mom. Sally's always wanted to be on-stage. Every year she sings — badly — at the community talent show.

Now she'll do what Lindsay says if Lindsay tells her it's her big break. She'll play Lindsay's mother. Ted's wife. A part-time — maybe one-time — job, for when the couple from New York come to the office to talk about the house. The husband's a Broadway producer. Does Sally understand what that might mean for their little town? How about . . . summer theater?

Lindsay makes Ben describe Emma:

Pretty. A little faded. Tired. Eager to please.

Not knowing more about the wife — there isn't much more she can ask — Lindsay takes a little risk and pays Heather, a girl she knows from town, thirty dollars to stand with her baby in the field and then duck down so the wife thinks she's disappeared, or that she hasn't really seen her. Lindsay knows it's counterintuitive. For her plans to work, the wife needs to be reassured not spooked. But Lindsay senses, judging from a few things Ben has said, that the wife is more likely to agree to something if she's a little scared. She's the kind who has to prove things. Lindsay could almost feel sorry for her if she could tap into the feeling of pity. The fact that Ben said "google me" is one of the things that keeps her from feeling sorry for the wife. What kind of woman is stupid enough to marry a guy who'd say something like that?

The wife is more or less exactly as Lindsay imagined. So Lindsay has the advantage. Emma hasn't been able to picture Lindsay. As far as she knows, neither she nor Ben has ever seen Lindsay before.

Emma has no idea what's coming for her. When she thinks about the future, she sees herself, Ben, and the baby. She is unprepared. It's not anyone's fault, it's a law of nature. Survival of the fittest. You have a nice person with no plans and you put that person up against a not-very-nice person with a lot of plans. Who's going to win?

Lindsay has hardly existed for Emma until Lindsay slithers out of her Prius in front of the house. The husband has spoken to Lindsay on the phone. That's all she knows.

Lindsay has told Ben to tell Emma that she sounds like a fourteen-year-old. Like a Valley Girl. Like an idiot. She encouraged Ben to say mean things about her, to tell Emma she isn't very bright.

Maybe he should have been an actor

instead of a producer, though Lindsay guesses the money is in producing. If she didn't know, *she* wouldn't suspect that Ben had ever met her or saw the house before Emma did.

He said everything he'd said the first time he saw it — and more. Wow the staircase, wow the rooms, double wow the theater! He couldn't believe how amazing! He'd never seen anything like it! He was blown away. If Lindsay didn't know, she certainly wouldn't suspect that he'd fucked her.

Oh, and he'd had the vintage stove installed, which at first Lindsay thought was excessive. But he must know his wife. Lindsay didn't discourage him. She sees it as another step toward his being okay with gaslighting a pregnant wife. Because the stove was *his* idea.

It worked. When Emma saw that stove, Ben told Lindsay, the approval rating in Emma's head flipped from a big maybe to a definite yes.

Lindsay plays super-solicitous. She's so glad that Emma and Ben are wearing sneakers. She'd hate for them to step in raccoon poo or on a rusty nail. She's super up front and honest. But she throws in a scary personal thrill for Ben, mentioning *The Shining,* which they watched in bed.

Ben doesn't flinch. Good for him. Once again, he's better than Lindsay expected.

Emma's going to go for the house. Lindsay can tell right away. Emma probably would have agreed even if Ben hadn't gone to all that trouble about the stove.

Lindsay wonders if Emma is going to ask her about Heather, the mystery girl in the field, and sure enough she does.

Lindsay says she has no idea who it could have been. The sun and shadow do strange things as they move over the fields. Sometimes the air seemed to shimmer and . . . you see things that aren't there. No, there aren't neighbors nearby. She doesn't know who it could be. What Emma could have seen. She must have had a little tiny . . . hallucination. No, the girl couldn't have walked here.

"One day," Lindsay says, "I thought I saw a billion frogs hopping on the road? I got out and stopped. And guess what?"

"What?" says Ben.

"There were no frogs on the road."

Adding that part about the frogs is exceptional. Awesome. Lindsay wants to high-five herself, she's so good at this. But she can't look at Ben. She doesn't want him to see how easily she lies to his wife. She thinks it might make him like her less. But she's wrong. He likes the frog thing, and he likes the other great thing she does, pretending to think the Madonna, the Virgin Mary, is the same as Madonna the singer. Playing dumb when she isn't makes him like her more, as she discovers the next time they meet at the hotel.

Lindsay wants Emma's life, or at least to have it offered to her, and then get to decide if she wants it or not. The husband, the baby, the house, the works. She'll find a way to bring in Beth. Lindsay likes the challenge. Meanwhile she's having fun.

At the real estate office Sally gets with the plan, and Ted just plays Ted. Lindsay's sweet old dad, asking Ben about the mileage on his Volvo. Ted wants Lindsay to make a sale. He thinks that selling the house will make her feel better about working for him. He has no idea. He thinks it's cute and just like his daughter when Lindsay says it would be good for business if Sally pretends to be his wife. The truth is, he's always liked Sally. He likes having her around. When all the fun stuff starts, with Sally pretending to be Lindsay's stepmom, Ted's happy to play along. It's the most interesting thing that's happened since Lindsay's mother died.

For now, the only problem is a big one:

the mega-renovations. Lindsay wants this to happen so much that she suggests JD, whom she mostly avoids. The fact that he's her half brother isn't necessary information. They might think she's throwing him a job, but the truth is she can't stand him.

By the time Emma is deciding, and Ben's pretending to decide on the house, any local builder capable of changing a light bulb is booked for the summer. The gossip is that JD had a huge job lined up, and the homeowners stiffed him and — surprise! — opted for Malibu instead of Sullivan County.

JD used to be a good guy, then something happened. No one knows what. He turned. He stole a few bucks from Ted and tried to steal from Lindsay, but she caught him rooting around in her backpack. He wasn't on drugs. It was something else. Ted even took him to a therapist who said that petty thievery was a cry for help. What did JD have to cry about? He certainly wasn't telling.

JD learned to hammer in a nail before he learned to snap two Lego pieces together. He's good at what he does. He's the best. It doesn't hurt that he looks like the hot contractor from central casting, and that he grew up with all the guys — the best plumbers, electricians, chimney cleaners — he needs to be able to call.

Lindsay calls and says, "I have a job for you. Young couple. New York. She's pregnant. Buying a big house. They're loaded."

He's surprised to hear from her.

"Where's the house?"

"Hideaway Home," Lindsay says.

There's a silence. A long silence.

Everyone knows that something happened to JD in that house. Junior year of high school, he'd gone in there on a dare. He and his friends got crazy drunk one night and made some kind of bet. The loser had to go into the house.

JD lost the bet. This was when the three crazy hermits still lived there.

He stayed for fifteen, maybe twenty minutes. His friends began to get nervous.

They were relieved when he burst through the front door. But they shouldn't have been.

Something happened. He saw something. Someone did something. He was never the same.

Lindsay has no idea if he'll agree to work on the house.

Finally, he says, "Let's do it."

"A couple of things," says Lindsay. "You need to keep your mouth shut."

"About what?"

"About everything."

"Like what?"

"Well, okay . . . I have a fake stepmom. Sally. She's pretending to be my step-mother."

"Why?"

"Good question. I'm not sure." The fact is, Lindsay isn't sure why she wants Sally involved. It might be a mistake. But she likes the power it gives her. If she preps Sally and gives her notes, Sally won't ask too many questions. And Ted seems to like it.

"Because," she tells JD. "Because I say so.

"Got it," says JD.

After Ben and Emma close on Hideaway Home, Lindsay goes back to having no clients. She has a lot of time on her hands, and so, it seems, does Ben, who can always find time to meet Lindsay at their favorite hotel. First they fuck, then they watch an old horror film. A weird romance, but what romance isn't? And besides, Lindsay doesn't believe in romance. She definitely isn't in this for the romance, which is why she sees no point in telling Beth about any of it. For now.

Meanwhile, she and Beth are having a good time writing the phony journal. Beth works for the historical society, so she knows a lot about the area, and she likes using that knowledge to (she thinks) get closer to Lindsay. When Lindsay has the brilliant idea of writing the fake diary for Emma to find, she doesn't have to invent much. It's a memoir, more or less. The sad story of Lindsay's failed acting career, of all the people who promised to help her, of everyone who disappointed her. Lindsay and Beth just have to change a few key details, backdate it, and do some research about Broadway hits to make the timeline work. *My Fair Lady* is perfect!

Beth doesn't know how the book is going to be used. No one but Lindsay knows. Beth thinks it's a fun project that she and Lindsay are doing together. She thinks they're having fun. Kind of like a short novel about a woman who lived in Hideaway Home. Maybe it will be a real book someday, maybe some kind of art piece.

Beth helps Lindsay make up the story that Lindsay writes in the notebook in that beautiful peacock-blue ink that you can't find online but can only get in one particular old-school general store in Ellenville. Lindsay remembers the ink from high school. The cool girl who wrote with it later went to an Ivy League college. Lindsay thinks that girl's luck might rub off on her if she uses the same ink.

Like Lindsay, the girl in the made-up journal was dying to act on Broadway. Maybe you could say she did better than Lindsay. At least she got to be in the chorus. And in another way she did worse, getting scammed by the lecherous Broadway pervert. Lindsay has known a few of those, but she was smarter than the journal girl, who let herself get pregnant and shipped off to have the baby in a loony bin upstate.

Lindsay has told Beth that she can never have children. And Beth has never said she wants kids. She is probably afraid to spoil their good thing by bringing it up.

Lindsay liked pretending to be someone whose life was worse than hers. It made her feel better about herself.

Now that she's gotten the lead in Ben's musical, she has it all over that imaginary girl, with her baby on the way, dealing with the creepy doctor and his wife conspiring to steal the baby. Sometimes Lindsay had to remind herself that the girl in the journal isn't real, that she and Beth invented her.

Lindsay thinks that Ben's a jerk for letting Emma do all the work, for having sex with Lindsay in the city while Emma makes all the decisions that go into a renovation. It's not Lindsay's problem, but it does confirm her view that people like Emma get what they deserve if they don't stand up for themselves.

When Lindsay and Beth finish the journal, Lindsay puts it on top of a box of crap salvaged from the historical society. She tells Beth: The book is all about Hideaway Home, and that's where it belongs. It's like putting a fallen baby bird back in its nest.

"The mother bird doesn't always take it back," says Beth.

"Don't be dark," says Lindsay.

Beth takes it to the house and asks JD to store it in the attic. They tell him not to mention it, which makes him suspicious, but he's grateful to Lindsay for getting him work. It's no skin off his nose to add a box of junk to the garbage already up there in the attic. Emma won't notice or care. And Lindsay has made him promise to keep his mouth shut.

JD has been pretty good so far. There was only that one night when he crashed the little dinner party Lindsay gave to show Ben how cool she was and that she was so in control, she could make him come to her house and act like he hardly knew her.

Lindsay would like everyone to forget that JD is her half brother, and not ask about

315

Sally, who, Lindsay realizes, she can't get rid of now without someone wondering what happened. JD almost blew everything when he claimed he'd dreamed about a blond girl and her baby in the field. He must have seen Heather poking around the house when Lindsay paid her and drove her there and hid down the road while Heather stood where Emma could see her from a window.

It was theater. It was fun. Maybe no one else would understand why Lindsay enjoyed it.

After JD plants the notebook in the attic, Emma finds it, just as Lindsay knew she would. Ben knows nothing about it. There's no need for him to know.

Plans work best when no one person — except Lindsay — knows everything.

After a while Lindsay tells JD that Beth needs the book back at the historical society, that a local donor noticed it missing. She and Beth were just being sentimental, thinking that a book about Hideaway Home belongs in Hideaway Home. The whole thing seems unlikely, totally ridiculous. But JD goes for it. Anyway, he decides not to object or ask too many questions. It's not worth a scene with Lindsay to refuse to do her a little favor.

If Emma happens to ask JD if he's seen the notebook, Lindsay counts on him not telling her that he's been adding and removing stuff from the mess in the attic. He probably doesn't think it's important, and it isn't, though Lindsay likes the idea of Emma reading the book and getting scared of something that supposedly happened at Hideaway Home. What would be creepier for a pregnant woman than knowing about another pregnant woman who was in danger — here, in her house?

Lindsay likes taking little sections from the journal and running with them. For example, the part about the pregnant actress eating all those oranges.

One afternoon, when Ben happened to tell Lindsay that Emma was on her way back from the city, Lindsay went to the house, left the door open, and left a bunch of orange peels on the front porch.

A little something extra.

Beth is okay with how the story in the journal breaks off in the middle. She's a fan of cliffhangers.

After they have sex, Lindsay and Ben take turns picking the films they watch.

One day, Lindsay asks Ben, "Have you ever seen *Gaslight*?"

317

"Not since I was a kid," says Ben.

"Let's watch it," says Lindsay.

"Sure," says Ben. "Why not?"

Does he suspect what Lindsay is doing? Probably not. He's not smart enough.

Lindsay monitors Ben's response as wicked Charles Boyer convinces his new bride, played by Ingrid Bergman, that she is going crazy. Years before, he murdered her aunt, but couldn't find the jewels he killed her for. When the newlywed couple move into the dead aunt's town house, objects start to disappear. A picture vanishes from the wall. Footsteps echo from the empty attic, the lights brighten and dim. Until, at the last moment, the hysterical wife, who now believes she's insane, is saved by a friendly police inspector before the evil husband can have her committed and get the house and the dead aunt's jewels.

Ben's gone silent — and tense. Lindsay can't read him, which she doesn't like.

Lindsay says, "The one thing I didn't think was so great was that the husband did it for the money. Bor-ring. So many things are more important than money . . ."

"Why else would he do it?" asks Ben.

"For the challenge." Lindsay reaches over and lightly rests a hand on Ben's thigh. "For the fun."

CHAPTER FOURTEEN:
BEN

First you think you're a good person, and then you're not. Something changes. What? After a while you realize you were never a good person. That time you didn't call your mom back. The little kid you punched on the playground because a girl you liked said he annoyed her. You were always the person you are now. You just couldn't admit it. Encouraging Ben to admit to his own badness is only one of the ways in which Lindsay has freed Ben to be who he really is.

The scariest thing Ben ever read in his life, scarier than any of the old horror films he loves — that he and Emma *used* to love — is a story about a guy who's being tortured: his cell walls keep moving closer, pressing in on him.

That's how Ben has started to think about his life. Emma has become all four walls closing in on him at once. They used to have so much fun. They laughed at the same things, liked the same music, loved the same films. Had sex. He remembers, sort of, but he's not feeling it. They used to talk. Then she got pregnant and turned into a different person: self-involved, humorless, rigid, and neurotic. All she can talk about is what's good or bad for the baby. Ben can't go to a restaurant without having to order something without mercury or toxins or parasites or whatever the hell she's afraid of. Something he doesn't even want. So she can have a taste of his. Which she never wants. She just wants to control him.

He's glad about the baby, he guesses. But he feels as if he's being asked to trade his entire life for the life of someone who hasn't been born and already doesn't like him, or anyway, who prefers Emma. The baby refuses to move when Ben puts his hand on Emma's belly. How unfair is that?

Of course they can't agree on a name. Ben's not going to like anything Emma comes up with.

Work had stopped being fun. Home wasn't fun. Nothing was fun anymore.

He spent his time at the office with the door shut. First he watched actual porn, nothing kinky, nothing violent, fairly standard stuff. Then, after he came, he switched to real estate porn. Multi-multimillion-dollar houses and apartments that not even his new money could buy.

One afternoon, when he felt like the walls were closing in so tight he could hardly breathe, he set the filter on a real estate site to "Over 10,000 feet. New York State." He scrolled through a few pages of abandoned nursing homes, schools, and churches. Living in a repurposed church seemed so . . . 1970s.

And that's when he found Hideaway Home.

It was love at first sight.

He's afraid to go there with Emma. She'll come up with a thousand things about the house that are impractical, impossible, and, worse yet, bad for the baby. He calls the Realtor. It's just an experiment. The Realtor sounds about twelve years old. Everything she says is a question.

When she asks what he does, he says "google me," something he would probably never say to another serious adult. He hears her typing. He can practically hear her reading his bio. She probably moves her lips when she reads.

She says, "When would you like to see the house?"

Later, he'll wonder if he knew just from the sound of her voice that he could fuck her if he wants.

He tells Emma he'll be in meetings all day. He'll be home late tonight.

It's a bitch of a driveway. There's one tree in particular, a giant oak, you really have to watch yourself not to run into it, head on.

But when he rounds that final curve, he has the strangest feeling: The house has been waiting for him. They recognize each other, Ben and the house. Is that possible? It seems to be happening now.

Maybe he's been here in another life, maybe he's been here in a dream. Maybe it's even stranger than that. It's his. He has to live here.

You're mine, says the house.

You're home.

It's a cool day, but the Realtor — Lindsay — is practically naked, in a little summer dress and a leather jacket that looks great but can't possibly be warm. Ben offers her his scarf. He was definitely right about the sexual invitation he heard in her voice on the phone.

Following Lindsay through the house, it's not that Ben remembers what happiness is. It's more like he *discovers* what happiness

322

is. Did he imagine he was happy with Emma? He can't remember what that felt like.

A beautiful house, a beautiful woman. This is where he belongs.

The walls have been closing in . . . but this house expands to the size of the cosmos. From the beginning, it's as if he and Lindsay are looking at the house together. As a place for them to live. Not Ben and Emma. Ben and Lindsay.

When he gets to the theater, he sits in one of the front rows. He never wants to leave. For the first time since he got here, he's unaware of Lindsay. He doesn't know where she is, or if she's watching him. His problems and conflicts vanish. He's where he's supposed to be. It's as if he's waiting for some wonderful play to begin.

By the time he makes himself leave, he knows he has to have the house.

Emma will ask about the kitchen. So he returns to the kitchen. And that's when he has the idea about buying the vintage stove.

He tries it out on Lindsay. She thinks it's brilliant. She thinks that everything he says is brilliant. Unlike Emma, who hardly listens or who disagrees before she even understands what he's saying. Lindsay says it's fine to buy the stove as long as he wants to pay for it, and it's legal. And they're consenting adults. He can't miss the way she says *consenting adults*. The way she laces it with double meaning and innuendo.

Why wait?

The next day he calls Lindsay. He books a hotel room. He's never done this before. And he'll never do it again. But how can you turn down something that's being offered to you, for free, with no visible strings attached — something you could have, maybe for the last time? Once the baby is born . . . . he'll never do anything like this again.

He knows it has something to do with the house.

The house is giving him permission.

He dreads coming up to see the house with Emma, but it's sort of fun, pretending he and Lindsay have never met and that he's never seen the place before.

He tells Emma about the house on her birthday, during yet another dinner at which they have nothing to say. He can't even order what he wants, and every sip of wine is supposed to make him feel disloyal. Sometimes he suspects Emma wonders why isn't *he* pregnant? Why isn't he the one who can't drink? Well, sorry! That's not how

Mother Nature designed it.

On the driveway, on this, his "first" trip to Hideaway Home, he again comes close to running into the giant oak, even though, this time, he knows it's there.

Emma says she sees a girl in the field. There is no girl in the field. There can't be. Great. Now she's hallucinating, in addition to everything else.

Lindsay arrives a few minutes after they do. As she slides out of her car and her dress rides up on her bare thighs, Ben feels a stirring that's half-anxiety, half-desire.

Lindsay says, "Pleased to meet you," smiling from ear to ear and shaking both their hands. At that moment Ben knows everything is going to be all right.

Lindsay totally nails it. She's an inspiration. She inspires him to pretend he's never seen the house. And in a way he hasn't. The house is even more amazing than he remembers.

Exploring the house with Emma, worrying that she'll trip and fall or inhale some harmful dust or fumes, isn't anywhere near as much fun as the walk-through with Lindsay was. For one thing, there isn't that buzz of sex in the air. Ben tries not to act as detached as he feels when Emma goes crazy for the plates and vintage crockery in the pantry. He imagines a dreary lifetime of her serving him one meal after another on rehab-clinic dishes.

Emma likes the house. Or anyway, she knows how much Ben likes it. She wants to like what he likes. She wants him to feel that they're in this together.

Well, at least for the moment, they are.

The stove is a major selling point. That *was* a brilliant idea. Emma's told him, a million times, about the stove she fell in love with. Okay, maybe four or five times. She's blithered on about how she's dreamed of a having stove like that. How could she not remember telling him?

Even as they're skirting the oak that seems to shape-shift from place to place, Ben and Emma agree on what Ben has already decided.

They're buying the house.

Ben keeps on meeting Lindsay. He makes time for it, in the city.

Lindsay keeps things interesting. Like that time she insisted — insisted! — that he and Emma come for dinner. At first Ben was on edge, but pretty soon he figured out that Beth didn't know about him and Lindsay, so why should Emma? Lindsay played it supercool. The girl could actually act.

And JD knew nothing about anything. Lindsay hated the way he barged in, uninvited, but Ben thought he was a useful distraction. A pretty boy Emma couldn't take her eyes off of. Well, fine. Ben wants her attracted to the hunky contractor. It makes him feel less guilty about sleeping with Lindsay. If it ever comes down to it, Ben can pretend to be jealous and turn things around on Emma.

The Christmas pageant might be fun. He and Lindsay will have an excuse to be together outside their hotel room, and he's always wanted to direct.

One afternoon, after sex, he tells Lindsay about a musical he's thinking of producing. An all-female version of *Peter Pan* that really takes on the question of gender.

Lindsay gets out of bed. She stands at the foot of the bed, facing Ben.

She's completely naked. She has a beautiful body, a little thin, a little boyish, but very sexy.

She sings the song from *Peter Pan,* "I Won't Grow Up." But she does it quarter time, super slow, like a torch song, sad. Her performance could have been terrible, but it's amazing. It's better than anything he imagined. By the time she gets to the end of the song, Ben realizes he's quit breathing.

"How did you do that?" he asks. "Where did you learn to do that?"

"Years of practice. Years of study. Years of imitating every actress I saw. Years of rejection. Years of hope and disappointment. So I guess you could say I've been working on this for years."

He feels likes the musical is the best idea he's had since *No Regrets*. He feels like the song was written with him in mind. Peter Pan was part of Ben's handle before he swore off social media.

Ben is trying to figure out how to tell Lindsay how much he loved her performance, when she says, "You know what would be awesome? While I'm singing that onstage, we could have photos of happy kids at play flashing on the wall behind me, so it taps into the audience's being all sad and tragic because they had to grow up, or whatever. If they ever did." She laughs. "I tried out for Peter Pan in community theater in Montclair or someplace. I didn't even get *that*."

Ben says, "What you just did . . . it's not community theater, that's for sure. But it might be something we can work with."

It's a crazy idea, he knows. Casting a

328

complete unknown to star in the musical would be risky and wild. Dangerous! But if Lindsay's good enough — and he thinks she might be, just on the basis of that one song — it could be a major publicity coup. Everybody loves the story of the diamond in the rough polished into something gleaming and bright. Lana Turner discovered in the drug store, Jean Seberg emerging from the crowds of girls auditioning to play Joan of Arc. It fuels everyone's fondest dreams: one minute you're waiting on tables, the next moment . . . your name in lights!

At first he worries that sex might be clouding his judgment. But no. Sex is sex, and work is work. He's never confused the two, and he's not confused now. He's never felt so sure, so clear.

One problem might be: What does he tell Emma? *Guess what, honey, I've cast our Realtor to play the lead in my new musical. Not just any Realtor — the Realtor I'm sleeping with.* Well, there's certainly no reason for Emma to know that part. And as for the casting . . . she trusts his decisions about these things. He's taken chances in the past, and they've succeeded beyond anyone's dreams.

Emma will find out when he wants her to. She'll find out *what* he wants her to. And if the show is a hit, she'll admire him all the more for this bold casting decision.

Things with Emma don't improve. Thanksgiving is a nightmare. She has nothing to say to his friends, who have nothing to say to her. When she does talk, her voice sounds muted . . . choked. No one has fun. It's all Emma's fault, not that he's blaming her. His friends can be snobby.

Maybe Ben will love the baby so much that he and Emma will fall back in love. But he doubts it. Staying up all night with a crying newborn isn't famously romantic.

The point is: His friends see the house. They get it. They understand the project. They love it. They envy Ben, even with his spacey wife. They understand he's a visionary, and that this house is part of his vision.

Ben wishes he were here with Lindsay, who is celebrating Thanksgiving with Beth, Ted, and Sally.

After everyone goes to sleep — Emma is snoring — Ben sits in the darkened theater and for the first time, after the tense day, he feels calm.

You belong here, says the house.

It was always Ben and the house. Everyone else is a minor player.

330

■ ■ ■ ■

One afternoon Lindsay says, "Let's watch *Rosemary's Baby.*"

"Sure," Ben says. "I mean, I've seen it . . ." The truth is that it scares him: the obsessed, failed-actor husband, the pregnant wife, the satanic cult with plans to steal the baby. It's freaky, given his current circumstances.

"You sound hesitant," says Lindsay.

She's testing him, and he knows it.

"If you don't want to . . ."

"I do," Ben says. "I do." Because the real truth is that it scares and excites him at once.

"Good, then," Lindsay says.

Simultaneously relieved and alarmed, Ben takes a deep breath.

Lindsay smiles at him. He's passed the test. As they're watching it, he wonders if this is something like what Lindsay has in mind. Not the satanic cult part but proving that Emma is unfit and taking the baby to raise as their own. It would be cruel, horribly unfair. But living in Hideaway Home with Lindsay is what he imagined from the day she showed him the house. He never wanted to consider how the baby would fit into that fantasy. But something about

331

Lindsay's suggesting they watch *Rosemary's Baby* hints at the possibility that she's given it some thought. It's her way of telling him something, of seeing how he responds.

As always — as she has been from that very first day — Lindsay is one step ahead, and Ben likes it.

CHAPTER FIFTEEN:
LINDSAY

Sometimes Lindsay screens, with Beth, the films she plans to watch with Ben. She doesn't tell Beth, obviously. That would turn the whole thing from something fun into something that's the opposite of fun. Together they watch *Rosemary's Baby,* and they both agree: the Mia Farrow character deserves what she gets. She's too trusting, too naive. One look at that desperate, pathetic husband and any halfway-intelligent female would know he couldn't be trusted.

If only Beth knew. If only Ben knew. Lately Lindsay's been thinking: *We could take Emma's baby.* It's not so much that she wants the child but that the thought of doing that raises the stakes so much higher.

It's exciting. It's a challenge.

Lindsay searches for a film with an interesting title and finds *Diabolique.* Too bad it's in French. She and Beth usually don't like films with subtitles, but Lindsay persuades Beth to stay with it. They love the scene where the wife is scared out of her wits because she sees her dead husband in a group photograph. That's when Beth and Lindsay get the idea of taking a photo of Heather and photoshopping it onto a picture to put in the historical society. A photo for Beth to show Emma.

Even though Lindsay told her not to, Beth considers telling Emma that the group photo of Hideaway Home is a fake, but Emma is so excited by it, Beth decides not to say anything. It would be weird to admit that she and Lindsay did it. And when Emma acts so snooty, wondering how someone like Beth could possibly have heard of Édith Piaf, Beth — she tells Lindsay — is glad she didn't let her in on their little joke.

Lindsay should have known. Beth isn't the kind of person who likes playing tricks on people. It was lucky she didn't tell Emma about the photo. That might have blown everything. It was Emma's fault — alienating Beth with her snobbishness — that Beth kept her mouth shut. Still, Lindsay dodged a bullet. She'll have to be more careful.

There's no reason for Beth to know that the plan — the rapidly evolving plan — is to gaslight the wife into thinking she's going out of her mind, then getting the husband, the house, and the baby.

Beth would never agree to that. She's too decent a person.

Meanwhile, Lindsay can't quite figure out where Beth fits into the plan. The absolute ideal would be to pitch their own reality show: *Two Girls, a Guy, and a Baby.* They'd have to fake the backstory of how the happy threesome got the baby. But so what? All reality TV shows lie. Everybody knows that.

Lindsay will think of something.

Lindsay likes it that Emma flipped out over the photo and asked why Beth was listening to Édith Piaf. Beth was insulted. Everyone knows who Piaf was. Didn't Emma hear Ben blabbing on, at that dinner, about his rip-off Piaf hit?

Emma's behaving erratically, in public. That's good for everyone to notice in case Emma's sanity is ever in doubt. Emma also had a pretty dramatic reaction to the photo in Sally's office, the photoshopped "dead daughter" that Lindsay told Sally to put there for Emma to see. Lindsay directed Sally to do an improv (Sally loves theater talk) about Lindsay's imaginary dead step-sister.

The last thing Lindsay wants is for Emma and Sally to get friendly. Beth can be

335

trusted, but Sally might slip up, and the whole sticky web will start to unravel. Involving Sally was a mistake. Lindsay should never have done it. She'd wanted to see how far she could take things.

Virginia, the Nibble Nook waitress, is Lindsay's second cousin. When Lindsay asks her about Sally coming in for lunch with that pregnant woman from the city who bought Hideaway Home, Virginia says they seemed very friendly. Like they'd been pals forever.

That's not part of the plan. Not what Lindsay wants to hear.

That's when Lindsay makes up her mind to protect her interests, Ben's interests, possibly the baby's interests. She needs to keep Sally from screwing up worse.

It's not the most original plan, but that's all right. Lindsay can live with that. Her idea is inspired by something she saw on TV, on *Better Call Saul.*

Sally has a condition for which she's taking a blood thinner to ward off a heart attack or a stroke or whatever. She loves talking about her health problems. She drones on and on.

Lindsay asks what meds Sally's taking. Sally's glad to tell her. She's thrilled that Lindsay cares. Lindsay looks up Sally's medication online and finds an over-the-counter pill that looks exactly like it.

One day when Sally goes to the bathroom, Lindsay finds her pills in her purse and switches them with OTC nondrowsy cold pills. She waits for the pills to work, maybe not to kill Sally, but at least make her sick — and get her out of the way.

Destiny wants this to happen.

Lindsay goes to Ben's rehearsal studio to perform, for his co-producers, the song from *Peter Pan* that she sang for Ben in their hotel room. It was better when she did it naked, but fine, this time she wears a little green slip of a dress. Not naked, but not exactly . . . concealing.

She and the woman, the producing partner, recognize each other.

Rebecca is Rachel.

She lied to Lindsay the whole time they were having an affair. She didn't even tell Lindsay her real name. But Lindsay's in no position to criticize anyone for lying.

For now it's just more evidence that this was meant to be.

What are the chances of meeting an ex-lover in circumstances like this? What are the odds of this kind of coincidence? When destiny is on your side, the odds are close to a hundred percent.

Lindsay is willing to swear that Rachel/Rebecca's husband, Avery, doesn't know about her extramarital affair. It's a little weird that Lindsay's been involved with a man and a woman who work together, one past, one present, two lovers both cheating on their separate spouses.

None of it means anything. It's temporary. A phase. You have youth and a body, so you use it, and then you do something else.

Rachel/Rebecca doesn't want her husband knowing about Lindsay, and Lindsay could probably prove whatever she said. She's seen Rachel/Rebecca naked.

At the audition, Lindsay sings the *Peter Pan* song the way she sang it for Ben, sad, slow, loaded with pain and regret.

Ben is ready to talk his partners into casting her, into taking a chance, a big gamble, riding the PR wave of the complete unknown. But they don't need persuasion.

Rebecca/Rachel isn't the brightest bulb, but she's smart enough to figure out what Lindsay will tell her husband if she says no.

Anyway, it's not really a problem. Because Rebecca/Rachel knows that Lindsay can do it. She'll be great in the part. She's young, she's sexy, she's appealing. Unknown. She's publicity magic.

Lindsay looks from Ben to Rebecca/ Rachel to her husband. Lindsay's already forgotten his name. Everything is as clear as could be. Lindsay has been transformed from failed-actress-country-Realtor to future Broadway star. The Broadway star she was always meant to be.

Thank you, Hideaway Home.

CHAPTER SIXTEEN: PERFUME

One evening Lindsay and Ben run into JD at the gas station when they're driving up from the city together. JD could blow the whistle on them, but he chooses not to. Maybe he's protecting Emma. Maybe he's protecting his job. It doesn't matter so long as he keeps quiet.

Except for crashing that dinner, he's been good so far. It occurs to Lindsay that maybe he likes Emma and would rather keep a big secret from her than possibly bring down everything so he couldn't be around her.

Lindsay's delighted when Ben tells her that Emma suspects him of having an affair with Rebecca. Hilarious! Lindsay was the one who had the affair with Rebecca.

"Here's an idea," says Lindsay. "Get me some of that disgusting perfume Rebecca wears, and I'll wear it when I stay over at your apartment. In case Emma comes to town, she can think she's right about who you're fucking. I don't particularly like the smell, but it'll throw her off our trail."

Every time Lindsay sees Ben, she hints that something is a little . . . off with Emma. Is he sure his wife is feeling okay? She doesn't seem right in the head. She isn't totally stable. Will she really be the perfect mother for a helpless baby?

They watched *Gaslight* together. Ben plays dumb, but they both know what they're doing.

Of course his crazy paranoid wife can't handle the responsibility. She's seeing things, hearing things, imagining things. What if she decides that the baby is the spawn of Satan?

Everyone loves the Christmas pageant. It's a huge success.

Lindsay finds it touching. She likes Ben's music. A little churchy but nice.

She adores the crazy spikes of emotion in Emma's face when she introduces her to Heather, and Emma sees the girl in the field, the girl in the old photo, and she figures out — or does she? — that she's just a local unwed mom. DNA explains it. Up here in the boondocks, everyone looks like everyone else, back through the generations.

Let Emma think she wasn't seeing a ghost,

or photos of ghosts, but a real young woman, probably the product of years of country inbreeding.

Let the snooty city bitch think whatever she wants.

It baffles Emma, which is helpful. It's a good idea for Emma to seem confused and out of control with a lot of people watching.

The sweet Christmas pageant makes Lindsay feel better about where she lives, more cheerful about the idea that she might live in the area someday, with more money and frequent acting jobs — starring roles — in the city. The jury is still out on whether she'll live with Beth or Ben. She goes one way and then the other on what they'll do about the baby. Sometimes she thinks she might actually like to have it. To bring it up as her own child. Have a kid with none of the bother. No stretch marks, no labor pains, no swollen leaky tits.

Let Emma have the baby and nurse it until Lindsay and Ben can feed it formula, and then they'll take things from there.

During the intermission between the Nativity pageant and the talent show, Lindsay is scribbling down names at the back of the theater. Sally hovers around, as if she's making up her mind, and then she asks if she can go last.

Lindsay figures why not.

But soon enough she sees: Why not. Absolutely why not.

Sally must have plotted this all along. She must have hidden the costume somewhere. The minute she comes out onstage, Lindsay senses something wrong, but it takes her a moment to untangle the twisted threads.

In between getting the journal back from JD and passing it on to Beth, Lindsay kept it in her desk at work for a few days. And now she realizes that Sally must have found it — and read it.

Sally's dressed like Eliza Doolittle. Like the woman in the Cockney chorus, the woman in the journal. No way this is pure coincidence. Sally is screwing with Lindsay's head.

Why is Sally bothering? She must think it's a clever way of letting Lindsay know that she knows what she's doing, a smart way of warning Lindsay to leave Emma alone.

Stupid woman, really.

Sally's performance is about the worst Lindsay's ever heard, and that's saying something after the talent to which they were just treated. But it's especially shaming, because Sally's slowed-down pace feels like a parody of the way Lindsay did the

Peter Pan song for Ben and his partners.

Maybe Sally's been drinking. Maybe she brought a flask to the pageant. She seems a little unsteady. Maybe Lindsay's switching her blood pressure medication is finally having an effect. Which would be fine. Lindsay hopes the damage happens sooner rather than later.

But Sally's performance has its good points. It's freaking Emma right out. She's radiating nervousness like some buzzy, jittery aura.

Of course Sally's read the journal. Lindsay knows it can't be coincidence. She can't figure out what it means. But it means something.

Who is Sally, and what is she doing?

Emma stands.

She steals the show, you could say. Upstages Sally completely. She solves Lindsay's Sally problem by screaming and screaming and then fainting dead away.

And then, just as they manage to partly glue Emma back together, Sally does the most outrageous thing of all. She sidles up to Emma and — using the exact quote that Lindsay and Beth gave to the old lady in the journal, the one who got "murdered" at Hideaway Home — warns her to leave, to get away. She says "they" made her sing the

344

song, when the truth is, Lindsay knew nothing about it. Sally must think she's doing more improv.

That's it. Sally has crossed the line. Something needs to be done. If the switched pills don't do their magic, Lindsay will have to act.

Oh, Sally, Sally. Lindsay feels worse than she expected. Sally deserved what she got, but still . . . Lindsay wishes she hadn't had to kill her pretend stepmother.

Lindsay's mother is dead. Her name was Grace. She was the cashier at Nibble Nook. She died of a brain aneurysm at work.

Sally took things too far. She went way off script. Warning Emma was really pushing the limit.

Maybe Lindsay wanted the feeling of having two parents, a father and a stepmother who wanted her to succeed. Who wanted her to sell a falling-down wreck, a monster white-elephant house, to a young couple — easy marks — from the city.

Once again destiny kicks in. Fate offers a helping hand.

The effect of switching Sally's blood thinner went to work that same night. The night of the Christmas pageant.

Ben and Emma had left for the city.

Lindsay and Beth, Sally and Ted were in Ted's living room, watching *Law and Order* reruns. Trying to relax.

Sally went into the kitchen to make tea.

Beth said she's seen this episode before, but Ted made her promise not to tell them who the killer is. Lindsay knew, but it was still entertaining.

They'd reached the final scene — the victim agrees to testify — before they noticed that Sally was still in the kitchen.

Lindsay found her lying on the kitchen floor. There was no pulse. Her face was twisted in a horrifying, crooked grin, as if she was enjoying some private joke.

The private joke was death.

Beth called an ambulance.

They went back into the living room to wait. The ambulance took fifteen minutes, not bad for up here.

Two men ran in. They strapped Sally to a gurney, but their grim faces — one of the guys gave Ted an almost reflexive head shake — delivered the bad news.

Sally wasn't a bad actress. She took it seriously. She loved it when Lindsay gave her the character's backstory, how she'd been born in Hideaway Home, and her mom had given her away to a local couple. The story

346

was she had no idea who her real mother was.

Lindsay should have found someone who could play a person who could keep a secret.

After Sally's lunch with Emma, Lindsay had a bad feeling.

It wasn't as if Sally knew everything, but she knew enough to chew a little moth hole that could start everything unspooling. And then came that warning.

That was bad improv. Really bad. Totally out of line.

Lindsay couldn't let that happen. There was too much at stake.

The pills — or the lack of — took a while to work. It was another lucky break that it happened the night of the talent show. Maybe the stress of being onstage was too much for Sally. Maybe God was punishing her for singing that song. Lindsay tells herself that Sally died happy. On the heels of a great stage success. All the high of opening night before the reviews come in.

Lindsay can't imagine what possessed Emma to come to the *Peter Pan* rehearsal. She can't imagine, but she thinks, *Bad idea, lady.*

That Emma has never shown up until now is a tribute to Ben, who'd convinced her that it was better for both of them if she kept her distance.

All the way across the rehearsal studio, Lindsay can feel Emma's shock and confusion.

Unless Emma is really stupid, she must have figured something out, or else she is doing it now. Probably both. Did Ben lie to her about the star of his show? Did he not tell her it's Lindsay? Did he say it was a big surprise that he was saving for when the show got closer to opening? Maybe Emma never asked.

Emma's obviously shocked, but glazed over, like someone who's had so many shocks that she can't feel them anymore.

"I need a doctor. Now," says Emma.

CHAPTER SEVENTEEN:
EMMA

Emma awakes on the floor in a pool of something. Something wet. She's wet herself. Her first response is shame. Then she remembers who she is, what she is, where she is. Ben's rehearsal space.

Her water has broken. She's going into labor. Ben's on the phone with her doctor.

Ben puts on his coat.

"Don't leave me," Emma says.

"I'm going to get the car," he says. "Avery and Rebecca will help you down in the elevator."

Emma has a million questions, but the contractions are coming faster than they should. They're supposed to start slow. You're supposed to be able to time them. A certain number of minutes apart, and it's time to go to the hospital. She can't remember the numbers. The intervals. These are coming quickly.

Is she — or the baby — in danger? She

will do anything she has to to save the baby. She will only think good thoughts. She will stay brave and positive. She will wonder — just once — why Ben and Lindsay went to all that trouble, forging that journal, involving Sally.

Sally's dead.

The girl in the field and the old photos — was that part of it? Was JD in on it too?

Emma asks herself these questions, just once, and then for the baby's sake she stops.

She will deal with all that later. None of that matters now.

Ben's got the heat in the car turned up all the way, and it feels good when Emma gets in the Volvo. He reaches across the console and takes her hand. It's painful to think that he used to do that all the time. He did it that first day they came up to look at the house. Maybe that was the last time he held her hand so tenderly. And now he's doing it again.

It makes everything simpler. Here they are, the two of them, the baby on its way.

A forged journal. An affair. An elaborate deception aimed at hurting her. She still wants to think it's possible that, once the baby is born, everything will get sorted out. She and Ben will leave that complicated, twisted world and enter a new one together.

She's afraid it's too late. But despite everything, she desperately wants to believe that something positive can still happen. She thinks, *You can believe anything if you want to, badly enough.*

Another contraction peaks and fades and disappears. She squeezes Ben's hand, which is now clutching the wheel.

Against all odds, she dozes off between contractions.

The next thing she knows, it's crowded and bright. She hears noises, voices. People are lifting her, pulling and pushing her, asking how she's feeling. She's fine, except that she's being pushed and pulled. Then comes another contraction.

A wheelchair, a cold room, lots of machines, a worried nurse coming and going.

"There's nothing we can give you at this stage," the nurse says.

"That's okay." There's nothing they have that Emma wants. She wants something they can't give her, though she can't remember what it is.

She wants to do everything differently. To start over. She wants to be another person. More like Lindsay. She sees that now. Too late.

■ ■ ■ ■

Dr. Snyder appears in scrubs. Her knight in shining armor. How happy she is to see his kindly familiar face! He won't let anything bad happen to her and the baby. He consults a beeping machine that's attached to her somehow. He presses a button and a ticker tape rolls out; it's like checking out at a supermarket with a very large order.

He frowns.

Then more hands lift her onto a gurney, and they're flying out of the room. Levitating, it feels like, but that can't be true. Her view is the ceiling, lights streaming past. Then they slam through a door and the light is blindingly bright.

Someone is holding her hand. All she can see are the eyes. It's a man. It's Ben!

Ben's wearing a mask and green hospital scrubs. He looks scared but also embarrassed, as if he's been made to dress up for Halloween in a silly costume. *Costume . . . costume . . .* the word scares her. Pain builds and crests and ebbs like a wave that picks you up and slams you farther down the shore.

A voice says, "Emma, push. It's almost here."

She hears a baby crying.

Her baby.

Someone says, "It's a girl."

They put the baby on Emma's stomach. Emma's weeping. Sobbing with love and joy and relief.

She wakes up and falls asleep again, until she's awoken again by a friendly nurse who asks if she wants to meet her baby. Emma can't read the nurse's tone. "Is she okay?"

The nurse says, "She's beautiful."

Another voice says, "She's perfect."

It's Ben. He's sitting in a chair.

For a moment she doesn't recognize him. Then for a moment she doesn't care. Then for a moment . . . what? She doesn't know.

All she cares about is her child. The baby fits snugly into her arms. Her arms know what to do. She puts her hand under the baby's perfect downy head, and the baby's perfect pink lips nuzzle at Emma's breast.

"See if she'll eat," says the nurse.

The baby's already latched on. The baby gulps like a little fish.

Emma feels overwhelming happiness, love, and joy. She has never in her life felt love like this, never in her life loved anyone like this, never . . .

Over the baby's head she sees Ben, smiling guiltily. The smile of someone who's done something wrong and wants to make it up to her.

That's when the truth comes rushing back. If the truth ever left.

"Iris," she says. "Baby Iris."

Ben will agree to the name. He owes her.

"We'll talk about it," he says. "Before we make it official."

"Iris," Emma says with all the strength she has.

"Okay," says Ben. "Okay. Hello, Iris."

His voice sounds hollow and forced.

"Hello, Little Person," says Emma.

The nurses say it's normal to be tired after giving birth. That's why they call it labor.

Every time Emma's awake, it's to hold and nurse the baby. Ben's always there, and she's superstitious about letting Iris hear her parents argue during her first days on earth. The baby's presence is a buffer, a wall over which they can only communicate with expressions and gestures. Every look that Emma gives Ben is a giant *WHY?* A silent, astonished *How could you?*

Emma still doesn't understand. She knows about Lindsay and the journal. She knows Sally is dead. But the rest is still a mystery. There must be a simple explanation. It can't

354

be as complicated — as wicked — as it seems. Why would anyone go to all that trouble? The journal. The photos. Sally.

She spends two nights in the hospital. There's some problem about how much their health insurance will cover, but Ben says he'll pay no matter what. And the nurse says it'll probably be fine.

Ben says he wants Emma to stay there until she feels strong enough to bring the baby home.

He tells this to several nurses.

"Of course," each one says. "Of course."

Ben goes home and is back in the morning by the time Emma wakes up. He sits in the chair. He helps Emma go to the bathroom. He holds Iris, staring into the baby's eyes. He seems totally enchanted.

One afternoon, while Iris sleeps in Emma's arms, Ben whispers, "I'm sorry. I made mistakes. I know that now. I love you. I want to be with you and the baby. Iris. I love the name. It's perfect for her. I want to be with you both. We'll go back to the apartment. We'll sort things out. I'll explain everything. I'll do whatever it takes for you to forgive me."

That Ben loves Iris's name cheers Emma. Or almost. She wants to hear his explanation. His version. But why does she look at him like he's the detective about to explain the mystery, when the fact is, he *caused* the mystery. He *is* the criminal.

Why did he pick Lindsay? She seems like such an airhead. And why does Emma have to ask why? Lindsay's young, she's pretty, she's sexy. She's free. She's not pregnant. And for a few seconds, at that nightmarish rehearsal, Emma saw that she wasn't just a country Realtor. She can sing. Emma watched her become Peter Pan: Ben's old Twitter handle made flesh.

The baby gurgles at Emma's breast.

Being patient, giving this time, not accusing Ben, not insisting he explain is the most difficult and strongest thing she's ever done.

Ben says he wants them home at the apartment. He'll work from home. He'll take care of them. He's found a perfect crib to put next to their bed. He's stocked the place with diapers and wipes and cloths and anything they might need. All of Emma's favorite foods. He'll cook her delicious meals every night. Until she gets her strength back.

Here's what's going to happen:

They'll talk this through. Ben will explain. She'll either forgive him or not. Lindsay. The journal. Sally. JD. Were they all plotting against her? Are they still?

She has to stay calm. She has to hope for the best. She has to prevent fear, mistrust, and panic from getting into the milk that baby Iris is so greedily, joyously drinking down.

Obviously, it's too early to tell, but as far as Emma can see, Iris has a sweet, easygoing nature. She's happy to be held, to be carried, happy to be sung to and rocked. If she cries it means she's hungry or needs her diaper changed.

Emma is ready to go home.

Passing the time until Emma's discharged, Ben and Emma avoid the painful subjects. But they talk constantly. It's been a long time since they were this close. They go over the list of things Ben has bought. Diapers, wipes, a changing cloth. Check. Little onesies. Check. A crib with the highest rating from every place that rates child safety, the most expensive infant car seat, even though, as Ben points out, they'll only be using it to get from the hospital to the apartment and then for six months or so until Iris grows out of it.

Six months.

He's turned *Peter Pan* over to Avery and Rebecca.

And to Lindsay, Emma thinks. But neither of them says that.

They're not ready for that.

They'll stay in the apartment. They'll order in and feed and change the baby and take naps and sleep when they can. They'll take baby Iris out for walks when it warms up a little. They'll bring Iris to the doctor for well-baby visits. Give her time to get strong. They'll let JD work on the house. He and Emma and Ben can discuss things on the phone. If there are choices, JD can send them images of the options. From now on, she and Ben will decide everything together.

A stream of social workers and nurses come through Emma's hospital room, making sure Ben and Emma don't have any questions about what to do when they get home.

Emma has plenty of questions — but none the social workers can answer. What is she supposed to do about a husband who's conspired with his lover to forge a journal and gaslight her in every possible way? A husband who's made her think she might be going out of her mind.

But now . . . Ben seems different. More like how he used to be. Maybe the baby has changed him already. Another miracle. He

358

couldn't be more tender or caring. His touch, as he helps her and the baby into the wheelchair that the hospital insists on, is the touch of a man who loves them both.

The baby adores her car seat. She waggles her tiny arms and legs in the straps as Ben fastens them. The nurse watching says how unusual that is. Most babies cry.

"She trusts us," Ben says.

Emma can't help thinking: *Why should she?*

Emma braces herself for Ben to complain when she sits in the back with the baby. He's always made fun of couples who do that. But Ben is beyond criticizing anything she does, no matter how sensible or (he thinks) neurotic.

It won't always be this way. This is the first time they've taken the baby out, even if it's just across town to the Upper West Side. Of course she's going to be cautious.

She stares into the baby's huge dark eyes. Iris can hardly see her, Emma knows, so why does it seem as if she does? Emma watches every flicker of expression that passes across the baby's face.

So she's slow to notice.

Ben should be driving across the park and north along Central Park West. But he's turned south onto the West Side Highway.

"Where are we going?"

"I've had a change of heart," he says. "I want to go upstate."

"I thought we were going to the apartment. I thought it was all arranged."

"The country house is just as good. Lindsay and Beth have gotten everything we need."

"Lindsay and Beth? *Lindsay and Beth?*" She hears her voice rising to a high, strained pitch. How can she be, at the same time, so furious and so numb?

How could Ben not have consulted Emma? How could he have changed their plans, just like that, without asking her?

Panic washes over her. Adrenaline speeds up her heartbeat. Something's wrong. Are she and Iris in danger? Or is she panicking for no reason? Her husband has changed his mind. People change their minds all the time.

Even as she tries to reassure herself, she's fighting the impulse to jump out of the car. She can't. Of course she can't. They're speeding along the highway, and it would mean leaving the baby behind. That's the last thing Emma wants to do.

It's impossible to process everything at once. For the moment, just for a little while, she longs to go back to the way things were, before she found out about Lindsay. She tells herself: This is Ben. Her husband, not her kidnapper. He's had a change of heart. Emma can go with it. She loves the country too. They'll be on their own, with the new baby. Ben will fall in love with the baby, and with Emma. Again. He'll regret what happened with Lindsay. He'll beg Emma to forgive him. They'll sort the rest out later.

"I got all duplicate stuff up there," he says. "The crib, the diapers, etcetera. Because, to be honest, I hadn't made up my mind."

His mind? *His* mind? What about *her* mind? What about what *they* want?

"I thought we'd decided." Emma's voice sounds weak. Well, sorry. She just had a baby!

"Not really," Ben says.

They're heading into the Lincoln Tunnel. There's hardly any traffic. What time is it? The lights on the tile walls strobe past.

Ben says, "If you squint, it's kind of like the candelabras in the Beast's house, remember Emma?"

Emma remembers, but she now thinks the lights look like prison-yard beams.

When they emerge on the Jersey side, she searches through her purse for her phone, but she can't find it. Whom would she call? Her old friends, the ones she's hardly seen or spoken to since she got pregnant and moved to the country? Her doctor? JD?

And if she called them, what would she say? Still, she wants to know where her phone is. "Where's my phone? Did I leave it at the hospital? Do you remember taking it?"

"I have it with me," Ben says. "I took it. You won't need it for a while. Just try to get some rest."

There's something new — something hard — in his tone. She hardly recognizes his voice. It's like they've wandered into one of those science fiction movies in which a familiar person has been taken over by an alien entity.

She and Iris are in trouble. And now Emma is really scared.

"Where are we going?"

"Upstate. Obviously."

Emma closes her eyes. Somehow that makes it easier to say what she has to say. "Ben, you need to tell me. Why did you and Lindsay do what you did — the journal, the photo at the historical society?

Ben says, "Emma, are you sure you're okay? I have no idea what you're talking about. What journal? The one you were looking for in the attic, the one you must

have thrown out and forgotten or maybe
—"

Unless Ben looks in his rearview mirror, she can't see his face. He's concentrating on the road. A safe driver. She's always loved that.

She remembers that first day they drove to the house. Now she wishes they'd never . . .

Iris is sleeping peacefully, but Emma can't let herself doze off. She needs to stay awake and aware. Vigilant.

At last they turn onto their driveway.

"Watch out for the oak," Emma says.

"I always do," says Ben.

Chapter Eighteen:
John David, AKA JD

Do I think a house can be cursed? Of course. That's why those haunted-house films are always popular. Everyone's scared of certain houses. Do the math. If your house is a hundred years old, chances are someone died there. Now divide that by whatever percentage of people you think — depending on your view of human nature — are evil. An evil person died in your house. Or several people died young. Children died. There were nasty accidents.

Someone was murdered.

Now let's take a house in which people suffered. I don't mean those houses where kidnapped girls were chained in the basement, but from the stories we heard about Hideaway Home, there may have been some of that. People drinking themselves to death, losing their families and jobs. Sad old actors down on their luck. Didn't their misery seep into the walls?

And those were the good old days.

After that, the three siblings.

Everyone in town knows something happened to me in that house.

High school, junior year. The usual story. Too much beer and boredom and too many girls to show off for. Anyone who took the dare and went into the house or even tried would get free beer for the rest of the night and the girls would look at him differently.

Girls liked me already. That was partly why I did it.

It was a hot July night. We left our cars down the driveway. The others hid in the bushes. The dare was that I had to get in the house and signal them by lighting a match they could see from an upstairs window.

It was a serious dare. Your basic horror-film dare. The first guy who goes into the haunted house is the first one who gets killed and flayed and hung from the rafters for the others to find.

But really, what could happen? Three old people lived there. No one knew. They never left the house. They had everything delivered. My friend's cousin delivered for UPS. Once he'd brought something that had to be signed for, and he couldn't tell if it was a man or woman. The person was old. Very old. With long hair and a beard. He said it could have been a woman with a beard.

I guess one of the old people could have shot me — and gotten away with it. I was an intruder. But I was too young and drunk to think of that. I wasn't thinking in the stand-your-ground mode but in the haunted-house mode. I was basically a nice guy, but it didn't occur to me that creeping around in some old people's house wasn't a nice thing to do.

All the lights were out. The house looked massive.

The three hermits were in there somewhere, probably asleep. All the windows were closed. The screens were torn. They didn't want bats or raccoons in their kitchen. Maybe they weren't so crazy.

The kitchen door was unlocked. I walked in very quietly. I navigated by moonlight. The place was a mess. There was a horrible smell: dust, sour milk, rotten cabbage, something sweet and rotten underneath. There were piles of junk everywhere. But no one was around.

I remember a hall and a lot of rooms. Little rooms with all the doors shut.

And now here comes the crazy part.

That's the last thing I can remember.

The next thing I knew I was back on the lawn.

I'd come blasting out the front door.

I've read about people who have been hit by lightning. One woman said her tongue sizzled like bacon. That's sort of what this felt like. Not that my tongue sizzled. It was more like my whole brain was being fried.

Fade to black, and then I'm on the lawn, blinking up at my friends.

No one believed I didn't remember. They thought I was hiding something. Holding out on them. Being cool.

Ted believed me. He believed I'd seen something awful that I couldn't remember. He believed it was screwing me up. Ted sent me to a therapist in Ellenville and even a hypnotist in Middletown, but nothing worked.

Before this happened I would have laughed at anyone who told a story like mine. I saw something. My mind went blank. Poor me, I had the shock of my life, and now my life is crap.

But when it happens to you, it's not funny.

After that, everything took what I'd guess you'd call a turn for the worse. My grades tanked. I stopped seeing my friends, I didn't apply to college. I quit the baseball team. I got into coke. I forged a small check on Ted's account. Lindsay found me going through her backpack — looking for what?

They didn't report me. They didn't have to. I was ashamed of myself. I left home.

I got busted for shoplifting a ripe avocado and some chocolate chip cookies from a supermarket in San Francisco. I was not in my normal state. I don't even like cookies.

I finally wrote to Ted for bus fare so I could come home. He sent me money, and when I got back, he insisted I go to a doctor. The doctor said I'm bipolar. I don't personally think that's true. He prescribed pills that I never took. By now I'd know if I needed them.

I work on houses. I bought and fixed up my own little house. I got a truck, a crew. I get good jobs. I'm good at it. Excellent. If I had a renovation to do, I'd hire myself. No more trouble. I keep supermeticulous records. I pay all my bills, my helpers, and my suppliers on time.

Lindsay knew it wasn't just any house she was asking me to work on. She wanted to see if I would do it and how much money it would take to make me work on a place where I'd had some kind of trauma — or whatever. Also, the fact was she needed someone who could take on a job that big.

Or anyone at all. All the other builders were booked for the summer, which I should have been, would have been, if my clients hadn't gone broke.

Lindsay knew that something had happened to me in that house. I guess you could say it was old news, but so little happens in our town, old news stays pretty young.

As soon as the house was officially empty and abandoned, and listed by the bank, I used to drive up that long driveway and park outside, waiting to see if anything came back to me. I didn't want to go inside, even when it was empty.

All that changed when Lindsay asked me to work there.

I liked the idea. Of course, it crossed my mind that maybe if I spent enough time there I might remember what happened. And, to be honest, I also liked the thought of taking a sledgehammer to those little rooms. To make something come out of the walls.

At the risk of sounding stupid, I thought, *I'm not just renovating a house, I'm exorcising demons.*

Plus, I needed a job.

Lindsay knew it was sort of a dare, a second dare that might reverse the bad effects of the first. Or something like that.

I never liked Lindsay. In high school she was a mean girl, one of those people who changed friends, ghosting old ones and making new ones on her way up the popularity ladder.

"Sure," I said. "I'll look at the house. See what we're talking about."

Lindsay said, "What are we talking about? We're talking about hundreds of thousands of dollars."

"Then that's what we're talking about," I said. What was in it for her? They wouldn't get much for the house. Her commission would be in the very low four figures.

The next time I drove up the road, I almost plowed into that giant oak.

From a distance, one word flashed through my mind: *disaster.* Closer up, two words: *major disaster.* A dead ash tree had fallen through the porch roof. I kept expecting a floor to cave in or a ceiling to crumble.

But just poking around the outside, checking the foundation, I could tell the house was more solid than it looked. Structurally, it was pretty sound. Someone knew what they were doing.

The systems had to be replaced. New furnace, new wiring, the works. A tear-down might have been cheaper. But that's not what the guy — Lindsay insisted on calling him "The Client" — wanted. He wanted the mystery, the history. The whole nine yards. A theater guy, Lindsay said. From New York. Pregnant wife. Starting a family. She winked. Did I get it?

I got it.

She said, "This guy sees the house as an extension of his dick." That's how Lindsay talks.

The job was transforming a horror house into an Instagram-ready, shelter-magazine-ready country paradise. As jobs went, it was interesting. *More* than interesting. Rewarding.

I was fifteen years older than I was the first time I'd been in that house. I was a grown-up by the time I started working there. I'd been around the block a few times. I could handle whatever it was.

Working in the house might provide the crucial memory jog. Everything would come back, the way it does in the movies. Who cared about my dark past? The job meant a lot of money. A lot. How could I say no?

The number worked for me.

The only thing that scared me were Lindsay's crazy rules. Don't talk about this or that. Pretend that Sally is our stepmom.

Lindsay was always a crazy girl. We knew

she had a hard time in the city. But still . . .
I was glad she'd finally figured out she was
gay and living with Beth. I thought it might
help Lindsay get over whatever her problem
was.

Lindsay was working for her dad. People
thought she'd settled down. They should
have known better. She got that crazy
wicked troublemaker look in her eyes when
she set all those conditions about what I
could and couldn't tell the client and his
wife.

Emma. I liked her right away.

Ben is a self-important pain in the ass,
but fortunately he's never there. Emma is
easy to work with. I want to help her. To
save her.

Is it normal to be attracted to a married
pregnant woman?

Emma has no idea who these people are.
Emma doesn't have a clue about what she's
up against.

Ben's all about the project, Emma not so
much. She just wants Ben to love her. Which
is not going to happen. Someone should tell
her. She's pretty and sad. Though maybe
I'm seeing a sadness that's still coming — a
sorrow that hasn't happened yet.

Right from the start I had the feeling there

was something going on between Lindsay and Ben, but I wasn't sure until I spotted them in a gas station off Route 17. I could tell they were driving up from the city together. The way they were standing, talking . . . you couldn't miss it.

When I told Lindsay I'd do the job, and Ben and Emma signed on, Lindsay gave me the key. She offered to show me around, but I wanted to go alone.

I kept looking for the place where it happened. Where something happened. I kept thinking something would bring it all back.

But nothing has come back.

It's as if I'd never been there before. As if it was all the bad dream I'd tried so hard to convince myself that it was.

It was dark the night I snuck into the house. I could hardly see farther than what my phone lit up. But I saw something. I know I did.

Maybe I should find an excuse to work at night. Maybe that would be helpful with the memory game I'm playing. But I'm tired at the end of the day, and so, I can tell, is Emma. She's glad to see us arrive in the morning and even happier when we leave in the evening and she can cook dinner on that stove that the husband bought and had installed before they even made an offer on the place.

Sometimes I run into Ben at the house on Fridays. He keeps out of my way. He says that everything looks good, better and better, and I say thanks, and we leave it at that. He's impressed by how fast I got the internet installed and the driveway graveled. There's nothing to do about the oak, of course. Everyone just needs to be careful. I warn the kids who work for me, and sometimes I catch myself holding my breath until they've driven safely past it.

I just know who to call, guys I knew from school. That's what being a local means. But it impresses Ben. He mentions it every time he sees me. *Good job on the driveway, good job on the internet.*

I don't know why I never trusted the guy. I always knew he was hiding something. He's the kind of guy who thinks he can sleaze by on pure charm. But his charm doesn't work on me.

I felt awful for Emma.

I began to notice that I knew exactly where she was in the house. I could tell what kind of mood she was in, without even seeing her.

And then, at that ridiculous Christmas

374

pageant, I sensed she was in trouble even before she screamed. I was the one who sprinted across the theater. I was there to catch her before she hit the ground.

Lindsay texts me to say that the baby is born. It's a girl. And then Lindsay texts: *Stand by for further instructions.*

Emma, Ben, and the baby are in the city. I assume Emma's still in the hospital, or just getting home.

The night after the baby is born, Ben calls and says he has a sort of . . . unusual request.

Could I put a lock on the outside of the bedroom door?

On the outside?

Yup.

Those are my "further instructions."

Unusual, all right. Who puts a lock on the outside of a bedroom door? No one, not unless you're planning to lock someone inside. Who are they planning to imprison? Is Ben — and Lindsay — scheming to lock up Emma and the baby? But why? That's the part I can't figure out.

I try to make it seem like he's joking. "Are you trying to turn this place into an asylum?"

He fakes a laugh. "Just another level of

security."

So really, I have two choices. I can refuse. It won't be hard to find someone else to do a simple job like that. Or I can agree, and keep an eye on Emma and the baby, just in case.

And then there's a third choice: I can install the lock and keep one of the keys.

That's when I know I'm going to have to help her. I'm going to have to break Lindsay's rules. I'm probably going to lose the job and the giant payout.

But I can't abandon Emma. I care about her. My real job now is to save her from whatever the creepy husband is planning.

The locked bedroom door.

I do what Ben asks. I put the lock on the outside of the door. I leave the key to the lock under the doormat, just as I tell him I will.

But I don't tell him I've kept a copy.

Emma

Lindsay is waiting for them at the house. When they pull up, she appears on the front porch.

Emma feels a searing heat pulsing behind her eyes, as if something is boiling inside her brain. How could she have been so naive? How could she have believed Ben?

376

How could she have imagined that things were going to be all right now that they have Iris?

Iris!

Emma dives in front of Ben when he tries to unbuckle Iris. She slips Iris out of her car seat and hugs her close to her chest. Iris had fallen asleep in the car, and now she snuggles against Emma for another little snooze.

Ben and Lindsay lead Emma and Iris to the bedroom. As if it's their house and she's their guest. As if she's their prisoner and they're taking her to her cell.

Emma assumes she and Ben are going to stay there.

There's a crib beside her bed. A changing table against the wall. Stacks of diapers and wipes.

"Call us if you need us," Ben says.

"Call you if I need you?" Emma's shouting now. The raw rage and panic in her voice wakes Iris, who begins to cry. Emma rocks Iris and, in her mind, tells the baby she's sorry. It makes her even more furious. Why should *she* be the one who needs to apologize? Every bad thing that's happened — that's happening — to her and Iris is Ben's fault. "Who are you, Ben? You're a monster! You're —" she's sputtering.

Lindsay cuts her off. "We're just down the hall." There's triumph in her voice. She's won, and Emma never even knew what a serious battle was being fought. How could that be a fair fight? Ben and Lindsay smile at each other. They don't care if Emma sees. Jealousy seems like a mosquito bite compared to the pain Emma's feeling. If it weren't for Iris, Emma would . . . what? Lunge at Lindsay, strangle her? How would that go? Lindsay is ten years younger, fitter, and Emma just got out of the hospital.

"Good night," says Ben. His face is blank, his voice robotic. Has Lindsay drugged him or cast a magic spell on him? Emma's kidding herself. Ben is a responsible grown-up.

"Good night?" Emma says. "Good night? What the fuck are you doing, Ben?"

And now Ben, her husband, the father of her child — he can't even look at her. It's as if his soul has been stolen. He might as well be a zombie. He follows Lindsay out of the room.

Emma hears the key turn in the lock.

She's their prisoner. And there's nothing she can do.

Maybe Emma has lost her mind, just as she feared she might.

She needs to stay sane for Iris.

The journal was a warning. This is what happened to the woman who wrote it. Except that there was no musical-comedy hopeful who got pregnant by a Broadway star. Lindsay wrote it. Actually, it *was* a warning. Whatever happened to the imaginary girl in the fake journal is what Lindsay is planning to do to Emma.

Emma takes a deep breath to steady herself. Iris is hungry, and Emma is reluctant to nurse her on pure milky terror.

It's Emma's room — her bed, her nightstand, her clothes in the closet — but it isn't her room. Nothing looks the same. She used to feel so safe here.

There's a bedpan beside the bed.

Iris falls back asleep.

They warn you about rolling over on the baby when you're asleep, but Emma can't imagine how that could happen. Iris fits snugly in her armpit. Emma knows exactly where the baby is. Iris has a healthy cry, strong lungs for a baby. She lets her mom know when she's hungry.

With Iris snuggled beside her, like a warm little peanut, Emma can slip her breast in the baby's mouth without having to move. It's so simple and so pleasurable that it's momentarily possible to forget that she's being held prisoner by her husband and his girlfriend.

She's a prisoner in her own house: a former mental asylum in the middle of nowhere.

What do they plan to do with her? Kill her and steal Iris? She doesn't think that's it. It seems unlikely. But what does she know? She never expected this. They need her now, to feed Iris. They're not ready to make their next move. Maybe they're deciding what comes next.

Why do they think Emma might want to run away? Because she *does* want to run away. She needs to get out of here. But where would she go and how would she get there? A woman with a newborn, without a car in the deep country in the dead of winter.

It was snowing lightly when they walked from the car to the house.

The girl in the field with the baby: that was a warning too.

Another warning Emma couldn't see. She'd thought it was her imagination.

It was never her imagination.

CHAPTER NINETEEN: THE LOCKED ROOM

JD

I have a bad feeling about Emma and the locked room. I try to text her, and when she doesn't answer, I tell myself she's still recovering. She's got a new baby.

And still I have that suspicion. Like a tooth that's just starting to throb. I decide to drive over to the house and see if anyone's there.

Just before I leave I get my shotgun and put it in the truck rack. I'm not sure why I feel the need for it, but I do. I never used it except once to kill a rattlesnake. No one admits we have them around here, but we do. I keep meaning to tell Emma to watch out.

The gun's unloaded, but the sight of it will convince Ben to back down from whatever he and Lindsay are doing.

Two cars are parked in front of the house.

Ben's and Lindsay's.

I can't risk pulling up near the house.

I park a short walk down the driveway. It's still snowing, but that's okay. I've worn my waterproof boots.

Of course, the door is locked. Big Brave Ben would never spend a night in the country without pulling up the drawbridge. I know every board on the porch, every splinter in the doorframe.

And I've got the front door keys. I inch open the door and creep into the hall.

It's dark. Pale moonlight drifts down from the skylight, but it seems to make everything murkier rather than clearer. I can't see in front of me. I feel as if I've never been here, though I worked here all summer and fall.

I hear something.

A baby crying.

A baby crying . . . all those years ago . . . something stirs . . . takes shape . . . like a picture coming into focus.

Then I remember. It comes back, piece by piece, like an image broken up into pixels, blinking on, lighting up, tiny square by tiny square.

First there was the smell.

The smell of a dead mouse in the wall. Of hundreds of dead mice in the wall. Mice and cats and death and rotting flesh.

And then the sound. The mewing, the *mewling,* on and on and on.

At first I thought, *Cats.* The house was full of cats. That was terrifying enough. What could be creepier than stumbling through a pitch-black house with cats hiding, lurking everywhere, ready to leap at me and sink their claws and teeth into my flesh? And yet I kept going, into the darkness in which, at any moment, a feral rabid cat could leap on my head and scratch my eyes out.

But it wasn't cats. It wasn't the sound of cats. The crying wasn't meowing.

It was babies. Crying babies.

More terrifying still.

I should have left right then. I should have turned and ran. No dare was worth it. Why did I care if my friends dared me to go inside the haunted house? What was in it for me? What was I trying to prove? I could have gone back out and made a joke out of it. The girls wouldn't have liked me any less. No one would have thought I was weak. They knew me better than that.

But I kept going. Following the sound of the babies. The crying babies. Were the babies in trouble? Was someone taking care of them? Did they need help? Was I supposed to save them? Was that why I'd been sent here — to do this?

Maybe that was what kept me going.

That's who I was. That's who I still am. The guy who wants to help. The guy who wants to save the ones who need saving. I'm the guy who runs toward the accident rather than away.

The sound got louder and louder. I made my way through the hall, past all the rooms with closed doors. It felt like a house in a dream. Like a house in a nightmare.

At last the narrow hallway widened, and the space opened up. I directed my flashlight up to see that I'd entered a large space. Sort of like a theater.

Not *sort of like* a theater.

A theater.

I was standing in the back of a theater.

The stage was dimly lit, not enough for me to see clearly, but just enough for me to make out indistinct shapes and movement. Something was happening onstage.

Inching closer, I saw a giant bed on the stage. Something was wriggling around in it. Under the blankets. Like worms. Like larvae in a hunk of rotting flesh.

Again, I wanted to run. And yet I needed to get closer. I needed to see.

Every cell in my body said *Run!*

Walking down the aisle toward the stage, I tripped over something — something hard. I looked down. A hunk of wood, maybe a stone.

I didn't care. I kept going.

The light was still hazy, bluish, faint, but at last I got close enough to see.

Three people were sitting up in the bed. All three were old. Very old. Pale and thin and withered. I couldn't tell if they were men or women. I couldn't tell if they were alive or dead. Which ones were wriggling and which were still.

There was a new smell in the theater. Rot and mold and corpses. Worse than a dead mouse in the wall.

Was one of the old people dead? Was that what I was smelling?

A little lamp by the side of the bed went on and lit them up. Half lit them up.

I wished it hadn't.

One of them had a face that was scarred and pitted, burned off, puckered down to a circular hole from which strange birdlike caws emerged. One was lying on its back. All three had nests of long gray hair flying about their heads. The three witches in a fairy tale.

Babies. I kept looking around for the

385

babies. Did these old people have babies imprisoned somewhere? That seemed impossible. How could they have gotten all those babies? How could they take care of them? No wonder the babies were crying.

Unless I was hearing the ghosts of babies that had lived and died in this place when it was an asylum. Didn't they say they used to send unwed mothers up here along with the old drunks? Maybe they'd killed the babies. Maybe I was hearing their ghosts. Maybe that's who was buried in the old cemetery that everybody talked about but no one was brave enough to look for.

A tape player — one of those gigantic old reel-to-reels — was on the stage next to the bed. A tape was playing.

The crying of the babies was a recording. It was playing on a loop, over and over. It was a recording of babies crying. The three ancient people in the bed were listening. Listening to it like music.

The one with the burned-out face was pretending to conduct.

The two who still had faces seemed to be smiling, or anyway, their faces were stuck in masklike grins. Then I looked past them and saw that the stage was covered with baby dolls, stuffed babies, rows and rows of moldy torn dolls, jammed together, several layers deep. Half the dolls were smiling, and the other half were partially rotted away, as if rats had been chewing them.

The three old people — alive or dead — lay in bed, listening to a tape of crying babies while doll babies were crowded around them.

I yelled, but it was more like I was hearing myself yell. Like the shout you make in a dream, the scream you think you're making at the top of your lungs, and then it turns out you're just making a turkey gobble sound to wake yourself from the nightmare.

I turned and ran. I knew they couldn't be following me, but I ran as if they were chasing me. As if they wanted to catch me and keep me in the house forever. But of course, they could never do that. They could never get out of bed. If they were even alive.

If they were even real.

I tripped again, this time over a hole in the floorboards. I fell and scrambled back up and kept running.

My head hurt.

I can still feel the pain.

I stumbled toward the air, toward the night outside.

I can still smell that dead mouse smell.

And then I was outside, and I fell on the ground. I heard, as if from a great distance, my friends gathering around me. Above me. "What happened? What the hell happened?" Their voices sounded wobbly. Underwater. I felt like I was at the bottom of a well, or a swimming pool.

"I don't know," I said. "I don't know what happened."

I kept hearing those babies cry.

In all its horror, it comes back to me now as I search the dark house for Emma. I hear a baby crying.

The sound brings everything back.

I'm there. It's as if I'm watching myself watching the three old hermits.

That's what happened to me. The house. The darkness. The sound of crying babies.

I remember.

I should turn around.

But it's different now. I'm older. A man. And I have a gun. And there's a woman and a baby in here. Emma and her child.

Maybe this is worse than what happened then. Those old people weren't going to hurt me. But Lindsay and Ben . . . who knows what they're up to? Who knows what they plan to do to Emma and the baby?

The bedroom door locks on the outside.

I have a key.

It's Emma's baby crying.

That sound, its cry, is what keeps me working my way through the darkness, trying to reach her, to save her, holding the gun with one hand and reaching into my coat pocket for the key to her room with the other.

CHAPTER TWENTY:
EMMA

Emma wakes from a deep sleep. Someone's touching her, touching her shoulder.

At first she thinks it's Ben, then remembers.

It's not Ben.

A man is standing over her bed. Her heart begins to pound, and she begins to pray.

Let the baby be okay, let Iris be all right and they can do anything they want to her. She doesn't care what happens to her, just let the baby be unharmed.

Emma knows this is where it's been leading, for whatever crazy reason Ben and Lindsay have done what they did — playing those mind games, writing the fake journal, locking her in the room. Are they planning to kill her and take Iris? Just let the baby be okay.

She smells wood chips and pine and soap. It's JD.

"Don't be afraid," he says.

She's more grateful than she will ever be able to tell him. Tears stream down her face.

He's come to save her. This is where it's all been leading. But neither of them knew it, exactly. Emma just knew that she liked him. She'd thought about him a lot.

Iris is crying again.

She rolls over to nurse the baby and Iris quiets down.

"Where are they?" JD whispers.

In the dim rays of moonlight shining in the window, she sees that he's carrying a gun.

"It's not loaded," he says. "I just thought we might need something extra."

"Extra?"

"Like maybe this is something we can't just talk through."

"With . . . ?"

"Ben and Lindsay?"

Emma flinches. His putting them in one sentence like that makes it all the more real.

As if on cue, someone knocks on the door.

"Why are they knocking?" asks JD. "If they had any brains, they'd just lock it again until they figure out who unlocked it."

"What should I do?" Emma whispers.

"Say 'come in,' " says JD. "Turn on the light, okay?"

Emma reaches over Iris for the lamp.

JD points his gun at the door.

Lindsay walks in, sees the gun.

"Is he fucking with you?" she says. "Is this asshole . . . ?"

"Wrong," says JD.

"How did you get in here?"

JD holds up the key and smiles. "You always did think you're so smart and everyone else is stupid."

He raises the gun. Emma believed him when he said it wasn't loaded. She still believes him. But what if . . . ?

"Wait," says Lindsay. "I mean it. Wait."

"I'm waiting," says JD. "No, you wait. I've got a better idea. Let's go find Ben."

"He's right down the hall," says Lindsay.

Emma remembers Ben imitating Lindsay, at the start. Was he lying then, too? She recalls the sight of Lindsay winding her arms around Ben's neck at the rehearsal studio.

"Excellent," says JD. "Let's go find him."

"Wait here," he tells Emma.

A few minutes later Ben appears. JD's following him. He isn't pointing his gun at anyone. He just has it, is all.

Ben looks disheveled, half-asleep, and so terrified that, for a moment, Emma's heart goes out to him. Too bad. No one's going to hurt him. And she's pretty sure that he and Lindsay were going to hurt her. They've hurt her already.

Her sympathy lasts less than a heartbeat. Who *is* this person? Her husband? She doesn't even know him. Maybe she never knew him. Who could he be, to have done the things he's done to her, to want whatever he wanted to do?

Emma starts crying and can't stop. The last thing she wants is to cry in front of them. To give them the satisfaction. She should be holding her head high. But tears are sheeting down her face. She wraps the baby's blanket tighter around her and holds Iris close.

JD puts his arm around her shoulders. Emma leans against him.

"I knew it," Ben hisses. "Slut."

"Knew *what*?" JD points the gun at him.

"Nothing," Ben says.

Coward, thinks Emma. How could Ben imply that there is something between her and JD after what he and Lindsay did? An affair with the hot contractor would have been nothing compared to that.

"Here's what's going to happen," says JD. "You guys are going to switch rooms with Emma. And you're going to give me all the keys. And I'm going to lock you in here. Emma's going to take the baby, and we'll go to one of the other rooms, and by tomorrow morning we'll have decided what to do with you."

JD pushes Ben just slightly as he herds him to the far edge of the room, far away from the door. Emma almost objects but doesn't.

"I need to take a piss," says Ben.

"Use this bedpan you've so kindly left for Emma. Or you can just piss out the window," says JD. "If you jump out, you'll die in the snow. But I assume you know that. You knew that Emma wasn't going to jump with the baby."

"We didn't want her to jump," says Ben.

"You didn't want her to?" JD's imitation of Ben is dead accurate and wicked.

Who's the actor now?

Ben is beyond shame. How could Emma have had his baby? Oh, poor Iris. This isn't what Emma wanted for her. But this isn't anything Emma could have predicted or even imagined.

"You're going to be sorry, Ben." Emma hardly recognizes her own voice. She's so angry she's hissing. "I don't know how or when, but you're going to realize what you've done. You're going to pay. You're going to suffer, really suffer. And I'll be cheering every step of the way."

"Go stand next to him," JD tells Lindsay. "And give me your phones. Both of you."

Ben and Lindsay huddle together. Their bodies know each other. Emma can't look. She checks on Iris, then glances up to see a long look pass between Lindsay and Ben.

She's seen that look before.

In the movies. The moment before the lovers decide to make a run for it.

Which is exactly what Ben and Lindsay do. Lindsay grabs Ben's hand and they rush out the door. Emma hears their footsteps on the stairs, then the front door slams.

She and JD listen silently.

A car starts up.

"They're taking the Volvo," says JD. "Should I go after them?"

"Why would you?" says Emma.

Why would he?

That's when they hear the crash.

It's the sound Emma has been dreading and expecting since the first day they drove up here.

First the cops come, then the ambulance. JD tells Emma to stay inside with Iris, it's too cold for them to be out. It's snowing too hard now for Emma to see. But JD, dressed for the weather and minus the gun, keeps coming back in to update her.

He knows one of the EMT guys from high school. The guy said it didn't look good. The crash victims (or so the guy put it) seem unlikely to recover.

"I'm sorry," says JD. "I'm so sorry."

"It's not your fault," says Emma. "You saved me."

JD's reluctant to leave, but Emma wants to be alone with Iris. He says he'll call Beth and Ted and tell them the news.

"Poor Ted," JD says. "Poor Beth."

Emma lies awake most of the night, trying to understand what's happened. The most she can come up with is that Ben and Lindsay were trying to make her think she was going crazy, to make her act unstable, and then claim possession of the baby.

The baby and the house.

What were they planning to do about Beth? Emma's sure that Lindsay must have had a plan.

Lindsay had a plan for everything. Too bad her plans didn't work out.

In time, Emma knows, she will grieve for Ben. Who knows if baby Iris will remind her of him? But she'll try to see in the baby the things she loved about her husband before Lindsay — and the house — took him away.

■ ■ ■ ■

JD comes back the next day, and the day after that.

Checking on Iris and Emma, he says.

The second night he stays for dinner.

The third night he stays. The pleasure of being in bed with him is almost overwhelming. They talk all night. Emma should be exhausted, but she's never felt so awake.

JD tells her what happened to him in the house, all those years ago, and how the memory only came back to him when he heard Iris crying. Emma tells him as much as she can remember, beginning with their coming to look at the house. When she tells him about the journal, he goes tense.

He says, "Beth asked me to put it up there. And then she asked me to get it back. I'm so sorry I didn't tell you . . ."

"Is there anything else you didn't tell me?"

JD doesn't have to think.

"Sally wasn't Lindsay's stepmother. She was a friend of Lindsay's mother."

"Why did Lindsay bring her in?"

"I don't know. I think she wanted a stepmom. And . . . okay, there's one more thing."

Emma whispers, "One more thing?"

"I didn't tell you how much I thought about you," says JD. "I thought about you day and night."

"Me too," Emma says. "About you."

JD says, "Sometimes bad luck has good luck hidden inside it."

Emma inherits the house and Ben's money.

Ted retires. The real estate business is shuttered. No one investigates Sally's death. She'd had a stroke.

Emma doesn't like to pass the historical society, so she has no idea if they get someone to take Beth's place. Beth is gone too. Just gone. Moved back to the city, according to town gossip.

Every so often Emma and JD and Iris and later, Sam and Max, the sons Emma and JD have together, drive past Lindsay and Beth's house. It's stayed empty. Sometimes she and JD talk about the first dinner they had in that house. So many things were going on. They'd had no idea.

The only thing they knew was that they liked each other.

After a while, on her own, Iris calls JD "daddy." He loves it, and then he makes it true. He adopts her.

Emma loves their life here, more than she ever thought possible that first day she and

Ben drove up the driveway. The problem was, she was coming here with the wrong person.

When the house is finished, it's featured in not one but two magazines, and after that JD has nonstop work. For a while Emma stays home with the kids but eventually she finds a job in a local public school, not unlike the job she had in the city before she got pregnant with Iris. Her children attend the school, though she's not their teacher. She sees them in the hallways.

Sometimes at night Emma lies awake, imagining that she can hear the ghosts of the people who lived here when it was Dr. Fogel's clinic. None of them scare her now that she's lying beside JD.

She tries not to picture the three hermits, the one thing she and JD never mention again.

Sometimes she thinks she can feel the spirit of the woman who left the journal in the attic, until she remembers that the woman wasn't real. Lindsay made her up. Maybe Lindsay was onto something. Maybe she was channeling something — something larger than herself.

Even when she was lying.

Because if that woman didn't live here, didn't hope and die here, stranded, then another woman did, or maybe someone just like her.

Emma snuggles close to JD. The house is quiet. Her children are sleeping peacefully, and she too drifts into a peaceful dreamless sleep.

CHAPTER TWENTY-ONE:
THE ACCIDENT

I wake up. Everything hurts. I'm in a hospital bed, but it's not the same hospital where I gave birth to Iris. It's different; the room is smaller. My whole chest feels bruised and sore, and my shoulder stings when I raise my arm, even a little.

Where's the baby? I want to shout, but my voice is rusty and hoarse.

Someone is standing at the foot of my bed. It takes me a moment to recognize Ben. His face is badly bruised. It's as if someone painted a broad purple stripe down the side of his cheek, and one eye is swollen shut.

"Emma," he says. "Thank God."

"What happened to you?" I croak.

"The same thing that happened to you," Ben says. "You went into labor, and I was so crazed with fear, trying to get you to the hospital, that I slammed into the oak tree. Thank God JD was there, working on the house. Her gave us a ride to the hospital."

Ben nods at someone standing in the corner of the room.

It hurts to turn my head.

It's JD.

He gives me a little salute.

I'm afraid to ask. But there's no choice. "Is the baby okay?"

"In the nursery. Sleeping like a baby." Ben smiles, though smiling clearly hurts him, and he winces. "Let's say it wasn't the delivery we dreamed of. Or planned for. But everything worked out okay. Mother Nature came through for us. The doctor's doing the standard hearing test. He'll bring the baby in soon."

"You were out for a while," says Ben.

"How long?"

"A while."

The rest begins coming back to me. Little snapshots of what happened.

"Where's Lindsay?" I make myself say.

Didn't she die in an accident? Lindsay and Ben. They hit the tree.

But now the accident seems to have happened to Ben and me.

Ben and JD look at each other.

"Who's Lindsay?" Ben says.

"Our . . . Realtor," I say, for want of a

402

better way to describe her. Where would I begin?

Ben just stares at me.

"Lindsay!" I repeat.

JD looks dumbfounded.

"Blond and young and —"

"Our Realtor was named Sally." Ben looks genuinely puzzled. "An older woman, very sweet, very honest about what the house needed."

Something strange has happened. I don't understand. This seems like a dream, but it's not. I can't . . .

A man in a white coat comes in, holding Iris. I expect to see Dr. Snyder. He'll straighten everything out.

I'm so sure it's going to be Dr. Snyder that it takes me a beat to realize it isn't.

It's Ted. Wearing a white coat. He keeps rubbing one hand against his jacket.

Holding the baby, he comes closer, close enough for me to read the name tag on his lab coat.

DR. THEODOR FOGEL.

Fogel. Dr. Fogel. The name rings a bell.

"Baby girl," says Ted, handing me the baby. "You're looking very well."

I take the baby and press it close. I feel an overwhelming happiness, love and joy. I have never in my life felt love like this, never in my life loved anyone like this, never . . .

But wait. Something's different . . . something about the baby.

Ben says, "Dr. Fogel calls all his patients 'Baby Girl.' Actually, it's a boy. Meet Sam. Baby Sam. My dad's name."

It's a boy.

It isn't Iris.

It isn't my baby.

"This isn't my baby," I say. "This is the wrong baby . . ."

As if from a distance, I hear a song running through my head.

All I want is a room somewhere . . .

Why am I thinking *Rapunzel?* Where did that name come from?

Through a fog I hear Ben and Ted murmuring about our accident . . . increased intracranial pressure . . . swelling . . . disorientation . . .

I look at JD, but he won't meet my eyes. He's staring at Ben and Ted.

"Your wife's a real hero," says Dr. Fogel. Ted. "Her whole body took a hit in that crash, and then she got through the labor. With flying colors. She'll be okay. She just needs some rest. My wife will give her something to help her sleep."

Dr. Fogel comes closer. He holds out his arms.

"We'll take the baby," he says.

ACKNOWLEDGMENTS

Thank you to my editor, Emily Bestler, and associate editor, Lara Jones.

ABOUT THE AUTHOR

Darcey Bell is the *New York Times* bestselling author of *All I Want, Something She's Not Telling Us,* and *A Simple Favor,* which was adapted into a critically acclaimed film starring Blake Lively and Anna Kendrick. Darcey was raised on a dairy farm in western Iowa and is currently a preschool teacher in Chicago.

The employees of Thorndike Press hope you have enjoyed this Large Print book. All our Thorndike, Wheeler, and Kennebec Large Print titles are designed for easy reading, and all our books are made to last. Other Thorndike Press Large Print books are available at your library, through selected bookstores, or directly from us.

For information about titles, please call:
  (800) 223-1244

or visit our website at:
  gale.com/thorndike

To share your comments, please write:
  Publisher
  Thorndike Press
  10 Water St., Suite 310
  Waterville, ME 04901